To Shirley—
With love,
Your friend
Jinx

THE TEXICANS

A NOVEL OF TEXAS

BY

ELIZABETH MAUL SCHWARTZ

Maddog Press
Sierra Vista, Arizona

The Library of Congress Cataloging-in-Publication Data
Schwartz, Elizabeth Maul
The Texicans/Elizabeth Maul Schwartz.—
1st edition
p. cm.
I. Title

813'.54—dc21

99-091819
CIP
ISBN 0-9677505-0-4
Printed and bound in the United States of America.
May 2000
First Edition
1 2 3 4 5 6 7 8 9 10

PUBLISHED BY MADDOG PRESS
P.O. Box 3891
Sierra Vista, AZ. 85635

This book is dedicated to the memory of my mother, Johnnie Ruth Coffey Maul, and my father, Fred Roy "Bud" Maul—two real Texans.

And to my husband, Robert Schwartz—an honorary Texan.

Acknowledgements

Every family has a history, but not all have the good fortune to have historians.

I am fortunate to have family chroniclers who have painstakingly researched the movements of Frederick and Katherine Stockman through historical documents. I have taken their combined efforts, did some of my own research, embellished the known facts with a hefty dollop of poetic license, and written a tale of early Texas.

I would especially like to recognize my cousin, Thelma (Dixie) Mandaville, for igniting my interest in family history, Lee Stockman and Judy for their dedication to the Stockman Family Newsletter, and Jim and Helen McMillan for their incredible lineage charts.

For my own research, I was assisted by the staffs of The Herman Brown Library, Burnet, Texas and the Sierra Vista Library, Sierra Vista, Arizona.

Help and support came from many friends—especially Sheran Vaughn and Mary Shroyer—and members of the High Desert Working Writers' Association: Katherine Baccaro (my helpful picker of nits), Leslie Clark, Gloria Fisher, Archie Taylor, and Holly Whitman.

And as always, my husband, Robert Schwartz, gave his love, unflagging patience and moral support. Without him, there would be no book.

Thank y'all.

A little rebellion now and then is a good thing, and as necessary in the political world as storms in the physical.—Thomas Jefferson

Wretches! Soon they will become aware of their folly.—Antonio Lopez de Santa Anna

TEXAS
Trinity River
NACOGDOCHES
NATCHITOCHES
TRINIDAD DE SALCEDO
NEUTRAL ZONE
El Camino Real
Opelousas Tr.
San Antonio (Bejar)
ATASCOSITO
ORCOQUISAC
NEW ORLEANS
TRINITY BAY
GALVESTON ISLAND
MEXICO
La Bahia
BARATARIA
MONTERREY
Rio Bravo (Rio Grande)
GULF OF MEXICO
SOTO LA MARINA
MEXICO CITY
VERA CRUZ
YUCATAN

CHAPTER

1

SPANISH TEXAS

Frederick Stockman didn't scare easily, but Texas worried him.

Five days in a leaky scow to get there didn't do much to ease his concerns. And the closer they got to that inhospitable wilderness, the more nervous the crew.

"Ease the sail. . .getting shallow. . .quiet!"

Snatches of whispered, anxious commands penetrated thick morning mists, betraying their arrival and increasing tensions onboard.

As the boat drifted towards shore and turned its bow into a slight swell, stiff sails were lowered, and the anchor splashed into brackish, chocolate-colored water. Passengers and crew cursed even these small sounds.

The anchor dug in as an incoming tide and a light onshore breeze pushed their stern to a halt within a few feet of a muddy beach. Only the burble of small wavelets slapping the hull divulged their presence.

But it was too late.

A pair of red-rimmed eyes watched them through the moss hanging from an ancient cypress.

Frederick slipped over the boat's gunwale into waist-high water, waded ashore, and stashed a bundle into a tree crotch. He paused to listen, and scanned the silent, swampy thicket.

Satisfied that no alligators, water snakes, panthers, renegade Indians, pirates, or marauding deserters from His Majesty's Army lurked, he slogged back to the boat. Still in the murky water, he shattered the silence, flushing a few quail with his deep voice.

"Looks safe enough, I reckon—ain't nobody shot at us yet. Don't see any sign of a fort, though. Are you sure this is the place?"

The boat captain looked slightly insulted.

"*Mais oui monsieur*," he sniffed, "of course it is. I have been here many times. What is left of the old fortress cannot be seen from here, but we are unable to cross the bar and navigate further up the Trinity River. You must *dèbarque*—disembark—here. Let us unload quickly, for I want to return to New Orleans on the evening tide."

"*¡Jesús y María!*" the hidden observer muttered under his breath. "He is staying."

His own voice pounded his ears, adding to the pain in his head. As he watched, Frederick took another bundle and worked backwards towards shore. Near the swamp's edge he lost his footing and turned suddenly to catch his balance. As he did, he locked eyes with the man peering from the forest. They both froze.

"*Alto. . .arrêté. .* .stop," the man on shore warned, using every language he knew. "I am armed."

“And my arms are full,” Frederick growled, in Spanish. “State your business.” As he spoke, he slowly shifted his burden to one arm and reached for his pistol, never taking his eyes from the figure in forest shadows.

“Speak up and come forward, or we'll blow you out of those woods.” Frederick gestured with his chin towards the heavily armed crew.

No one moved for several seconds, then a small man clad in a filthy brown robe doddered forth. His arms trembled as he struggled to level an antiquated musket almost as long as he was tall. After a few steps he stopped and, unable to support the gun's heft, lowered the muzzle and slumped against a pine tree.

Frederick sloshed to the beach while keeping a wary eye on the priest. He bent, placed his load carefully on a log, then straightened, pistol in hand.

He did not need it.

The priest's full attention was on the bundle, which began to rise. Then, as he gawked, it threw back its hood and an angel with emerald eyes blinked at him in surprise and smiled.

“Oh, Padre,” she said, “I am so happy to see you. Please bless my child.”

Sunbeams broke through the mist, bathing her red hair in a brilliant halo and illuminating the toddler she held in her arms.

Dizzied by shock, relief, and fever, the lonely, sick old monk was so overcome he broke into tears and croaked, “Welcome to Tejas, my child.”

CHAPTER 2

Padre Solano awoke the next morning to find he had two things to thank God for: both his malarial fever and the miserable fog were gone. He wished his headache, the soreness in his bones, and the intruders were.

He lay still for a minute before gingerly pushing himself from a buffalo skin mattress. Days of soaring body temperatures had tenderized his skin, making his rough-woven robe an instrument of torture.

Once upright, he made his way to a rotting pine door and wrestled it open, glowering at its stiff and stubborn cowhide hinges. Sunrays, dove coos and something seldom heard in this place greeted him: laughter. It did not please him. The scow had sailed, but the foreigners remained in their camp a few yards from his decaying room in the long abandoned fort.

Did I not, months ago, inform the Bishop in Monterey of the illegal norteamericanos arriving in unwelcome droves? And that our ill-equipped and undermanned army in Tejas could do little to stop these interlopers?

An impoverished priest, he was without means to provide food and shelter. He clucked disapproval. *What is a poor servant of God to do?*

His Majesty's government had made it quite clear these treacherous *norteños* were not welcome, but still they came. On the run from something or someone, they thought to hide in Spanish-owned territory. Surveying the camp he admitted that, unlike most—those who came ashore like half-drowned, starving dogs—this new family had arrived with more than just the clothes on their backs. But no matter, they had to go.

"This time," he muttered, "the King's soldiers will return and despatch these trespassers back to their own kind."

A burst of giggles called his attention to a group of children. The foreign and mission Indian youngsters were playing a game involving an inflated pig's bladder. In addition to the small child he'd seen in her mother's arms yesterday, he counted three more and frowned. *This is no place for white children. Nor Indians, but they won't leave.*

Solano's musings were interrupted when he heard the red-haired woman call her family to breakfast. His stomach growled. *Perhaps this would be a good time to enter them into my ledger? After a bit of breakfast? No, I'd best keep my distance. Is that roasting pork I smell? Well, maybe just a little food, then I shall tell this family that it is not safe here. They must return to New Orleans. I will eat, then I will warn them off. It is the least I can do for a good Catholic woman.*

The woman beamed a sunny smile when she saw him coming.

"Father, it makes us so happy to see you feeling better. There is even a touch of color in your cheeks," she said, stepping from under the waxed-hide roof of her makeshift kitchen.

Padre Solano, having recovered sufficiently to regain his officious manner, was not to be diverted from his Royal duties—and hot food—by cheerful pleasantries. "Señora, I must speak with your husband," he sniffed.

Smiling wryly at the shabby little priest's poor attempt at hauteur, the tall man asked, "What can I do for you, Padre?"

"I should warn you, sir, I represent His Majesty's government here and you are trespassing on Spanish land. When the soldiers return there could be. . .problems. These soldiers might be. . .uh. . .somewhat undisciplined." Solano glanced uneasily at Katherine.

"I don't reckon they'd molest us with a representative of His Majesty right here to keep 'em in line. Tell you what, let's have some breakfast and then you can try to scare us off.

"But first, let me introduce myself. I'm Frederick Stockman and this here is my wife, Katherine." He pronounced it "Katrin," his slight German accent skipping the *h*.

"That big one over there," he pointed, "is our oldest, George, and these are Henry, David, John and Peter," Frederick said as he waved his hand in the direction of the other boys. "I can't hardly keep 'em straight. The baby there is Margaret, and we're all Spanish subjects with a passport issued by the Crown. Have a seat here on my log here and let's eat."

The padre, caught flat-footed, was, for one of the few times in his life, speechless. He stood open-mouthed for a few seconds, then, recovering his comportment and voice, he intoned, "In that case, Señor Estocoman, perhaps after we have eaten we can complete the formalities. I shall bless our food."

A hearty breakfast of Johnnycake and pork chased away some of the priest's reserve, and curiosity got the better of his practical nature.

"Señor Estocoman, I see you have no horses or oxen. How do you propose to move your family to your land grant?"

"I was gonna ask you the same thing, Padre. We were told we could buy some here."

"Oh no, not here. Perhaps in Nacogdoches—a far walk. There are only poor Indians here and they have no animals."

"Padre, since there's no mission or fort, what in holy Hell are you doing here?" Stockman boomed.

Katherine frowned at her husband for cussing in the priest's presence, but Solano appeared to take little notice.

"I came to this not-so-holy-Hell to minister to what is left of these Indians. Although the mission closed long ago, they refuse to leave. I had an escort, but when I fell ill the soldiers continued their patrol and left me to heal. Or die. I do not think they cared which."

"When're they coming back? Maybe they'll sell us a horse or an ox. I have money."

"They were to return days ago, I think. I lost track of time. No matter, they will come. But, señor, these soldiers will not sell you a horse. If you had a horse they might take it. And oxen are more valuable than silver here in Tejas—or as you say in English, Texas."

"I guess I'll just have to come up with another idea then. Thanks for the information though. And we're glad you could join us for breakfast. I'll get those papers you want."

Later that day Padre Solano unpacked his quill pen, precious ink, battered red leather ledger embossed with the gold Spanish Royal Crest, and dutifully recorded the Stockman family's arrival.

Frederico Estocoman *57 años*

María Katrina Estocoman *35 años*

He paused and smiled after this last entry, which would be his private joke. In his fevered state yesterday he had, for that moment when the bright sun illuminated Katherine and her child, thought he was looking upon the reincarnation of the Virgin. And, after all, many married women of pure character were addressed as "María."

Xorge *20 años*

Enrique *14*

David *12*

Juan *9*

Pedro *6*

Margarita *3*

Señor Estocoman is a native of Germany, holds a valid passport and immigrates to Tejas Territory as a loyal Spanish subject. They are of the King's faith and speak the King's Spanish. March 6, 1806.

He did not make note of the furs, skins and dried beef that were loaded onto the New Orleans-bound scow. Nor did he deem it necessary to mention the new blankets the local Indians—and he—now possessed. The King's tax collectors took a dim view of foreign traders.

CHAPTER 3

Katherine stared at a patch of diamond-studded sky through a frame of tree branches. A none-too-distant mountain lion's scream quickened her pulse and she reached over to check on little Margaret. Mountain lions, or panthers as they called them in Texas, were known baby stealers.

Satisfied, she burrowed deeper under her quilt and closer to Frederick. Straining to hear more from the cat—hoping not to—she finally softened against her husband's side. His light snores, accompanied by cicada and cricket chirps, comforted her. But soon the things she had learned from the priest about her new country stalked into her thoughts and kept her from sleep.

Padre Solano, replete with crawfish stew for supper, had held the family spellbound with praises—and condemnations—of this province he knew so well.

"Texas," he'd told them, "is a bountiful land, with much game, wild horses and cattle. Vast herds of bison blanket the plains and where there is water, multiple crops can be harvested each year. If God were to create an Eden in the Americas, Texas would surely be it.

"But," he warned, "there are serpents in this garden. You will find few legal residents here—only scattered settlers, priests, and soldiers. And Indians. We have some peaceful ones, but then there are the Comanches. They are fierce and cruel beyond belief."

Sensing his talk of Indians made Katherine uneasy, he thought to comfort her, but only made matters worse by adding, "But the Comanches seldom come *here* because this place is not healthy. That is why the Mission failed."

Katherine's eyes widened.

"Oh, dear, I am a foolish old man. I have distressed you."

Katherine assured Solano she was interested in all aspects of their new country. Besides, it was the first time in her life she had engaged in a strictly social conversation with a priest and she was reluctant to discourage him. He was a clever storyteller as well as chock-full of local knowledge, even though some of it was disquieting. No stranger to living in the wild, Katherine was nonetheless disturbed to learn this part of Texas was even more isolated and perilous than most.

She sighed. *Have we made a mistake by coming here?*

"What are you thinking about, Red?" Frederick whispered, startling her. "Are you fretting?"

"I thought you were asleep. No, I'm not fretting. Well, a little. I try not to, but what about the children? Will we be safe? How long do you think we'll be stuck here? We can't expect to take the little ones far without horses or oxen. What will we do?"

Frederick gathered her in his arms. "Now don't you peeve yourself, honey. You leave the worryin' to me. Haven't I always taken care of you and the children? You're tired, Red. After a good night's sleep, tomorrow'll look brighter, you'll see."

Frederick yawned, turned over, and was soon snoring again.

Katherine lay awake for a long time. She was not so sure things would be brighter. Not at all.

Day three at El Orcoquisac, as this place was called, dawned brightly, indeed.

The children brought Katherine corn and salt, gifts from the Indians. Grinding the corn into meal, she added honey provided by Padre Solano, rolled the mixture in damp corn shucks and buried them in hot ashes to bake.

David caught catfish and Katherine prepared a hearty meal without using precious provisions brought from New Orleans. The repast took on a festive air and once again the priest entertained them, between bites of ash cake, with tales of Spain, Mexico and Texas. A benign Texas.

Katherine slept soundly that night, lulled by the sighing of tall trees and the smell of campfire smoke. *Perhaps*, she thought as she drifted off, *I worried for naught.*

"Mama, those Indian kids told us there are giant man-eatin' Indians across the bay," David said matter-of-factly as they ate breakfast the next morning. "They're called Karankawas and they live on an island. And sometimes they paddle over in dugouts, steal the women and kids, and eat the men."

Katherine, striving to remain calm in the face of this fresh piece of disastrous news, looked beseechingly at Frederick. He broke out laughing.

"Son, let's not worry about a few pesky, horse-thievin' Injuns. They may scare the puny locals, but they sure as hell don't want to tangle with the likes of the Stockmans. Besides, Davey my boy, they'd probably figger you was too hard to clean," Frederick teased.

David grinned his little half-smile while the family fell into raucous laughter and side slapping in appreciation of Frederick's well-delivered quip.

Katherine, too, enjoyed Frederick's joke. She smiled at the man she'd married twenty years before. With his imposing height, hazel eyes and graying hair and beard, Frederick was handsome in the rough, healthy way of frontier men. Well past middle age in a land of disease and danger where few men lived into their sixties, she noted he still cut a fine figure. For an old rogue.

David, slightly embarrassed to be the brunt of Frederick's tease, concentrated on his venison and biscuit breakfast. Mama had used some scarce wheat flour to make both bread and biscuits this morning and he liked that. But she'd baked extra, and that usually meant his Pa was leaving. Like back in Louisiana, when Papa and George left to trade goods along the Mississippi. He was right.

"Children," Frederick said, "your Ma and I have decided that unless we want to be stranded here forever, I'd better go on up river and find us a horse or something so we can move. We also think I'd best go alone, leaving George here to guard the home fires and keep game on the table."

George looked less than pleased to be left behind, but before he could say anything, Frederick added, "George'll be in charge. Well, I guess your Ma will really be in charge, but he'll take care of my chores."

Brushing biscuit crumbs from his beard, Frederick rose. "I reckon to be gone only a week or so. The priest expects his soldiers back real soon, so if I'm delayed you'll have some extra guns about. I expect you to look out after each other and help your Mama and George with the chores. And I'll be back before you know I'm gone. Right, Red?"

Katherine, not convinced this was one of Frederick's better plans, nodded all the same and quickly turned her back. She blinked back tears as she gave the appearance of being engrossed in the business of wrapping salted venison, biscuits and bread in cloth and putting them into Frederick's satchel. She'd cry later. Alone.

Each time Frederick left—and there had been many such partings—Katherine feared he would not return. She knew if anyone could survive this danger-fraught wilderness, Frederick could. But she had deep misgivings about his trip, for this time he was leaving her and the children in a forlorn swamp.

CHAPTER 4

Nine long days after Frederick left, ten soldiers—leading mules and led by a corporal—returned for the padre.

Solano, while thankful his escort had finally come to claim him, was dismayed to see several kegs of *aguardiente* strapped to the mules. Not one to resist a dram of strong drink for himself, he was nevertheless fearful of the tough young soldiers' rowdy behavior under the influence of so much alcohol. While the men were occupied setting up their *campo*, Padre Solano stole away.

Following an animal path along the Trinity River's bank for a quarter-mile north, he then cut through the thicket to the Stockman camp. Once he left the river there was no path, for the Stockmans were careful that no signs were left, no path marked.

Frederick had picked the spot for his family before he left and, to the priest's thinking, he had chosen well. The high-ground location boasted a freshwater stream, and dense woods for a windbreak and protection from probing eyes.

When the family had moved, Padre Solano was disappointed to lose them, but now he felt relief. And though Frederick had said nothing of his mistrust for soldiers, the padre knew Frederick's choice for his concealed camp was no accident.

"Señora María," he blurted, out of breath, "the soldiers are back. Perhaps we should not make it known your husband is gone. Actually, there is no need for your family to talk with them. If necessary, I will talk with the *capo* (corporal). I will tell him you are legal immigrants on your way north. *If* they see you, that is. And I don't think they will. . . ." The priest was babbling and he knew it.

Katherine, troubled by the padre's obvious agitation, called the children to her. Smiling, she told them, "The soldiers are back and they are tired from their trip, so I want you to be very quiet and stay close. George and Henry will return from hunting soon and then we'll have an early supper. Your father will be here in a day or two and he'll be real proud to hear you didn't pester the nice soldiers."

David, a bright child, immediately piped up, saying, "The Indian kids told us some soldiers ain't so nice. They take their food and make the men work. I betcha them Indians have skedaddled by now."

The priest nodded and Katherine frowned.

"David, with George and Henry out hunting, you're the oldest man, so I'm making it your job to keep John and Peter quiet. And nearby."

Proud of his responsibilities, David herded his younger brothers to a clearing in back of the camp. Picking up a pile of smooth stones, he divided them up among his siblings and they began pitching them at a stick pounded into the ground.

Katherine walked back to the river with Padre Solano, out of the children's hearing.

"Now, Father, what's the problem?"

"Oh señora, they brought much *aguardiente,* confiscated from a smuggler. I fear they will drink the evidence. Sometimes I have seen soldiers do. . .uh, things with Indian women when they are drunk. I have never seen *these* soldiers behave poorly and I truly do not believe they would molest a white woman of good standing, but perhaps it would be wise to take certain. . .precautions."

"*Gracias,* Padre Solano, for your concern. We're accustomed to dealing with problems of this sort, having lived many years amongst unruly types. My boys are plenty handy with a firearm, but I'm confident a confrontation can be avoided. Surely your soldiers will behave themselves with a representative of God and the King so near."

She smiled and added, "But, we'll stay out of sight, as you wisely suggest. Now, perhaps you had best leave before they come looking for you."

Katherine watched the back of the priest's partially bald head until he disappeared from view, then she sprinted back to her campsite and sprang into action. She unwrapped Frederick's Brown Bess musket, "Old Bessie," from its oiled-hide pouch, loaded it, and propped it nearby.

Around her head she tied a dirty rag, covering her hair. She put on several layers of clothes to pad out her slim frame and rubbed soot from a burned log into her gums and teeth, then smeared ashes over her pale complexion. There was little she could do about her green eyes.

She broke out a jug of corn whiskey and mixed some of it with honey.

She was ready.

There would be no campfire tonight, so she was preparing a cold supper when George and Henry returned to a mother who appeared to have lost her mind.

"Mama! What happened to you?" cried Henry when he saw her. "Are you hurt?"

"Shush, Henry. Keep your voice down. We have a little company nearby and we would just as soon not make their acquaintance," Katherine said, emphasizing the 'not' while keeping her voice light.

The boys listened carefully to their mother as she explained their situation. Raised near the rough-and-tumble settlement of Bayou Pierre on the Mississippi River, they were no strangers to the seamier side of life on the edge of civilization. Nor were they ignorant of the effect of too much liquor on otherwise sensible men, especially in a place where there were few ill consequences for a man's actions. They knew what to do.

The sun set and, without a fire, a chill fell on their camp. A full moon brightened the forest, but not their spirits. Katherine thought the moonlight unfortunate, for darkness is a fugitive's friend.

While the family huddled together in their rough wooden shelter, George kept watch on the river path. Katherine hated for him to be out there alone, but tonight it had to be.

"Henry, did I hear the baby whimper? Of late she's been a little restless and I'm afraid she'll wake and cry. Keep her warm."

"She's dead to the world for now, Mama. You get some sleep."

Katherine closed her eyes, but felt she couldn't possibly sleep. She was astonished when cheerful bird chirps and sunrays woke her. After checking on the baby, who was gurgling happily in Henry's arm, she rummaged in her stores for something for breakfast.

"Sorry, no fire this morning, we can't afford it. But I have nice smoked fish for breakfast. Did you know that many people in Europe have this for breakfast every day? It's considered a delicacy," she brightly told her children.

"Somehow, Mama, I can't get too danged excited about the fashion in Europe. I could use some good ole fried salt pork and quail eggs," Henry groused. The others agreed, but ate their fish in silence.

The Stockman camp-turned-prison, with Katherine as warden, started their day not only with cold food, but further unwelcome restrictions.

"No running, noise, or wandering away," she dictated, and for the most part, it worked. Until midmorning, when Margaret began to wail and Katherine reluctantly fed her sweetened whiskey. The baby fell into an alcoholic slumber.

George and Henry took turns guarding the river path while Katherine did her best to entertain the bored and restless younger boys. She read to them from her Bible, embellishing the stories to make them more relevant to their lives. She changed her voice to bring the characters to life in a Texas swamp. She softly sang hymns and ditties, letting the children join in if they kept it low. When her voice gave out she silently prayed.

"Mama, do you smell tortillas? And roasting meat?" David asked as a southerly breeze wafted into the Stockman camp, carrying aromas and sounds from the Royal Mexican Army encampment. Katherine cursed the Spaniards, resenting the hot food and boisterous laughter denied her children.

For the second night in a row they had no fire and Katherine began to worry about keeping her family fed while they holed up like rabbits gone to ground.

Please, please, let Frederick come home tomorrow, she prayed. *We can't hide like this much longer.*

It was getting harder and harder to control the children and she deplored keeping little Margaret drunk. *What on earth will Frederick think when he returns to find his baby drunk and his wife transformed into a soot-blackened hag? Serves the old s.o.b. right.* In spite of herself Katherine giggled, then settled in for another long night.

Six hours later sporadic gunfire sent frightened children scurrying to her side.

"What is it, Mama? Indians?"

"Not in the middle of the night, I'd wager," George said. He had just returned from watch to give Katherine a report.

"Most likely drunken soldiers letting off a little steam. Nothing to worry us," Katherine soothed.

Clinging together in the moonlight, straining their ears to determine the direction and proximity of the shots, they heard men singing. The chorus confirmed Katherine's suspicions.

"See, the soldiers are just having a little *fiesta.*" *And getting rid of the aguardiente,* Katherine added to herself. *Tomorrow they'll be hung over, but quiet.* "I don't think we need worry tonight. But just to be sure, I want both you and Henry to stand guard, George."

Katherine gave the boys some jerky and sent them to the riverbank to watch the path leading from the presidio ruins.

And that's how Padre José María Morales y Solano nearly lost his life at the hands of a fourteen-year-old boy.

The old priest, taking advantage of his inebriated escort's songfest, decided it was a good opportunity to check on Katherine and the children.

Creeping along the river as stealthily as his age and physical condition allowed, he cursed his limited abilities. He stepped on a brittle tree branch and cringed when it cracked loudly and a twig lodged painfully between his toes. He froze, but discomfort forced him to bend over to remove the offending wood from his sandal. As he struggled to reach his foot, a ball of lead whizzed along his scalp, flattening him.

For the first few seconds following Old Bessie's roar the forest fell eerily silent. Soldiers stopped singing and Katherine stopped breathing.

Henry, knocked to his knees by the musket's mule-like kick, struggled to stand and reload. His ears were still ringing from the gun's bellow when he heard the priest wail, "*¡Jesús, María y José! Save me!*"

Katherine heard the cry and bolted from camp in the direction of the priest's pitiful lament, yelling, "Boys, don't shoot! Don't *anyone* shoot! George, help me with the padre. Henry, stay where you are and guard the path."

They half-dragged, half-carried the hapless monk back to camp.

"Light a fire, George, and use some gunpowder to get it going. Throw in some bear grease. . .I need light and water, *pronto.* It's too late to hide. Even the drunkest soldier had to hear that shot.

"Henry, when they come up the path, don't shoot. Holler for them to stop and then I'll talk with them. Don't show yourself. They may be wall-eyed soused, but they're still trained professionals."

Cradling the dazed priest's bloody head in her lap, Katherine sobbed, "Oh, Padre Solano, please forgive us. Henry didn't know it was you."

Solano, bewildered and in pain, struggled to figure out what happened. *Did I fall?*

"Can you hear me, Father? It's Katherine. . .María Katrina. You've been shot. There's blood on your head, but the ball seems to have only cut your scalp. Be still and let me clean the wound."

Returning with more spring water, George told his mother, "I can see a parade of torches along the river path, Ma. And the padre here probably left a trail to our camp a mile wide, so they'll be here real soon."

"Call Henry back. I want everyone to sit here in the full light of the fire. All except you, George. You hide in the woods behind camp. Take the weapons with you and station yourself so you have a good view of us, especially me. Don't shoot unless I pull off my scarf, but if I do I want you to kill as many of them as you can. Hurry, I can hear them."

With her family gathered around the fire, Katherine leaned over and whispered, "Father Solano, I'm going to sit you up. I need you to hold the baby. Do you think you can do that?"

The padre nodded and wished he had not. He groaned in protest when Katherine jammed a battered hat stuffed with moss on his aching, tonsured pate and positioned him so he would be the first seen. He was seated on a log, propped up between Katherine and Henry, when a soldier crashed out of the woods and reeled to a tipsy stop. Befuddled, he waved his pistol in the air, then gawked at the people sitting calmly around a fire.

Katherine, never taking her eyes from the soldier, snaked her hand to the edge of her scarf. She pictured George taking aim. "Wait, George, wait," she whispered under her breath.

The young soldier squinted, as though seeing double, then spied the priest, who, for some unfathomable reason, was holding a baby.

"Padre, what are you doing here?" he slurred. "And who are these people?" As he talked he clumsily stuffed his pistol back into his belt and appeared close to doing grievous harm to his privates.

Katherine relaxed and lowered her hand to the priest's shoulder, careful not to snag her scarf as she did so. "The young man asked you a question, Padre Solano," she said loudly, giving the dazed monk's shoulder a hard squeeze.

Solano, his eyes slightly crossed in an effort to see clearly, vaguely wondered why he was holding little Margarita. Focusing on the soldier, he grinned crookedly and announced, "Welcome to Tejas, my child."

For what seemed an eternity, only the crackling fire and men rustling through the thicket disturbed the hushed tableau vivant. Then Katherine broke into a guffaw appropriate to a Louisiana saloon. The children sniggered and the Spanish soldier joined in.

Padre Solano smiled. He was pleased these people were amused, but wondered what he said that was so funny.

The other soldiers arrived to find an old hag, a Franciscan monk wearing a straw hat, several children, and their fellow soldier engulfed in spasms of laughter.

Whatever these people were drinking, they wanted some.

"Doña Katrina, I must speak with you," the Corporal said when he visited the next evening.

"Of course, *Capo* Rodriguez. How are you feeling?"

"Sober, with a headache, thanks to the *aguardiente*. It is no wonder they call it 'water with teeth'. But I will recover, as will the priest. It is of him that I wish to speak with you."

"Sit down, please. *Café*?"

The Spanish corporal settled onto a log by the fire, accepting a cup of coffee that he suspected was his own. His soldiers were overly generous with his provisions.

"As you know, we came to escort Padre Solano back to San Antonio de Béjar. When he can travel we must go. He is reluctant to leave you here, but I am not certain you are willing to go with us."

"You are correct, young man. I'll wait here for my husband."

"That is the problem, Señora Estocoman. I cannot. Leave you here, I mean."

"I don't understand. Will you force us to go with you?" Katherine asked, keeping her voice light.

"It is not my wish to do so, but I will if I must. Perhaps your husband will return in the next few days and the problem will be solved."

Katherine nodded and smiled, but her heart was racing. *Surely they won't make me leave. What will Frederick do if he returns to find us missing?*

All watched anxiously for Frederick the next few days. The enclave of unwilling inhabitants in the insect-and-reptile-infested swamp settled into a routine as they awaited the padre's recovery from a convenient relapse that the corporal suspected was a delaying tactic.

The soldiers, many with children of their own back home, gave the Stockman youngsters treats, told them stories, and allowed them to ride His Majesty's mules.

Miguel Gonzales, the first drunken soldier to stumble into the Stockman encampment, was assigned as protector of the family against alligators, snakes, mountain lions, renegade Indians—and drunken soldiers.

A Spanish aristocrat born in Mexico, Miguel was serving his military duty before going to Spain to study law. His fair skin, deeply tanned in the Texas sun, accentuated bright blue eyes and white-blonde hair. Although a lowly private, his demeanor and appearance made it obvious he was of the upper classes.

Two years younger than George, and six years older than Henry, the eighteen-year-old soldier soon became their friend, reveling in the familial warmth of the large, fascinating,

Stockman clan. His own family had returned to Spain, expecting him to follow, but Miguel, more interested in the New World, was not looking forward to going to the old one.

"Jorge, it is my dream to go to New Orleans. And to see the Mississippi River. Is it as large as the Rio Bravo?"

"I never saw the Bravo, but in some places you can't hardly see across the old Missisip. And New Orleans. . . ." George launched into a glowing description of that town. Sitting in an isolated swamp, it seemed unfathomable that a city like New Orleans was only a little over three hundred miles away as the crow flies. The boys figured they could make it on a good horse in less than a week. They talked a lot about horses—with which they had much experience—and of girls—with which they had almost none.

Miguel recounted the events of his less-than-satisfactory career as a soldier in His Majesty's lancer unit, The Second Flying Company of Alamo de Parras, at San Antonio de Béjar. For a few days life was relatively pleasant at Orcoquisac.

Until the storm hit.

And it was a toad strangler.

Torrential rains swelled the Trinity River into an ugly reddish-brown threat spilling over its banks. The downpour indiscriminately soaked soldiers, settlers, and servants of God.

Katherine and the children moved into the fortress ruins, as did the soldiers. Over their consolidated camp they stretched every tarp, blanket and animal hide they could find over makeshift roof repairs, but their lives remained miserable in the face of inescapable dankness.

Under their poor shelter Corporal Ruiz, Padre Solano and Katherine passed the time discussing the dilemma in which they found themselves.

"I've thought this through, *capo*. If I leave here before my husband comes back, it will be in chains," a defiant Katherine told them.

Padre Solano raised his eyebrows in alarm, but the corporal smiled. "I have no chains, señora. Nor would I be willing to put them on you. I have a better idea. I shall leave Private Gonzales here to protect you until your husband returns. Then he can escort your family to your new home."

Katherine beamed. Then she frowned. "Could you look around for Frederick? I mean, he should be traveling south, and if you are going north. . . .?"

"Of course we can," Padre Solano interjected. "We could follow the river north to El Camino Real instead of taking the Opelousas Trail, can we not?"

The corporal eyed the priest. "Would that choice of route perhaps aid in your recovery?"

Solano smiled and nodded.

Ruiz sighed. "Then we will take the long way home and, now that the padre has been miraculously cured of his fever, we will leave as soon as this weather has passed." Katherine suppressed a smile.

Twenty days after Frederick left to buy some horses, Katherine, small children gathered around her, watched the soldiers ride away. A tear slid down her cheek and over her upturned chin when Padre Solano waved good-bye. For all her bravado, she was immensely relieved that Private Miguel Gonzales was staying behind until Frederick returned.

But where *was* Frederick?

CHAPTER

5

Frederick didn't know where he was.

He did know the miserable rain had ceased, for it no longer ran into his nose and mouth. This thought reminded him of an old joke about people who were so purse proud their upturned noses threatened to drown them when it rained. He started to laugh, but the pain in his head checked him in mid-chortle.

He pushed himself to sitting and looked around for his horses. To his vast relief, he saw them grazing nearby. He vaguely remembered hobbling them before the fever flattened him, but had no idea how much time had passed since then.

He tried to stand, but his head reeled and his stomach lurched. "Hungry," he croaked, and collapsed back into the mud, out cold.

Hours later, the whinny of horses and an insistent tug on his boot brought him to. When his body began to slide down the slimy mud bank towards the river, he bellowed a curse, sat up abruptly, squinted to clear his vision, and found himself looking into the ugliest set of yellow eyes this side of the Devil's own.

What in tarnation? Damned gator!

The mammoth bull alligator dragged Frederick to within a few feet of the swollen river before he was able to do anything about it. He knew if that big son of a bitch got into the water, there was no way a man, even a healthy one, could fight him. He kicked with his free leg.

Startled to find his intended dinner suddenly come to life, the alligator almost lost his hold on Stockman's boot, but then clamped down harder, tearing a hole in the water-softened cowhide. Stubbornly maintaining his toothy grip, he backed toward the water.

Frederick grabbed desperately at roots, logs, anything to stop him, but nothing held. Then, as he slid over a large rock he managed to hold on. And as much as he hated to lose a perfectly good boot—what with the cost of things—he clung to that slippery rock and pointed his toe. The boot slid off, freeing his foot. He wasted no time shinnying up the steep, quaggy bank and grabbing his gun.

The alligator, realizing he'd been duped, spit out the boot and writhed up the embankment behind Frederick with astonishing speed. But not before Stockman grabbed his rifle from its wet oilskin.

"Come on, you slimy bastard," he yelled, hoping the damp weapon would fire.

The alligator lunged and clamped down on the first thing in his path: the gun barrel. Frederick fired but, even with half his head missing, the gator kept coming.

Kicking, sliding, attempting to back-paddle in a foot of mud, Stockman managed to stand, then fell flat on his back with a *whoosh*, his lungs knocked empty. Gasping for air, he scrambled to escape the thrashing tail, thinking, *More'n one man's been killed by a danged dead gator.*

Using his weapon as a club, he bludgeoned the animal, screaming, "Die, you ugly son of a bitch, die!"

And it did.

Half a mile downstream, Corporal Ruiz signaled his men to a halt.

"Did you hear that?" he whispered.

Padre Solano nodded, frowning in the direction of the shot and shouts. Getting his bearings, he nudged his mule to a trot.

"Padre, wait! You could be riding into danger," the corporal warned.

"And I might be on my way to help a soul in need. You stay, but I must go."

Cursing under his breath, the young Spaniard reluctantly waved his troop forward.

"That senile old fool," he muttered. "He'll get us all killed one day." He made a mental note to complain to Captain de la Garza back at Béjar. *If we survive the priest's good intentions, that is. Man of God or no, he is very unwise to rush towards the unknown. Especially in Texas.*

Catching up to Solano, the corporal saw he had dismounted and was hurrying—as fast as his peculiar hitch step allowed—towards a bloody heap near the riverbank.

"Padre, wait. It could be a trap."

The priest ignored him and kneeled in the quagmire next to the unmoving form. Convinced that Frederick was dead, he wailed, "Oh, poor María Katrina. Whatever will she do?"

He touched Frederick's bloody forehead, expecting the worst. "*Dios mio,* he's still alive! Quickly, bring water. He's burning with fever."

Taking less care than was his norm when ministering to the infirm, Padre Solano threw cold water onto Frederick's hot face. Thinking himself under attack again, Frederick spluttered, flailed around for his gun and knocked the priest onto his rump. Solano sat in the mud, trying to catch his breath while the corporal suppressed a smile.

Frederick growled, "Lord, Padre, please don't tell me I'm in Heaven, 'cause it sure looks like Texas. Or did I make it back to Orcoquisac? Where's Katrin?"

Corporal Ruiz handed Stockman a water gourd and pulled Solano to his feet. The priest huffed, "Believe me, you are far from Heaven. But only a few miles from your family. Señora María is quite concerned for your welfare. You gave me a fright, all covered with blood, which, thank God, does not seem to be your own."

Frederick eyed the soldiers. "I see your escort found you."

"*Sí*, we are on our way to San Antonio de Béjar. María Katrina asked us to look for you, as you have a habit of taking up with those of questionable character. I see she was wise to worry." Solano, smiling, nodded towards the dead reptile at Frederick's feet.

Frederick grimaced and aimed a weak kick at the twenty-foot monster's tail. "As usual, Katrin's right. That big son of a bitch tried to steal my boot. You know, it's gettin' where you just can't trust nobody these days."

"*Adios*, Corporal. *Vaya con Dios*, Padre. Thanks for coming to look for me and everything," Frederick told them as they prepared to leave the next day.

"Our pleasure, Señor Estocoman," Ruiz told him, a hint of irony in his voice. "And please, send Private Gonzales, the young man guarding your family, back to us in San Antonio when you reach your new home. He may need an extra push, as he is greatly enjoying your wife's cooking. *Adios y hasta luego.*"

Frederick watched the troop leave, then tightly rolled the alligator skin and, to the dismay of his horse, tied it behind his saddle. Cured, it would make a fine pair of boots. *Serves the evil boot-stealin' bastard right. The only good gator is boot leather.*

Katherine heard the approaching horses at the same time as she realized that most of the Indian children had scampered into the woods. Dropping the shirt she was scrubbing into her wash pot, she grabbed Old Bessie and herded her own children and one leftover Indian toddler behind her. Using a tree limb for support, she shakily aimed the heavy musket at the clearing and waited. *I probably can't hit a danged thing with this cranky ole musket, but I can raise a ruckus that'll bring Private Gonzales and my boys on the run.*

When the rider entered the clearing, Katherine, overwhelmed with relief, chucked the musket and bolted from her hideout.

"Frederick, oh, Frederick—you're home. You're safe!" She rushed into his arms and all the rancorous thoughts she had harbored vanished with his embrace.

Supper was a celebration.

"Chocolate. And fruit. Manna from Heaven," Katherine mumbled around an orange slice.

"Naw, Nacogdoches—and believe me, that village is a far cry from Heaven," Frederick quipped. "And everything would'a been a far cry fresher if I hadn't gotten caught by that storm." Then he told a rapt audience of his brush with death from fever and a toothy monster. The children's eyes grew wide when he displayed the mutilated boot and unrolled the huge alligator skin.

Then it was the children's turn.

Henry took a ribbing about shooting the dangerous padre and Miguel elaborated on the tale, telling of his surprise when he stumbled into the Stockman camp. As he told Frederick of the *bruja vieja* he found there, he smiled apologetically at Katherine for describing her as an old witch. His English was surprisingly fluent, his proficiency improving daily under the tutelage of George and Henry.

When Miguel stopped talking Henry said, "Papa, Miguel ain't so keen on army life. He says there's talk among some of the soldiers about how's maybe Mexico would be better off without some ole King in Europe taking all their money and telling 'em what to do."

"Yep," Miguel said.

The children giggled: Miguel was picking up Henry's accent and favorite words.

"My family came from Spain," he said, "but I was born in Mexico. They call me a *criollo*—Creole in English. It means a Spaniard born in Mexico. But I consider myself Mexican."

"I thought they called you *gachupín*," David blurted.

Katherine blanched and Frederick swatted the boy, but Miguel laughed. "Some do. It is all right David, but you must be very careful not to use that word in front of other Spaniards. It is a terrible insult."

David blushed and smiled his shy smile, grateful to be forgiven, but, characteristically, curious. "Miguel, what exactly does it mean? Why is it bad?"

Miguel shrugged. "In the beginning, when Cortes and his conquistadors first came to the Americas—almost three hundred years ago—the Indios who lived here had never seen a horse. They thought the men, dressed in armor and carrying spears, were part of the horse. Like a Minotaur. . .in reverse."

Miguel then spent the next ten minutes telling everyone about the mythical Minotaurs. He was well educated, having studied with private tutors most of his life in preparation for taking his place in Spanish society.

"All right," Henry said. "So these soldiers were supposed to be half-man, half-horse. . .how did they get that name: *gachupín*?"

"*A gacha* means 'on all fours,' but for some reason *gachupín* actually means 'those who have spears.' "

"What's so bad about that?" David asked.

"Nothing really. . .but over the years the Spaniards—especially the early conquerors—have become despised in the Americas, so *gachupín* now means four-legged, spear-carrying tyrants. And many want us out of Mexico."

"Politics ain't none of our concern," Frederick growled. "We'd best stay out of it. 'Course if the Mexicans want to toss the King out on his royal rear end that's their business. I've already fought in one revolution, and except for Old Bessie there that I took off one of them redcoats, I ain't got squat to show for it."

The subject was closed.

Frederick turned to Katherine and patted her hand. "Red, I think you'll like your new homestead, even though I'm told there's not much there. Just a few soldiers watching the Opelousas Trail for smugglers."

Miguel snorted in derision. "Yes, so they can steal their goods. It keeps the army in beef and horses. We would do better to allow free trade and force the real thieves—the ones running things in Mexico City—to earn an honest living."

Frederick beamed. "I'm real happy to hear that, because. . . .

Katherine interrupted him. "What was called trading in Louisiana is smuggling here," she said, shooting a frown of warning in Frederick's direction. *Miguel might not consider himself a gachupín, but he's a Royalist soldier.*

"We came to ranch, Frederick. I think you'll make a fine *ganadero*—a stockman."

The family laughed at Katherine's play on words, but Miguel looked confused.

"Miguelito, let me explain," Henry said when the laughter died down. "In English our name is Stockman, and the Spanish word for stockman—one who takes care of animals—is *ganadero*. Therefore, Papa will be *Ganadero* Stockman. Stockman Stockman."

Miguel grinned in delight. "Ah *si*, *Ganadero Estocoman*. Yes, it is very amusing,"

"Now, I say we get some sleep. We have a long day's ride tomorrow," Katherine said as she rose and dusted off the back of her skirt. "I'm really looking forward to seeing our new place. By the way, Frederick, what's it called?"

"Atascosito."

"That's a beautiful name. What does it mean?"

"Little Boggy," David chirped, and was rewarded with a stricken look from Katherine and another cuff from his Pa.

CHAPTER

6

ATASCOSITO 1808

Frederick was gone. Again.

Katherine's hopes that her adventuresome spouse would settle into ranching had vanished, along with Frederick, only weeks after moving to Atascosito. And worse, during the past year he had expanded, rather than reduced, his trading route.

I should have known better, she told herself, *once a trader, always a trader.*

Blowing some bothersome strands of hair from her face, she set her shoulders, viciously snapped a peapod in half, and pushed the bright green peas out with her thumb.

No sense feeling sorry for myself. After all, I have a somewhat sound roof overhead, healthy children, plenty to feed them and, for the moment, no screaming war parties threatening to swoop down on us.

Holding the bowlful of peas in one hand, she used the other to launch herself from a pine and rawhide chair and waddled across the room. A few of the peas escaped, bouncing in all directions across the hewn cedar floor. She looked down at them in exasperation. *They'll just have to stay there until one of the children comes.* She picked up her thoughts instead.

In truth, their life at Atascosito was downright bliss in comparison with some of the Hell-on-earth places before. Their ranch boasted a large herd of horses and cattle and even a few milk goats. As Padre Solano had predicted, her garden was bountiful and had practically erupted overnight with produce from the seeds she'd brought from New Orleans. The rich soil along the Trinity River was a gardener's godsend, the herds of wild mustangs and cattle a treasure trove for ranchers.

So what more could a woman want?

She stirred the bean pot, banged the wooden spoon harder than necessary on its iron rim, and growled, "A woman could want a husband. One who stayed around to help with the ranch and the birth of his own children, that's what."

"Mama did you call me?" Maggie asked as she ran into the kitchen.

"No, honey, I was talking to myself. Round up those peas I dropped, Baby."

"All right, Mama. Hey, David said Señor Pedro is a *con-tra ban-der-o*. What's that?"

"David would do well to mind his own business, and you would do well to not repeat everything you hear, young lady. Gossip is the Devil's friend. Señor Pedro is our friend and a rancher. That's all you *or* David need to know. Now, be a good girl and get me some onions from the shed."

Katherine was rolling biscuits when Henry, bone-tired weary and covered with red dust, stomped into the kitchen. In his vaquero garb, he looked a decade past sixteen.

A wave of sympathy for her son, tinged with anger towards his father, surged through Katherine. With Frederick and George off 'on business,' the bulk of the dangerous and all-consuming ranching duties fell to Henry. He loved the work and strived hard to keep up with the demands on him, but it was a lot for a boy his age.

Even with help from the few local soldiers, it was an almost impossible task for Henry to protect the Stockman herd from Indians. The cattle were prone to stampede at any small provocation. And an animal separated from his herd was easy pickings.

Adding to the workload, the Spaniards required a great deal of paperwork. In a land with little paper. The Governor of Texas demanded detailed records for each of His Majesty's horses and cows rounded up and branded with the Ganado Stockman *fierro y marca* (brand):

Katherine bestowed a mother's approving smile upon her dusty son. "Enrique, in the two years since we came here I swear you've grown a full head taller. Tall and handsome, just like your ole Pa. Thank the Lord you didn't get his disinclination towards ranch work."

Henry returned her smile, and she added, "You look all grown up, boy. Next thing I know you'll be looking for a wife and a place of your own."

As she said this, a feeling of uncharacteristic despair overtook Katherine. *I'm thirty-seven, with grown sons, and expecting a baby. I should be expecting grandbabies.*

"Mama, you look awful tired. Why don't you let me finish up supper and you go sit down. David'll help me out when he gets done fishin'. I sure hope he got plenty of catfish today, 'cause I'm hungry enough to eat one of them mustangs if they wasn't so danged ornery and stringy," Henry said, removing his grimy hat. "Fried mustang. Yum."

Henry's antics, as usual, lifted Katherine's spirits and she giggled. "I'll be all right, son. But could you have a word with David for me? He listens to you. That boy's been talking about things he shouldn't. . .told your sister that Pedro Procela is a smuggler."

"Well, heck, Mama, he is. So's everybody else in Texas. If they was to kick every smuggler out of the territory wouldn't *be* no Texas. Pa always says that as long as those Spaniards running things in Mexico City interfere with free enterprise he'll be able to keep us in beans."

Henry moved around the room tossing spoons and plates onto the table as he talked.

"Pa says God invented the Louisiana border to reward the traders, and that as long as those government types make sure everything coming here from Mexico costs ten times what it should, traders'll make the most of it. Even if we wanted to play by the *gachupín* rules, we Texicans don't have any money to pay the bastards with."

"Language, son. Your father had best be careful talking about what God put on this earth. They aren't on real good terms as far as I know."

Henry laughed, glad to see his mother regain her sense of humor.

"And son, be real careful what you say about the officials, because you just never know when a soldier might overhear. A few speak pretty good English and I suspect they understand a lot more than they let on. I know many of them are your friends, but never forget they're in the Royal Army."

"Yes, Mama," Henry said softly. "But a lot of soldiers don't give a hoot about Spain. I mean, it ain't as if the Royal Army treated 'em like human bein's or nothin'. Whoever heard of an army where the soldiers have to pay their officers for the food they eat? Hell, most of 'em would starve to death if it wasn't for handouts from us settlers. And you know and they know that those handouts didn't get to Texas through Mexico—they were brought here from the United States. And that's smugglin'."

"You've made your point, Enrique, but you just hold your water when it comes to talking about it outside of this house. Or even in it. We have too much to lose. It's bad enough that your father. . .oh, never mind. Go whistle up David, it's getting late."

David had been a busy boy and, like most twelve-year-olds, his curiosity and energy knew no bounds, and his judgment was sometimes lacking.

He loved to fish, and his uncanny skill for smelling them out had led him to a new backwater where he hoped the big ones lurked under marshy banks. He was seldom wrong.

Bits of chicken skin, a fat worm or a freshwater clam generally landed a cat or a bass, and fish guts in a slatted trap yielded crawfish. He loved the crawdads best of all. His mouth watered when he thought of the stews and pies his Mama made with the little critters.

Hearing Henry's whistle, David reluctantly picked up his pole and a bouquet of wild irises he'd picked for Katherine's medicine chest. The Indians said the roots were good for toothaches, and besides that, she liked flowers.

He loped downstream towards the catfish he'd strung to a submerged log in three feet of murky water. *If I hurry,* David thought as he trotted along the path, *I can set a crawdad trap with fish guts before supper. But first, I've gotta skin them cats.*

David was not the only one thinking about catfish.

Floating just below the surface in the murky water, submerged except for his big, unblinking, yellow eyes, a huge bull alligator watched the boy run towards him. The reptile was hungry, but not hungry enough to tackle a half-grown boy. His mind was on catfish and he could see them break the surface of the water occasionally, trying to free themselves from David's gill twine.

David splashed into the water, reached in and grabbed the string, causing the catfish to struggle frantically and futilely to escape.

Excited by the thrashing fish, the alligator launched eighteen feet of pure muscle towards his prey. His powerful jaws, filled with filthy, jagged teeth, overshot the fish and snapped shut, with tons of pressure, on David's arm. The immense creature immediately went into a death spin designed to disorient and drown his victim.

The force of the attack would have knocked the boy clear out onto the bank had the beast not had him by the arm.

David, rendered almost unconscious by the blow, gasped for air. Though dazed, he was still fully aware of what had happened. And what had him.

Desperate to know what to do, he remembered his father's story about the alligator and the boot. But there was no boot. *If I don't get my arm loose from that gator, he's gonna drown me. What would Pa do now?*

Time seemed to go into slow motion. Recalling what the Indian children had told him about alligators, David took a deep breath, gathered his courage, and willed his body to go limp. The reptile, sensing victory, stopped spinning and began to tow his dinner towards deeper water.

David knew he'd only have one chance. He let the alligator drag him freely for a few feet, until he felt a submerged log under him. Summoning the last of his strength, the boy planted his feet against the log and, with gargantuan effort, yanked his body weight away from the animal. And was free.

The alligator, satisfied for the moment, silently swam away with most of David's lower arm clamped in his smiling jaws.

"Henry, something's wrong. David should be here by now. Let's go look for him, right now, while we've still got some light."

"Mama, let me go. You don't need to be wanderin' around out there in your condition. I'll go find him and be back before you know it. Come on Furface, let's go get David."

Henry's dog looked up expectantly and wagged his tail when he heard his name.

Katherine knew Henry was right. She was in no shape to go on a search. She waited one frantic hour, but when Henry didn't return by dark, she sent Peter to fetch soldiers.

Carrying torches, a small search party combed the woods along the riverbank until ten, when, after several close calls with dangerous animals and quicksand, they called off the search until dawn.

Furface found David near the backwater that night and stood by him. The alligator glided back around midnight but, warned off by the dog's warning growls, took the catfish and left. And when Henry resumed his search just before first light, Furface's barks guided him to his little brother's cold body.

Katherine knew David was dead even before Henry returned that morning. Throughout the long night the mysterious, spiritual connection many mothers have with their children had ebbed with her son's life. Tearless and pale, she stood by his grave holding what was left of a wilted bouquet of wild irises.

After a few words spoken by Henry, she bent and added the flowers to the seashells and red dirt covering her boy's body. When she tried to straighten, agony surged through her, knocking her to her knees. A scream of pain and grief she recognized as her own echoed though the pines.

"Mama!" Henry yelled, rushing forward and picking her up.

Katherine, her face ashen, groaned, "Enrique, you'd better get me into the house. Fast."

Stunned mourners barely had time to help Henry carry his mother to the house before Joseph Anthony Stockman, who would be known as José Antonio, made his Texas debut.

The moment Katherine laid eyes on her new baby she fell in love, and that love would be a special bond between them as long as they lived.

She had loved all of her children at first sight, but this time, perhaps because of the loss of David, her protective instincts bordered on obsessive. The crib she had carefully prepared lay empty as she guarded her new son in her bed.

Henry also felt a special link to José Antonio. The baby could not replace David, but it almost seemed José's early arrival was, well, wondrous. *Maybe*, he thought, *this was God's way of sayin' I shouldn't be angry with Him for taking David. I'll try.*

Katherine, on the other hand, was very angry, but not with her God. *No, it isn't Him I'm angry with. When Frederick finally gets home, there's gonna be some changes around here.*

CHAPTER

7

"Pa, I can't hardly believe he's gone," George said as they stood by David's shell-covered grave near the path from Trinidad. They had stopped to pay their respects before going on to the ranch house.

"I know they told us in Trinidad that he was dead, but it seems like we could walk down to the river right now and find him fishing."

Frederick straightened the wooden cross and looked towards the river, then at the cabin. Smoke curling from the chimney was the only sign of life.

"I know, son. It ain't fair. With all the evil sons-a-bitches running loose in Texas, why'd this happen to our David?" Frederick handed his horse over to George and turned from the grave to find and comfort his wife.

Katherine heard Frederick attempting to scrape mud from his boots before coming into the house, and waited for him by her cook table. Joseph Anthony, three weeks old, slept in a cradle next to the fireplace.

Hat in hand, Frederick strode in, then stopped and held his arms wide.

"Red, I'm sorry as hell about David. He sure didn't deserve this. George and I'll leave early tomorrow morning to hunt down that goddamned gator."

Katherine, instead of rushing into her husband's arms for comfort, stood her ground. She picked up her baby and glared at him.

Dropping his arms and taking a hesitant step forward, a confused Frederick asked, "Uh, what did you name that little critter?"

"His name is Joseph Anthony, after the saints. I thought of naming him David, but it didn't seem quite right. And Frederick, if you leave this ranch again I swear to God I'll never speak to you again as long as I live."

Frederick, who had started forward to see the baby, stopped in his tracks and stared, dumbstruck, at the strange woman who had just screeched at him.

"What did you say?"

Katherine, flushed and trembling with emotion yelled, "You heard me, Frederick Stockman. I've spent most of the last twenty-some-odd years waiting for you to come home. While I waited, I birthed babies, fought Indians, and hid out like a rabbit gone to ground more times than I can recall. I've lain awake too many nights trembling with fear. I won't do it anymore. You only come home long enough to make another baby and take off again. Well, no more."

Never, in all their years of marriage, had Katherine raised her voice at him in anger and he was stunned by the force of her fury. *What on earth was going on here?*

"What do you mean, *no more?*" he asked, barely controlling his own building temper. When Frederick was angry his voice became very low, his speech exacting. "Just what do you think you would do without me? Do you think I'm off at the horse races on these trips? I haven't told you all I do because I don't want you to worry, but it ain't no promenade in the damned plaza. Me and George deal with men who'd just as soon slit our throats and steal our goods as to look at us. We risk goin' to prison. And all," Frederick slammed his hand loudly on the table, "so I can put food here."

The baby flinched, startled by the loud rap on the table, but Katherine didn't even blink.

"Katrin, I won't have some woman telling me what to do. Even you. What's gotten into you? Now, I'm real sorry our David's gone, but me bein' here wouldn'ta saved him from that gator."

Katherine didn't back down. "No, maybe not. But at least you would be here when I need you. When we came to Texas, it was to ranch. That's why they gave us a passport. Your so-called 'trade' business, which is nothing more than smuggling, endangers us every time you go to Nacogdoches or God-only-knows where else. If we lose our passport, what will we do then? I'm sick and tired of living alone, in fear. If you leave here again, just don't bother coming back, you, you. . .*outlaw!*"

Frederick stared incredulously at his furious wife, then said quietly, "This *outlaw* is your husband, and you need me, Red."

Katherine shook her head violently.

"No, I don't. Henry and I can run this place just fine by ourselves. We've *been* doing it. And with no help from you. If you want to keep on traveling, you go ahead. At least we won't have to worry about *when* or *if* you decide to grace us with your presence."

"You aren't the girl I married anymore, Red."

"Child, Frederick. I was a child. And you're right; I'm a woman who won't be treated like a child. Now you just make up your mind if you're man enough to live with a woman, dammit."

The children, drawn to the house by their mother's loud voice, grew round-eyed and afraid when they heard her cuss.

Henry and George, realizing the situation was turning serious, shooed the children to the barn until the verbal storm blew over. They had heard plenty of loudly contested disagreements in their lives, but never between Ma and Pa.

Children and chickens scattered from Frederick's path as he stormed angrily into the barn.

"Saddle my horse, George, I'll be leavin' now. And most likely won't be comin' back. Your Ma has lost her damned mind and I won't be sticking around to have some loco woman scream at me."

"Pa, I'm sure she's just upset, what with losing David and having the baby 'n all. She'll be better tomorrow. Please don't leave. Sleep out here tonight and in the morning things'll be a danged sight better," Henry pleaded. He wasn't at all sure he was right, what with his Mama so lathered up.

"Please, oh please, don't leave, Papa," wailed Margaret. Her five-year-old mind could not quite grasp what was happening, but she *did* know her Papa had just gotten home and now everybody was yelling and Papa was leaving. And even before she had a chance to ask him what he'd brought her.

Margaret's tears drained Frederick's anger. He scooped her up, hugging her tightly. Her tiny body shook with sobs as she wrapped her chubby arms around his neck and clung to him.

"There there, little one. All right, I won't leave today, I promise. Tell you what, you go tell your Ma I'm sorry, and if she'll let me back in the house I could use a good meal."

Margaret, beaming through tears, took off for the house with her good news. She found Katherine, also teary-eyed, sitting at the table.

"Mama, please don't cry. Papa wants to come in. He says he's hungry. And sorry."

Damned sorry, Katherine thought. Her private joke made her smile and, wiping her eyes, she leaned down to hug her tiny peacemaker.

"You go tell Papa you talked me into it."

Supper, usually a boisterous gathering, was an abnormally subdued affair. The children sat straight in their chairs, no elbows on the table, and used their Sunday dinner manners, saying "please" and "thank you." They didn't even spit on their biscuits so the others wouldn't steal them.

Their uncommon behavior was not lost on Katherine and she felt a pang of guilt.

Frederick didn't eat much. He hadn't had time to adjust to the empty chair and place at the table Katherine continued to set for David. With foreboding awareness of impending further loss, his eyes moved around the table, studying his surviving offspring. Henry and little Maggie favored their mother, even down to the red hair and freckles, while George and John were dark, like himself. Peter, blonde, as David had been, seemed to have been given a look-alike in Joseph Anthony, but it was too soon to tell. Frederick feared he might not be around to find out unless Katherine came to her senses.

After supper Katherine washed the dishes and put the children to bed while Frederick secured the barn. George and Henry decided to do a little night hunting in case the fireworks started again, so Katherine was alone when her husband returned.

Sitting in front of the fireplace in her long white sleeping gown, her copper hair glowing in the firelight, Frederick thought she looked like the thirteen-year-old girl he had married so many years ago.

Until she turned to look at him.

In the set of her shoulders Frederick saw uncompromising hardness, and knew Katherine would stick by her ultimatum. He sat down facing her and said, in a soft voice, “Katrin, I am an old man—nearly sixty. All my life I've tried to live and let live. Maybe that's a fault of mine. If I've let you down, I didn't do it on purpose. You've gone and thrown me for a fall here. I don't know for sure what to do about it. But I do know I can't just up and change overnight. Rightly or wrongly, I have my pride. It ain't my nature to let someone tell me what to do.”

He rose, and added, “I'll sleep in the barn tonight and be gone in the morning. George'll stay. He knows who my partners are, so when you need money he can find me. I don't think the children should suffer from lack of money because their Ma's got a burr under her saddle.”

Katherine stared steadfastly into the fire.

Frederick walked out the door, hesitating in the dog-run. When Katherine said nothing to stop him, he shut the door and continued to the barn.

Katherine rocked and cried for a few minutes, then went to bed. She had a lot to do tomorrow.

CHAPTER 8

"I've got him! Hurry up, get him tied—he's a lively little stinker!" Katherine bellowed, just a little louder than the calf. She knelt with both knees on a terrified calf's front legs while Henry expertly bound the animal's flailing back legs together just above the hooves. They held on while George did the branding.

Katherine averted her eyes, lifting her arm to wipe dust and sweat from her forehead onto her filthy shirtsleeve. The branding was over in seconds, leaving the stench of seared fur and flesh, and echoes of the calf's pitiful bawls.

Katherine's compassion for the frightened animals was overridden by practicality: she needed her brand or earmark on every hoofed critter they could round up if her ranch was to survive.

The freely roaming wild cattle—called mavericks or *cimarrónes*—of East Texas bore little resemblance, in physique or temperament, to the British-origin stock Katherine's family had raised on the East Coast of the United States.

In Texas, the most prized—and most dangerous— were called "blacks." They traced their ancestry straight back to Spanish bullrings. The long horned "browns"—freckled or light-brown in color, some with donkey-like crosses on their backs—were smaller, but no less dangerous to round up.

Katherine liked to say that her *cimarrónes* gave "mean" a whole new meaning. These formidable breeds had survived more than two centuries in hostile territory by forming a circle or wedge and counterattacking any bears, wolves, mountain lions, men—or women—that threatened them.

During the year following Frederick's huffy departure, Katherine had adopted a bullheadedness of her own. Backbreaking work and smart herd management earned Ganado Stockman the grudging respect of the authorities in San Antonio de Béjar.

The success of the ranch bested the naysayers—those Spaniards in government who harbored nothing but disdain and distrust for non-Hispanic settlers. Padre Solano had initially opened a few doors in the Governor's Palace, but the priest had returned to Spain, and Katherine was determined to hold the Crown's high esteem without him.

The day Frederick left, his pride smarting from Katherine's hissy fit, George and Henry had returned from their hunting trip with a huge alligator skin. Katherine refused to look at it and no one in the family dared discuss it.

Nor did they discuss Frederick's absence for several days. George was the first to mention his father.

"Mama, Pa left us a sack of silver. What do you want me to do with it?" He poured the coins onto the kitchen table. "It's a smart sum."

Katherine almost swooned with relief. "So I see. Well, I'm sure not too proud to use it. First, we need to hire a Mexican couple.

I'll need the woman to help cook and watch the little ones while I learn the stock-raising business."

"Ma, why don't you just let me buy a couple of slaves to help me'n Henry with the ranch, and you can take care of the house," George implored. "There ain't no use in you having to do a man's work."

"George, you know how I feel about slaves—it isn't Christian to own another human being. I know your father didn't... doesn't...feel the same, and has done some slave trading, as well as horse-trading. He probably even has one or two of those unfortunate souls stashed away somewhere."

Seeing a blush rise from George's collar and rapidly reach his cheeks confirmed Katherine's long-held suspicions as to Frederick's slaver status.

"It's all right, son, I don't hold you at fault. Your Pa chose not to teach you the difference between right and wrong. But now you'll listen to me. We won't have slaves on this ranch as long as I draw a breath of fresh Texas air.

"And as far as me doing 'man's work,' I'd just like to know what makes men so damned special? What is it you and your father can do that I can't?" Katherine asked with mock indignity, then added, "Except maybe make babies. And pee standing straight."

"Aw Ma, I didn't mean it that way. I. . .we just don't think you ought'a be ridin' in all that dust and spending time around a bunch'a ole smelly cattle, mustangs, and vaqueros. Me and Henry can attend to that part. I didn't mean you *couldn't* do it, just maybe you *ought'n* to."

"And what do you have to say, young man?" Katherine asked, turning her attention to a silent Henry, who had apparently found something of great interest near his boot.

"Well, Mama," Henry drawled, his head down, "George and me just think roundups might be a little dangerous, what with you being a woman'n all. And some vaqueros might get the wrong idea, even if you are old."

Katherine burst out laughing and the boys exchanged uneasy looks.

"So kind of you to notice," she told them. "And boys, I appreciate your concern, but as head of this ranch, old woman or no, I need to learn the details of our business. I don't plan to spend all my time out on the range, but I need to know what's necessary to keep the place going. Now let's go rope something."

Rope they did. And brand. And pull calves.

Pulling a calf from a wild cow in labor was no easy task, but when a heifer was in trouble trying to calve, they had to help her if the animal and her offspring were to survive. After corralling the distressed cow, Katherine undertook the decidedly unpleasant and dangerous task of reaching up into the cow as far as she could to tie ropes around the unborn calf's legs. The boys then took a wrap on a post and gently pulled until the calf plopped free.

Henry and George grudgingly admitted their mother had a way with the cows, and she didn't seem to mind this job considered distasteful by the vaqueros.

On the other hand, Katherine abhorred branding the stock, especially the horses, and pooh-poohed the widely held belief that they felt little pain. But she recognized the necessity.

Unmarked animals, even though on Stockman land, could be rounded up by soldiers and claimed as the property of His Majesty. Without fences, Katherine's livestock roamed freely, subject to Indian, Mexican and Anglo rustling. When the army recovered stolen animals, her brand gave Katherine some chance to get them back. Unless the soldiers needed a meal or a mount.

George traveled to Nacogdoches every other month for supplies, and although Katherine never asked whether he saw Frederick, she suspected he did; George always returned with little treats for the children and small presents for her, reminiscent of Frederick's gift-bearing reappearances.

Some days her grief for David was almost overwhelming—a pain that hit her like a physical blow and left her in deep despair. When that happened, she wondered how Frederick was coping; he had, after all, lost his entire family. Was it as hard for him?

And some nights after supper, when the household was quiet and she lay in bed alone, she wistfully listened for the sound of an approaching horse.

CHAPTER 9

The lone rider, hidden behind a stand of pines near the barn, watched the lanterns go out one by one.

He had watched all day.

The Stockman men and their Mexican cowhand rode away mid-morning, and he had followed until satisfied they didn't intend to return, then he doubled back.

He waited throughout an almost unbearable afternoon. First, tantalizing kitchen smells wafted his way, torturing his empty stomach, then a frigid wind blew in. Just before sunset the clatter of dishes from the house bespoke a table piled high with hot food he could practically taste.

Dishes were washed, children protested bedtime, and the Mexican woman left for her own cabin. Finally, fires banked and lanterns out, all was quiet.

He was free to proceed.

Dismounting, he tied his horse to a tree branch, crept to the barn and opened the creaking door a few inches. Warm air bearing the aroma of fresh hay pulled him inside a little too quickly. The door squeaked and a chicken squawked. He froze.

When the hen settled down he tiptoed in—feeling his way cross the dark barn—to a pile of straw, where he collapsed. Before he drifted off he thought, *When the moon has set, I will make my way to the house for food and money.*

Katherine slept fitfully, awakened several times by whistling wind and groaning trees. During the late morning heat, dark blue-black clouds gathered on the horizon, then the breeze freshened to announce the onset of a Texas blue norther.

She and Lupe had piled extra blankets on the beds, certain they would be appreciated before the night was out. They were right.

The norther hit with a gust of chilly air that sent the temperature plummeting more than forty degrees in as many minutes. By midnight the clouds had scudded through, whipped out of existence by furious wind, which, as if sated by conquest, lulled. A three-quarters moon emerged in the frigid night sky, bringing brightness, but no warmth.

Lying under a pile of quilts, Katherine heard a chicken squawk. She drowsily hoped a snake hadn't gotten into the roost, or the stupid hens weren't smothering each other to death trying to keep warm. Burrowing further under the heavy blankets, her mind wandered to what she should do the next day.

Me and Lupe'll unpack and air the buffalo skins. If this is the beginning of storm season, we'll need 'em. And I'll get the children to pick any fruit or vegetables ready to can, just in case we get an early frost.

Her thoughts turned to George and Henry, out in this weather, and she prayed they found shelter and were not sleeping in the open. Turning over to go back to sleep, she heard the chickens again.

"Dammit! I don't need this tonight," she groused, forcing herself from her nice warm bed.

Her bare feet burned when they hit the icy wooden floor of her unheated bedroom. Grabbing an armload of clothes, she sprinted for the great room, where a banked fire afforded some warmth. There, she quickly slipped on two pairs of heavy woolen socks, then went into Henry's room off the kitchen for a pair of his pants. She hesitated, shimmied into a second pair, and then added two heavy shirts, a doeskin jacket and boots.

At the porch door she jammed a hat over her ears for extra warmth, and grabbed a loaded gun from its rack.

If that's a snake or a coon in the barn trying for a chicken dinner, I'll blow him into Louisiana. I hope.

Reaching for a lantern, she decided against it. There was one in the barn, and the moonlit yard was bright enough for her to see her way. She considered getting Lupe to accompany her, but shrugged off the thought. *No need for both of us to freeze our butts off.*

By the time Katherine reached the barn door her teeth were chattering. She paused outside to listen. Hearing nothing, she pulled the heavy wooden door open a few inches, and slipped inside. *If there's a varmint in here, those ole squeaky hinges'll scare it off. Unless it's deaf. Do snakes have ears?*

All was quiet, except for a little contented clucking. Katherine breathed a sigh of relief, turned to leave, and was roughly grabbed from behind. Her attacker covered her mouth with one gloved hand, partially pinning her arms with his other arm.

Although startled, Katherine reacted on instinct. She swung the musket's heavy stock into his shinbone, just above his boot top. Yelping, the man let go long enough for Katherine to wiggle loose, but—as she dashed for the door—she tripped over a pile of buckets and fell heavily onto the hard earthen floor.

A cacophony of sounds erupted in the barn. Chickens squawked, horses whinnied and kicked at stall boards, and goats bleated. But Katherine no longer worried about her stock. She was afraid for her life.

Struggling to her feet, she lunged for the door and grabbed the edge, only to be seized again. This time she lost the gun. She was taking a deep breath, trying to calm her thoughts for one more escape attempt when the man spoke.

"*Señor, por favor,* I mean you no harm. Please, I only needed a place to sleep. I swear before *Jesús y María,* I am telling the truth. I am not a *bandito.* Take me to Señora Estocoman—she knows me. *Por favor,* please, stop fighting."

Katherine went limp.

"Then let me go."

The man released her, stepped away, and drew his pistol.

"Please, light the lantern and do not make fast moves," he said. "I am not an evil man, but I am a desperate one. I will defend myself, if necessary."

The normally comforting glow of the lard lamp did little to stop Katherine's heart from trying to escape her chest. She turned to face her tormentor and gasped as she found herself looking into the cornflower blue eyes of Miguel Gonzales, the young soldier who had escorted them from Orcoquisac.

"Miguel? You just about scared the devil out of me. Shame on you!" she fumed and slapped his sleeve.

Miguel was equally astounded. "*Señora* Estocoman, is it you? The first time I saw you, you had black teeth and were an old woman. Now you are dressed as a man. Forgive me. I had no idea. . . ."

"Oh, shut up and let's go to the house. You must be freezing out here. And probably hungry. Come on, let's get warm and maybe, just maybe, I'll feed you. Then I think I'll shoot you." Katherine took his hand to pull him towards the door, but he balked.

"I cannot, Doña Katrina. It's too dangerous—for both of us. You cannot be seen with me, and I simply cannot be seen. The Mexican woman—do you think she still sleeps?"

"Yes, Miguel, evidently she sleeps very well. We made enough noise out here to wake the dead. And even if she did wake up, she won't hurt you. She's only a little grandmother for God's sake. Come on."

"If you say so. I am very hungry. I promise I will not stay long, as I do not wish to endanger you. That is why I watched and waited until Jorge and Enrique left. I will explain."

"Explain over food. Let's go," Katherine ordered through chattering teeth.

While wolfing down corn bread, beans, and stewed beef, Miguel told Katherine of his plight. "I could stay no longer in the army of Spain, for I believe the Spaniards— even though I am one—are enemies of Mexico. They have no right to be in Texas or Mexico. There must be no New Spain. My fellow compatriots and I will drive them back to *Europa* where they belong."

He gulped heavily sweetened coffee and continued.

"For three centuries the *gachupín* elitists have lived in luxury, claiming God-sanctioned right to rule. Mexicans starve and are held in bondage—slavery."

His eyes glowed from both firelight and revolutionary fervor. For an hour he recounted atrocities perpetrated on the Mexican people by the hated Royalist Army, then, exhausted by his own tirade, he suddenly remembered David.

"Oh, please forgive me. I have not expressed my sadness over the death of your son. When I heard, I prayed for his soul. David was a good boy."

Katherine, fatigued by his fervor, their earlier wrestling match, and lack of sleep, said softly, "Thank you Miguelito, I miss him. David thought of you like a brother. . .said he wanted to be a soldier like you. But now you've deserted the army and if they find you, they'll hang you. Where are you going and what'll you do? Can we help?"

"Doña Katrina, if you could give me food and lend me a small amount of money, I will be gone by dawn. I cannot tell you where I am going, for this knowledge would be dangerous to you. I will only say it is not in Texas."

"Of course I'll help you, Miguel. I don't have very much money, but I can let you have a little. Señor Stockman doesn't live here any longer, and I'm too tired to explain why, but it means that we have fewer *pesos fuertes* now. Stay one more day and get some rest. George and Henry will be back tomorrow afternoon and they know where Frederick lives. That ole man knows just about everybody in the territory. He'll help you."

Miguel opened his mouth to protest, but was silenced when a miniature Katherine tottered into the room, rubbing sleepy eyes and dragging a blanket.

Margaret made a beeline for Miguel, climbed into his lap, smiled, yawned, and fell asleep. The adults laughed and Katherine shook her head.

"I guess that settles it, Miguelito. You've got to stay. If Miss Maggie wakes in the morning to find you gone, there'll be hell to pay. Put your horse in the barn and get some sleep. You'll be safe for tonight."

She gathered some blankets from a trunk, then frowned. "Is your horse branded?"

"*Sí, señora.* Unfortunately, my horse bears the brand of the mission at San Antonio de Béjar. I am a horse thief as well as a deserter."

"You're a mess, that's what you are. All right, hide your saddle and gear in the barn and turn that horse loose. Be sure to give him a good hard whack on the ass so he knows he's not welcome. We can't take a chance on having him found anywhere near here. We'll give you a new mount."

She held out her arms. "Hand over Maggie and get moving, it's almost dawn. You can sleep in there," she said, pointing to the quilt partitioning off Henry's "room."

Henry, George and Miguel had a joyful, albeit potentially dangerous, reunion when the Stockman boys returned the next day. The young men talked of the old days at Orcoquisac, their first meeting, and the padre.

Little Maggie dogged Miguel's every move, turning adoring green eyes and all her charm on him.

After supper, when Miguel said his good-byes to Katherine and the children, the little girl cried and clung to him until he promised to return soon. And to bring her a gift when he did so. He said he would, but even so, Katherine had a hard time comforting her seven-year-old.

"Mama," Maggie whimpered, "when I grow up, I want to marry Miguel."

"Sweetheart, Miguel is a grown man, almost George's age, but I guess it's possible that he'll wait for you. After all, your father was. . .is. . .twenty-two years older than me. Don't cry, honey, you'll see Miguel again soon, I'm sure," Katherine soothed, thinking, *But I hope not too soon.*

George, Henry and Juan followed Miguel to the barn, where he saddled one of Henry's tamed, but unbranded, mustangs.

"So, Miguelito," Henry said, "tell us what's really going on. Where are you headed now?"

The deserter glanced nervously in Juan's direction, but Henry told him, "You don't have to worry none about old Juanito here, Miguel. He ain't got much use for the King, or his army—'bout like the rest of us Texicans around here."

Miguel cinched his saddle, grateful that Henry had broken the horse. Some mustangs required breaking anew every day, but not when Henry did the breaking.

"Many Mexican rebels, *norteamericanos,* and Royalist Army deserters are gathering in the Neutral Zone and think the time is near to liberate Mexico and Texas. When we are ready, we will attack. Be warned, my friends, you will be caught in the middle and have to choose sides. Now, I must go, for there is a certain *Capitán* de la Garza who is eager to stretch my neck."

He swung into the saddle. "I will see your father and return your horse to him. Adios, my brothers."

Juan was the first to speak after Miguel disappeared into the night.

"Señores, this is very bad. Spain has a large army and they are merciless to traitors."

George frowned. "It don't sound good, does it? Don't say anything to your wife, Juan. Lupe and Ma are thicker'n them blue flowers in spring and there's no sense in us getting those two all upset.

"Hellfire, someone's always coming into Texas with bright ideas about making it a State of the Union or a free country, but all's happens is a bunch of folks gets killed and nothing ever comes of it. Henry, don't you go getting all hotheaded over this neither. It ain't our concern—yet."

Juan walked to his cabin, frowning and mumbling, and the Stockmans returned to the main house.

"Miguel get on down the trail?" Katherine asked when her sons entered the kitchen.

They nodded.

"Did he say where he was going? He wouldn't tell me. I hope he'll be safe, because he's a good boy. Lord, I hate to see him all alone like this."

"Hell, Mama, he won't be alone," Henry said, drawing a warning look from George.

"What do you mean?" Katherine asked.

"He don't mean nothin', Ma. Sometimes he jest talks to hear his head rattle," George replied as he stretched, yawned, and tried to look nonchalant.

"Honestly, George, sometimes I think you think I'm simple or something. Now *talk*, Henry Stockman."

The boys knew that tone of voice, and surrendered. Between the two of them they told her what she wanted to know, and as they did Katherine felt a chill of unease. She had never heard of anything good coming from the notorious strip of land between Texas and Louisiana called Neutral Ground, or The Zone.

Under neither Spanish nor American jurisdiction, the Zone was a lawless hotbed of hotheads, ruffians, freebooters, thieves and murderers. The no-man's-land, initially set up to ease tension along the border, had become a haven for smugglers. And now revolutionaries. That this den of scoundrels was getting themselves organized to invade Texas was most alarming.

Katherine sat quietly for a few minutes the said, "George, I want you to go to Nacogdoches to see your Pa. Give Miguel time to go ahead, because I don't want you riding with him. I need to know how dangerous the situation really is, and Frederick will know if it's all talk. You can leave after breakfast tomorrow. Now let's get some sleep."

The next morning, however, Katherine looked like she hadn't gotten much rest. And neither had Lupe. None of the men, it seemed, held their tongues in the face of female interrogation.

When George came to breakfast, he was not dressed to ride. Unwilling to discuss her concerns in front of the younger children, Katherine said nothing. George ate with little of his usual enthusiasm, then walked out on to the porch, knowing his mother would follow.

"George, why aren't you ready to go to Nacogdoches? I need you to talk with your father about what's happening with these invasionists."

George, shuffled his feet, refusing to look his mother in the eye. Katherine put her hand to his cheek and asked softly, "Son, what is it?"

"Ma, Pa ain't *in* Nacogdoches," he blurted. "He's in Villa Trinidad de Salcedo."

Katherine, surprised, huffed, "Why, what on earth is he doing there?"

"I can't tell you, 'cause I promised I wouldn't. I can't say no more, Ma, and don't try to make me. You gotta come with me and find out for yourself." George stubbornly set his jaw and Katherine knew she would get no more information.

"George, it's at least a four-day ride to Villa Trinidad. I would be gone too long. . .the children. . .the ranch. . .I just can't. . . ." Katherine looked ready to cry.

"You've got to, Ma. I can't say why, but you just got to. Juan, Henry and Lupe'll watch things around here. Please, Ma?" George pleaded.

Katherine, visibly upset, mumbled, "I'll have to think about it."

Katherine walked to her thinking spot near a bubbling spring and sat on a favorite rock to ponder. The norther had passed, leaving warm weather in its path, so she pulled off her boots and weighed the pros and cons of a trip north while wiggling her toes in cool grass.

An hour later she stood up, brushed aside her reluctance along with the leaves on her skirt, and began looking forward to the prospect of the journey.

Trinidad village, founded three years before, had a population of nearly one hundred people. After over three years in the wilderness, Katherine felt a surge of excitement. *There's a store. An honest-to-goodness mercantile. The smell of new goods! Not that I can afford to buy anything, but won't it be fun to look?*

Back at the house she announced her trip to the family, then went to dig in her trunk. Finding her best dress, a green cotton, she thought, *What the hell*, and threw it into her satchel.

She found herself looking forward to seeing Frederick. Surprised, she sniggered and whispered to herself, "Even though, in all probability, the old reprobate is a guest of His Majesty's in the hoosegow at Villa Trinidad."

CHAPTER 10

Katherine lowered her saddle to the ground, untied then unrolled her blanket, flopped down, and fell instantly asleep. When she woke at dawn—their third morning on the trail—the *escolta* was almost ready to ride. She groaned.

Just hours before she and George departed from Atascosito to find Frederick, the local military commandant decided he preferred that Señora Estocoman travel with a military escort—an army patrol heading north towards Trinidad. Since the Stockmans couldn't travel without the commandant's approval, there was nothing to do but join the fast-moving detachment.

Katherine sprang to her feet and began gathering her belongings.

"George," she scolded, "why didn't you wake me? Now we don't even have time for breakfast."

"Ease up, Ma, we ain't in no hurry. The soldiers say we're so close to where we're going that we can do the last leg without 'em.

I think they feel bad 'cause you're so worn out. You've got all the time you want."

"Oh, thank the Lord. Let's put on some coffee and then I'm going to wash the dust out of my drawers."

Katherine waited for the sun to move higher in the sky, then went to a nearby stream to bathe. She found a manmade pool; some past stranger had dammed the creek, then lined the water hole's bottom with flat stones. It was, she thought, the kind of thing Frederick would have done.

The water was cold, but she didn't care. Using a piece of French soap hoarded since New Orleans, she washed her hair and wrapped it in a rough cloth. Dressed in her green cotton outfit, she returned to the campsite to dry her hair in the sun while she drank coffee.

"I feel like a colt in spring, George. Now, you go on and take a nice bath yourself."

"Awww, Ma, I just had me a bath last week. A man could catch his death in that ole cold creek," George wheedled, hoping his mother's sense of survival would override her need for him to clean up. "I mean, you're the one's always worryin' about our health."

"You'll live. And don't try fooling me by splashing a little water on you. I want you scrubbed head to toe. Then I'll fry some quail eggs and pork. Go on now, no heel dragging."

George reluctantly did as he was told, even changing his underwear. He rejoined his mother, poured a cup of coffee and grinned sheepishly. "I hate to say it Ma, but I do feel better. I just don't think it's a good idea to wash off all that protection too often."

Two hours after they broke camp George veered off the main trail.

"George, where are we going? Isn't Villa Trinidad straight up the river?"

"Yep, but there's something here I want you to see. It's just 'round the bend."

Katherine shrugged, wondering what could be so interesting. She followed him through a clearing to a large house that was still under construction. Even in its incomplete state, she could see the structure was far superior to the usual frontier "two-pens and a passage" design, called a "dog-run" in Texas. The basic layout— two square buildings connected by a breezeway where the dogs hung out—was the same, but there the similarity ended. This house was three times the size of most settlers' dwellings.

"Now this is a house of a different color," Katherine quipped. "Oh my, look. Real windows!" As they drew nearer she saw the windowpanes were not of glass, but a diaphanous material.

"Ain't it grand, Ma?" George asked, dismounting.

"Very. Somebody's put a lot of work into this place. Do you think they'll mind we're here?" Katherine asked. She swung off her horse and walked towards the house.

"Naw, he's used to people dropping by. Folks been hearing about these windows and coming around like there was a prayer meetin' or a social taking place. Come on inside."

Walking through an open door, Katherine was impressed with the amount of light the windows allowed into the interior. Staring up at them, she asked, "What are those panes made of? They don't look like any glass I've ever seen."

Amber light streamed through the windows, illuminating Katherine's shiny red hair. Her green dress intensified the emerald color of her eyes, and George was struck by his mother's beauty as he backed out the door.

"From here I'd say they're made of crushed diamonds and sent by angels to shine on one of their own," answered a familiar gruff voice.

"Frederick! What are you doing here?" Katherine exclaimed as she whirled around.

"I live here, Red," came Frederick's soft reply, "and so should you."

CHAPTER 11

W*hat,* Katherine thought to herself as she kneaded a batch of biscuits back in her kitchen in Atascosito, *do I really have here?*

She looked around the ramshackle cabin and grinned. *Not much in the way of a house, that's for sure. But it's mine. My home. My ranch.*

Katherine was proud of her accomplishments. She had, with the help of her boys, accumulated several hundred head of cattle. *But cattle can be moved. Not easily, of course, but we could, with help, get them to Frederick's place.*

Frederick's place. That had a strange ring. *If I move north, how long will it take to quit thinking of it as 'Frederick's place.'?*

Henry stomped into the kitchen, dripping from a spring shower that had begun to fall. He looked at the puddle around him and shrugged. "Sorry, Ma."

"It'll dry. Not much can hurt this old floor. Get into dry clothes before you catch your death."

Henry pushed the quilt aside and entered his "room."

Katherine stared at the quilt. *Seven people living in two rooms. 'Course, now that spring's here, George and Henry will move to the barn, but still. . . .*

"Henry?"

"Yes, Ma."

"Have you thought about what we talked about?"

"Yes, Ma."

"And?"

"Your decision, Ma.

"No, Henry, it's not. Not entirely. You and George have worked hard on this ranch. You have a say."

Henry stepped out from behind the quilt. "We just want you to be happy, Mama. If movin' north to live with Pa will make you happy, then me'n George are all for it."

Happy. I'll have to think about that. What's happy mean? I want to be safe. I want us all to be safe. Frederick doesn't think there will be a problem with rebels soon, but. . . Aloud she said, "Well, Atascosito isn't as safe a Villa Salcedo. They don't have much in the way of Indian problems up there."

"That's so, Ma."

"And your Pa promised to settle down and not go off tradin' any more."

"That he did."

"And he misses you children."

Henry dried his hair with an old shirt, covering his face. "Uh, huh."

"Just how hard would it be to move our herd?"

Henry dropped the shirt and beamed at his mother, his quick smile and twinkling eyes telling her what she wanted to know. "Shoot Ma, nothin' we can't handle."

No lightning flashed, no thunder roared, no mountain lion screamed. Maybe it was the full moon.

The cattle, after meekly—as meek as wild cattle get—allowing themselves to be herded north from Atascosito for two days, began to mill and low in the middle of the night. Henry, instantly alerted to trouble, yelled, "They're gonna stomp!" jumped on his horse and rode off into the night.

Katherine quickly saddled her horse, with Frederick following her lead—a new modus operandi he'd adopted since they'd hit the trail to move the herd to their new home near Villa Salcedo. It had become quickly apparent to him that his wife was the cattleman in the family.

"Stay next to me Frederick, and when I say so, start firing your gun," Katherine yelled, untying a bullwhip from her saddle.

"Let Henry and the vaqueros handle it, Katrin. It's too dangerous."

Katherine threw her husband a grin, booted her horse, and sped after Henry, thankful that the full moon lit the landscape so well.

"Damn that woman," Frederick growled, grinned, then followed.

In just the short time it took the drivers to saddle up and give chase, the herd had stopped milling and was in full stampede.

A thousand frenzied animals thundered away through forest and clearings, destroying everything in their path save large trees. If they weren't stopped they would run to the next river and losses would number in the hundreds.

Catching up to the frantic herd, Henry led a three-rider wedge that rode to the front edge of the stampede and began firing guns and cracking whips. The rest of the vaqueros, led by Katherine, flanked the charging cattle and, after a harrowing hour, succeeded in driving the cattle into circling back on the outside of the herd.

The stampeding bovines slowed, milled in confusion, then stopped as suddenly as they had started and began grazing as if nothing had happened. By some miracle, no one was hurt. Only a few head of cattle, and a day on the trail, were lost.

"My god, Katrin," Frederick said as they rode back to camp, "how did you learn to do that?"

A wide smile glinted through the red dust coating Katherine's face. "Shoot, Frederick, that wasn't even a righteous stampede."

Frederick, enchanted by his wife's newfound confidence, fell in love with Katherine for a second time—and this time for the woman she was, not the dewy-eyed promise of a girl he could mold.

Settling into the new house Frederick had built, Katherine and her husband frolicked and cooed like newlyweds. Their romantic antics were a slight source of embarrassment to their children, even though they were thrilled to have the family reunited.

Katherine was ecstatic in her new home. By some standards she still lived on the teetering edge of civilization, but for her the newfound security of having a solid house, a husband committed to reform, and a bright future in Texas was more than she could have imagined. She even had visitors!

Folks came from miles around to meet the Stockmans, see their home with the gypsum windows, and share food and conversation around her enormous pine plank kitchen table. As one of only a handful of non-Hispanic families in Texas, they were a curiosity, and as successful ranchers, a source of both admiration and envy.

The busy kitchen's fireplace boasted four iron cranes for cooking pots and several built-in bread ovens. Lupe and

Katherine could bake up to six loaves of bread at a time when flour was available.

The house's windows, mounted high, just below the ceiling, were protected by massive cedar storm shutters with heavy timber drop bars that closed from the inside. In case of hail, violent winds, or Indian attack, they formed an impenetrable barrier. Open, they could be used as handy gun ports.

The Stockman children loved showing off trap doors in the ceilings that allowed access to the roof. Four-foot parapets around the entire roof sported more gun ports, allowing the family the ability to repel an attack with little risk to themselves. And if barricaded in, they could access both buildings by crossing on the roof instead of through the open breezeway.

This ingenious design, along with an inside water well, permitted the comfortable family dwelling to be converted into a fortress within minutes. Frederick, after the loss of David, had left little to chance in the protection of his reunited clan.

Edmund Norris and his family, colonists who had been in Texas a year longer than the Stockmans, were frequent visitors. The Norris and Stockman children formed friendships that would last their entire lives, much of that time as in-laws, and, at times, fellow outlaws.

"That's a bunch of bull," little Johnny Norris yelled, "them windows didn't come from no *Nuevo* Mexico."

"Yes they did," Maggie sniffed. "My Papa said so. He bought them from a trader who brought 'em here. They're made of something called jip-some, from a mine in New Mexico." Miss Margaret Stockman wasn't easily bullied about by some ole boy.

"I bet you don't even know where New Mexico is," John challenged, moving the conversation to safer ground. "I saw a map once and it showed right where Santa Fe is."

Thinking the children had bickered enough for one day, Katherine called, "You two stop pestering each other and come here. Sounds like you both need a nap. Unless, of course, you'd rather help Papa survey."

The children ran to the porch where Katherine was shelling pecans. "We wanna help! We wanna help! What can we do?"

Frederick trotted his horse into the yard, leaned from the saddle, and handed Maggie the end of a rope.

"Hold onto this end real tight, Maggie, and stand here by your Ma. I've stepped the line off so it's as close to fifty *varas* —yards—as we can get. Johnny boy, follow me."

Frederick rode slowly north, playing out the heavy horse hair rope. When the entire length lay stretched along the ground, he gave Maggie the signal to let go of her end and told Johnny to rewind it into a coil.

Maggie ran to the coiled line, took the end, and Frederick repeated the procedure. The children soon tired of the tedious work and went off to play, leaving the rest of the one hundred rope-stretches to George, Henry, and Frederick. At the five thousand vara-north mark, Frederick finally drove a stake in the ground.

The same routine, followed over several days, was duplicated to the south, east and west, painstakingly staking out the Stockman *suerte* or farm grant.

Once the farmland was marked, they loosely surveyed their grazing land. The 105.7 acres (caballeria) allowed for each head was a nebulous number, as herd strengths changed. These demarcations were of little importance since the few settlers were scattered well clear of their neighbors. Disputes rarely arose.

In later years, this would not be the case.

CHAPTER 12

"Pa, we just might have us a little problem," George said between bites of fried rabbit. He was enjoying a home cooked meal after days on the trail.

Since Frederick had settled down and become respectable, George and Henry took turns going for supplies and, Katherine suspected, running a few illegal goods. George had, that day, returned from one of these trips.

"What now?" Frederick asked, sounding weary. *It seems like damned near every day some new bother came along to set a man to worrying.*

"Well, I ran into a fellow in Nacogdoches who heard a bunch of those Neutral Ground rascals talking about this new Governor, Manuel Salcedo. Seems this Salcedo is a might easier to get on with than that uncle of his, but he's still gotta dance to Mexico City's fiddle."

George reached for another piece of bread.

"Anyhow," he said, "there's talk of cleaning up Neutral Ground and rousting out those troublemakers what's plotting to take Texas away from Spain. But that ain't our problem. Our problem is Miguel Gonzales, Mama's pet deserter."

"Oh Lord, let's discuss this later," Katherine moaned, cutting a dangerous look in the direction of her husband and son.

"Yes ma'am," George said, bending to his food.

After supper, Katherine ordered the younger children outside to do chores. Margaret, whose ears had perked at the mention of Miguel, stomped out only after losing a whiny bid to stay and listen.

"I'm sorry, Ma, I didn't mean to upset you," George apologized. He looked at Katherine's swollen waist and thought, *No wonder she's a mite addled. Expecting again at her age. It would put any woman in a lather.* "You needn't hide bad news from me, George Stockman. Just, please, don't bring it up in front of the younger ones. Our little rabbits have big ears," Katherine admonished.

"And bigger mouths," Henry added. Lupe and Juan, also called in on the family conference, nodded in agreement.

"What exactly did you hear, son?" Frederick asked quietly.

"Well sir, it seems our Miguelito and those freebooters in the Zone have been running guns to Mexican rebels near San Antonio de Béjar. Miguel got hisself caught, but was lucky 'cause he was arrested by his old army troop, and they managed to let him accidentally escape."

"That's a relief, but what's this got to do with us?" Frederick demanded.

George blew an exasperated breath.

"One of the soldiers who let Miguel escape deserted and went with him. He was the one who put a bug in Miguel's ear that *your* name came up when the Commandant at San Antonio was telling the new Governor about possible troublemakers amongst the *norteamericano* settlers."

Lupe crossed herself and Katherine sucked in her breath.

Frederick tensed, then willed himself to relax and grin. "Me? A mischief-maker? Why, everybody in Texas knows I'm a fine upstandin' rancher. Hell, I'm surprised the King hisself hasn't told ole Governor Salcedo to make me a member of government."

Everyone except Katherine chuckled. Cheeks flushed, she fumed, "This is no laughing matter, Frederick Stockman. We can't afford to have scandalous gossip flying about. And when those rumors, true or not, reach the ears of the man who literally holds our lives in his hands, we could be in danger."

Katherine stood and added, "I want you to *do* something and do it *now*!" She whirled and stomped out.

Frederick followed, catching her around her bulging middle.

"Whoa, Red," he said, pulling her close to him. "I was just makin' a little joke. I promise everything'll be all right."

Katherine looked doubtful, so Frederick explained. "I'll go see the commandant at Trinidad tomorrow morning, first thing. Him'n me's pretty tight, you know. We keep him in perfumed soap for his lady friends, good ole Virginny tobacco, and the best medicines that can be smuggled in. Hell, he's practically my. . .uh. . .George and Henry's business partner. We Stockmans don't trade guns or talk treason, so there's nothing to worry about. I know what I'm talkin' about here."

"Frederick Stockman," Katherine said quietly, "I cannot believe that you are so incredibly simple as to think you have given me any comfort by telling me that the highest authority in Trinidad *knows* you're a contrabander."

That said, she stormed away, leaving Frederick to puzzle over how he had messed up so badly.

Comandante Felipe de la Garza's face lit up with anticipation when Frederick entered his office.

"Frederico, what a pleasure to see you. It has been much too long. How is the beautiful Señora Estocoman?"

"Even more radiant than ever, especially for someone who looks like she swallowed a watermelon seed. She is beautiful, but, of course, no more so than your lady," Frederick replied diplomatically.

"Which one?" the Spaniard asked, laughing and slapping Frederick on the back. It was a local joke to talk about the ladies of the area as if there *were* any. Female companionship was a rarity for a Texas soldier.

De la Garza motioned for Frederick to sit by the fire. "So, my friend, what brings you on such a cold morning?"

"Hopefully nothing important, Your Excellency. Just a small problem for which I need your advice."

"I am flattered, Frederico. Now, tell me, what is so grave as to bring you so far?"

"I've heard, through. . .sources, that my name has been bandied about in San Antonio as a *filibustero.* You know me and my family, Felipe—I may not be perfect, but I'm no traitor," Frederick said with a smile.

Felipe frowned. This was not good news, nor was it a problem he wished to be involved with. He did not know the new Governor well, but knew the man sympathized with the settlers' and soldiers' plight, turning a blind eye to petty smuggling. But filibusters were another matter altogether.

De la Garza had heard that those filthy *norteamericano* invasionists—villainous pirates all—were joining with Mexican rebels and amassing in the Neutral Zone with a mind to invade Texas.

Governor Salcedo and his military forces in Texas were preparing to lop the heads from that nest of vipers soon. Even the American government was concerned about the lawlessness in the Zone. Or so they claimed.

"I can see why you would be concerned with this taint to your good name, Frederico. These unruly insurgents who threaten the Crown should not be mentioned in the same breath with our loyal settlers who have sworn allegiance to the Crown."

De la Garza glanced at a portrait of King Carlos hanging over his mantle and wondered if he was still in power. Unrest seemed to be plaguing Spain and Spaniards everywhere. He sighed.

"I shall speak with the Governor," he told Frederick. "He has asked me to prepare a list of loyal Spanish subjects in my district, and I will make special mention of you." Then he added carefully, "I trust there is nothing I should know in connection with this, uh, hearsay?"

"Well," Frederick said, "there *was* one small incident.

De la Garza cocked an eyebrow and waited for Frederick to explain.

"A soldier who deserted your army, Miguel Gonzales, was the same soldier who escorted us, under your army's orders, from Orcoquisac to Atascosito some years back. Perhaps this prompted the despicable slander."

Frederick watched as de la Garza's facial expression turned from concerned to darkly furious. Perplexed, he waited to see what he had said to upset the Spaniard so.

With great effort de la Garza regained his composure. "Frederico, this Gonzales is a notorious traitor. A scoundrel without peer in the eyes of His Majesty's Army. It had escaped my memory that you were. . .acquainted. However, it is not your fault you have the misfortune to know him."

The commandant strode to a table and picked up his sword. "Personally, I plan to hunt down Miguel Gonzales and put him to the sword for crimes against the Crown. And for deserting while under my command."

"Well, sir," Frederick drawled, "if I see that dastardly deserter, I'll tell him you're lookin' for him."

De la Garza's eyes narrowed as he tried to discern whether Frederick was toying with him. He made his decision, then smiled, saying, "Bueno, I shall take care of this matter immediately. Consider it a thing of the past. Now, perhaps a brandy? I would offer you a pipe, but alas, my supply. . . ."

"Then perhaps you would accept this with my compliments," Frederick said quickly, handing him a pouch. "If you need more, Henry can get more on his next trip. He will, of course, see you for his travel permit to Nacogdoches—and beyond."

"I shall, as always, be delighted to see your fine son. Please give my regards to Señora Estocoman."

"I will. *Hasta la vista, comandante,*" Frederick replied.

CHAPTER 13

"How do I look? Is my hair all right? Oh, Frederick, I'm so nervous."

"Dang it Red, it ain't the king coming, just the governor. You look wonderful, the house is grand and the children. . .are clean. What more could you want?"

"Nothing, I guess. Frederick, I want you to know how very proud of you I am."

"It ain't nothing. Besides, it wasn't my doin', but yours."

Following his alarming brush with scandal, Frederick proved himself the very epitome of a loyal Spanish subject engaged in the business of ranching. While others sympathized with would-be liberators of Texas, the Stockman family leader voiced his loyalty to Spain long and loud.

Felipe de la Garza was so pleased with Frederick's accomplishments he invited the Governor to visit the Stockman ranch while on an inspection tour of Texas Territory.

"Welcome to our home, Your Excellency," little Margaret lisped in perfect Castilian Spanish, curtsying as taught by de la Garza's staff. The lisp was natural, but the Governor had no way of knowing that.

The Spaniard, captivated by the red-tressed child, smiled and kissed her hand. "The pleasure is all mine."

Turning from a dazzled Margaret towards Katherine, Governor Salcedo nodded towards Felipe de la Garza and said, in halting English, "My *comandante* thinks very highly of your family. Your ranch is a fine example of what loyal settlers can accomplish with hard work and good faith. You and your family are to be commended."

Katherine blushed with pleasure and dipped into a half-curtsy. "You are too kind, Your Lordship," she told him. "We are delighted you took time to visit our home during your tour of the provinces. Would you care for some refreshments?"

"*Gracias*, Señora, but I must decline. We have many leagues to ride, and I am eager to return to my wife and daughter. My long weeks of travel to the eastern settlements are at an end and I long for my home in San Antonio. Please, however, accept my gratitude for your kind offer."

Katherine nodded her approval at his sense of family, and the Governor turned to Frederick.

"Señor Estocoman, perhaps you would accompany us back to Villa Trinidad so we can discuss the fascinating business of ranching in Texas."

The Governor bowed one last elegant sweep to Katherine and gracefully hoisted himself into his ornate silver and leather saddle. As if by theatrical cue, his entire entourage did likewise.

Margaret, awestruck by the Governor's frilly shirt, gold embroidered vest, plumed hat, and cavalier gestures, whispered loudly to her mother, "Mama, he's just about the purtiest man I ever did see."

Following a moment of stunned silence, George and Henry started to laugh and Katherine looked flustered.

"What did she say? My English is not so good," Salcedo asked de la Garza.

Felipe de la Garza, a little unsure of the governor's reaction to the child's description of him, hesitated, then decided to directly translate what the child said.

Salcedo laughed heartily and said, "And you, your little sister and mother are surely the prettiest ladies in this part of Texas."

The Governor was still smiling as they rode north along the Trinity River.

"Your Excellency, I apologize for my little girl's behavior. Her Mama teaches her reading, writing, and numbers, but we don't get many highborn visitors. Except ole Felipe here."

Salcedo was slightly amused with de la Garza's obvious discomfort at Stockman's familiarity. *It is,* he thought, *always a problem to befriend the lower classes. In Spain, the rules are simple, men know their places. In Texas, where strength is king, all of the fancy titles and gold frills mean little. Men like Stockman and his sons will one day rule Texas, not some Peninsular like myself, sent to govern in the name of a Sovereign in Europe.*

"You are too kind, Señor Estocoman," said Felipe de la Garza, interrupting Salcedo's darkening thoughts. "My station in life can hardly be compared to that of his Lordship. But of course you *norteamericanos* address little importance to that sort of thing. In fact, you rid yourselves of the British royals who tried to subjugate the colonies, no?"

"Yes, that's true. But I didn't care much for the new brand of 'royalty' we got for our efforts," replied Stockman.

"Very interesting, Señor Estocoman. I had no idea you were North American. I thought you to be German," Governor Salcedo commented.

"I was born in Germany, but my family immigrated to the British Colonies. I was a young man when the colonials got into it with the Redcoats, and I just naturally sided up with my friends. After the revolution I realized I wasn't much cut out for crowded places, so I decided to go somewhere a man could breathe, and found Spanish Louisiana. But then the United States bought up Louisiana from the French, and I'm damned if it didn't start to crowd up. I guess I ain't cut out to be a *norteamericano*. I was sure glad when you folks allowed me to come here, and I plan to stay."

Frederick grinned at Governor Salcedo. "Unless, of course, you've a mind to sell Texas,"

Felipe de la Garza, fearing Stockman had gone too far, held his breath. The sale of Louisiana Territory to the United States by that upstart Frenchman, Napoleon, was an outrage. Making light of Napoleon's blatant theft of Spanish lands was an insult.

Salcedo, however, seemed to be enjoying the banter.

"As far as I know," he said lightly, "our King has no plans to part with this territory, but," Salcedo's face clouded, "perhaps there are some who would take it by force."

"Well, I ain't one of 'em, Your Lordship. All we want to do is raise stock and farm. We've no use for those who'd muddle it up for us."

"That is very comforting, sir. I will accept you at your word as a gentleman," the Governor replied.

Felipe de la Garza, made uneasy by this conversation, wished for a change of subject. He almost dared to interrupt, but was saved when Frederick stopped his horse, causing the Governor to rein in as well.

Looking the Governor of Texas straight in the eye, Frederick said, "Your Lordship, my wife would question that 'gentleman' stuff, but I give you my word about one thing: I will not personally get involved in any uprisings. That pretty much puts me on your side of the table, as you Royalists hold all the high cards.

"Now Governor, what do you want to know about mustangs and wild cattle, other than they're ornery as hell?"

While the Governor and Stockman discussed *mesteños and cimarrónes,* Felipe de la Garza mulled over what Frederick had just said.

Texicans were so direct they could usually be taken at their word, but somewhere in Frederick's words de la Garza detected some double talk. He just could not put his finger on it. *Damn these people,* he thought. *I dread the day we have to fight them.*

And we will.

On the surface, Stockman seems to pledge undying loyalty to Spain, but, on the other hand, the old bastard never really said so. Damn them all.

CHAPTER 14

In the Fall of 1810, on a visit to Neutral Ground, Henry found Miguel Gonzales enflamed by the revolutionary fervor of a Mexican priest-turned-radical, Father Miguel Hidalgo y Costillo.

Hidalgo, who was being compared to George Washington, Paul Revere, and any other number of American Revolutionaries by his followers, had issued a *grito*: a call to arms for Mexicans and their allies to toss Spain out of the New World.

Hidalgo certainly had the support of Miguel and his fellow Mexican rebels, as well as many pseudo-rebels with less patriotic intentions.

"Henry," Miguel expounded, his exuberance bouncing off the walls of his dilapidated dog-run cabin, "surely you must see the importance of Hidalgo's revolt within the very heart of Mexico. Nothing can stop us now."

Henry bit the inside of his cheek and thought, *How about the entire Spanish Army of Mexico? I'd hardly call that nothing.*

As if reading Henry's mind Miguel said, "Of course, the Royalists will be savage in their defense of Texas, but we will win, for God is on our side. But we need the Texicans, too. Henry, your father fought for the freedom of the United States and now Mexico needs his help. And yours."

"Miguelito, you know we secretly support Mexico, but Pa's dead set against us getting into this fracas. What can I do? He's my father and I just can't go against him."

"I do not wish you to openly defy your father. But you could tell us of the Spanish troop strength in Texas," Miguel suggested.

Henry frowned, but said, "I can, *if* Commandant de la Garza keeps renewing my travel papers."

Encouraged, Miguel pushed. "Would you also be willing to deliver messages to certain of our friends in Texas? Mexico will not forget you when we are free."

"Miguel, I'll do what I can, but I won't do anything I think will cause trouble for my family."

"I would not want you to. I know you cannot give my regards to your parents, but I think of them often."

"It ain't no problem me sayin' I saw you, Miguel. Ma and Pa both like you a lot, they just don't want us involved in your revolution. Oh, by the way, Pa said *Comandante* de la Garza's got a real bad hankerin' to see you. Dead."

"You have my permission to tell the *gachupín* bastard that I feel the same. Of course, if you do, he will surely hang you, so perhaps it is wise to wait until I can tell him personally. Godspeed, my brother. We will contact you soon. *¡Viva Mexico! ¡Viva la Revolution!*"

"Like I said, I'll do what I can, so long as Pa don't know. And," Henry warned with a sarcastic grin, "I'd watch those "*¡Vivas!*" if I was you, or you won't *viva* long enough to fight any revolution. If the wrong ears hear you, it could cut your *viva* right short." He opened the door and looked back over his shoulder.

"And a Mexican with a short *viva* ain't much good to the *señoritas, compadre*."

"Henry Stockman will help us, but he will not join our Army of the North," Miguel told his Captain.

"Until we are ready to strike he will be a valuable source of information of the troop strength in Texas. His family is known to be Royalist, and they are free to travel throughout the territory. When the time comes, though, the Stockmans will join with us. Of that I am certain."

James Gaines, another rebel, nodded in agreement. "What Miguel says is true, Cap'n. I know the Stockmans. When the fight starts they'll side with us. The old man is a mite long in the tooth, but he's a tough hombre. And don't forget there's other families like them in Texas who'll throw in with us once they see we're winning."

"Yes," Miguel proclaimed, "when they see the Heroes of Mexico conquer Governor Salcedo and liberate them from the injustices of the King they will support us with their very blood."

Gaines held his hand out to stop Miguel.

"Oh for Christ's sake, Miguel, don't start all that *Viva Mexico* crap. We all know why we're in this fight. Land. And the right to run it without Spanish taxes. We'll chase the Spaniards south until they run into Hidalgo's bunch, catch 'em in the middle, and squash 'em like *cucarachas*. Just remember, when those cockroaches are dead we Texicans want a say-so in the new rules."

"Si amigo. I put the cart before the *caballo*," Miguel said quickly. "When the Republican Army of the North meets with Father Hidalgo's Army of America, Mexico will be free. Then we will run Texas as we wish." He gave James a sly grin. "On our own land, of course."

Gaines laughed and slapped Miguel on the back. "There's another thing you need to talk to Gutierrez about, Miguel."

"What?"

"Land grants, Miguel. Spanish ones. As the chief Mexican in the Army of the North, Gutierrez needs to understand that if we want people like the Stockmans to support us, he's gotta guarantee that new Republic of Mexico won't take folks' land when we oust Spain. Otherwise, what reason have the settlers got to help us win?"

"An excellent point, Jaime. I will seek assurances that land claims will be honored for the Heroes of Mexico. Now, I must get some sleep, so I will see you *mañana. Buenos noches, caballeros,*" Miguel said as he waved and left, with nary a *¡Viva!*.

With Miguel out of earshot, one of the men asked, "Does that Meskin really think we're gonna risk our necks so's a bunch of chili chompers can tell us what to do?"

James Gaines growled, "I'd watch what you call Miguel if you value your scrawny neck. He's a friend of mine. He and I are in this fight so we can live in Texas in peace."

"Think that'll ever happen?"

Gaines shrugged. "One thing's for sure, something's gonna happen, and it ain't gonna be pretty. I just wish we'd get on with it." He spat on the floor and rose to leave. "Meanwhile, I can use the forty bucks a month."

"Yeah, me too," another man said. "I been wondering though—where do ya figger the Meskins is getting the money to pay us? It damned shore ain't coming from Mexico,"

Gaines grinned and drifted towards the door. "What the hell do you care, just so's you ain't in jail like usual,"

The man slapped his sides and laughed. "Yeah, not only did these Meskin heroes git me out of that New Orleans jail, they're paying me to hang around and do nothin', which is just fine with me as long as we don't run out of whiskey. And I have to admit that you dog turds are better company than those in the jailhouse."

"Well, this dog turd needs some shut-eye," James Gaines yawned. At the door, he turned and yelled "*¡Viva Texas!* And the devil with everybody else."

"Enrique, my friend, how was your journey?" Felipe de la Garza asked when Henry walked into the warmth of the officer's study at Villa Trinidad. "And what news do you bring from Neutral Ground?"

Henry, wind burned and chilled to the bone after bucking a blue norther all day, gratefully accepted a mug of hot chocolate from the *Comandante's* Indian servant.

"Oh, sir, the usual: outlaws outlawin' and ne'er-do-wells doing what they do best. Most of 'ems sitting around telling tales about that earthquake up the Mississippi. They say a giant wave came down the river as far down as Bayou Pierre. It must'a really been something to see," Henry replied.

"Yes, we received reports of many drowned or killed by falling rocks and trees along the banks. Great crevasses swallowed men and their wagons. Tell me, is the earth still angry?"

"They say there's still a rumble now and again," Henry answered.

"And what of the human rumbling in the Neutral Zone?"

"Human rumbling? Don't rightly know what you mean," Henry answered, feigning a casual attitude to match the Spaniard's. Stalling, he took another mouth-puckering sip. He preferred his hot chocolate Texican style, laced with sugar.

Smiling at the Spanish officer to cover his grimace, Henry downed the rest of the bitter drink like a dose of quinine.

De la Garza half-smiled, his sly eyes never leaving Henry's face.

"Perhaps, Enrique, I should be more direct. It is important to me, and to your family, that I am made aware of any problems threatening the tranquillity of Texas."

Stockman choked back a guffaw. Calling Texas tranquil was like calling a bull alligator a horned toad.

The officer intensified his stare. "We hear disturbing rumors of an invasion plot by *filibusteros* in the Zone. Perhaps you heard something of this while there?"

Henry held de la Garza's gaze. He knew better than to try to play dumb. "Well, sir, like I said, there's the usual bunch of rabble-rousers—maybe a few more than usual."

"Perhaps I haven't made myself so clear, Enrique. It is in the interest of Spain, Texas, and the Stockman family that when you are allowed to travel into the Zone, you return with as much exact information as possible about the activities of the so-called Army of the North."

Henry, an accomplished gambler, did not blink, but his heart dropped into his stomach. He was glad his face was whipped crimson by wind, for he felt a warm flush traveling up his neck.

Pouring more hot chocolate to buy time, hc put the cup carefully on a table, smiled widely and declared, "Yes, sir. I do understand. You want me to spy for Spain."

The commandant broke into a hearty laugh, slapping Henry on the back.

"I am always amazed by the candor of you Texicans. It is a charming trait I have come to appreciate. *Sí*, Enrique, I wish you to 'spy,' as you call it, for Spain. But not just for Spain. Surely you realize the consequences for the legal residents of Texas if there is an organized attack by insurgents?"

De la Garza lost his smile and added, "Spain will not tolerate such an insult and retribution would be swift and deadly."

Putting his arm on Henry's shoulder, he guided him towards the door.

"Now, enough of this unpleasant talk, Enrique. I am sure you are eager to return to Ganado Estocoman. Please convey my compliments to your parents. You and I shall talk more before you go once again to the Zone. *Vaya con Dios*."

"I saw Miguel," Henry said casually, taking down a bale of hay for the livestock. "He says *'hola.'* " He and George were in the barn, finishing up some chores after Henry's homecoming supper.

"Well, you tell him 'hello' back when you see him again. Or maybe I'll see him when I go to the Zone. I 'spose it's about my turn," George replied.

"Your turn to do what, George?" Frederick asked, entering the barn. "Do some work around here?"

"Awww, Pa. I been my working like a slave around here while Henry was gone. I figger I'd go on the next run to the border. Henry tells me he saw ole Miguelito."

Frederick frowned. "Henry, I don't think it's a real good idea to be seen hanging around Miguel, much as I like him. By law you could do six months hard labor for just knowing him."

"I know, Pa. I'm careful."

"I'm sure you are Henry, but word has it Miguel's joined up with a real bad bunch, so we'd best stay away. I hope he doesn't think he can trust those filibusters. Most of those cow patties will slit your throat for a swig of whiskey. There ain't no tellin' what they'd do for land in Texas."

Henry drew a deep breath.

"Pa," he said, "we've got to talk. *Comandante* de la Garza wants me. . .us. . .to spy for him. He made it damned clear he wants information on Miguel and his bunch, or he won't issue us any more travel papers. What'll we do?"

Frederick glanced at the open barn door. "Shut that door, and take a look around while you're at it."

The barn secured, Frederick talked in a low voice.

"Looks like we got ourselves between that ole rock and hard place, boys. I guess the best we can do is oblige both sides, but real careful-like. We're bound to get caught in the crossfire unless we outfox the whole lot. Maybe it would be best to not take any more trips east for awhile."

"Pa, it ain't that easy," Henry said. "It's just a matter of time until all hell breaks loose. Miguel's bunch is gonna invade Texas, and the Spaniards know it."

"Are you sure?"

Henry nodded. "De la Garza even knew about the Army of the North. Word is the Mexican rebels down south, and those here in Texas and in the Zone, are all part of the same group now. I don't know who's gonna win, but it'll be one heck of a fight and we'll have to choose sides soon. What are the other settlers saying?"

"The ones I trust, like the Norrises, secretly favor the rebels," Frederick replied, then fell silent. After a few minutes he took off his hat and slapped it against a post.

"Dammit all to hell, boys, I hate revolutions, even when I end up on the winnin' side. As sissy as it sounds, I think we'd best hunker down and wait to see which way the wind blows."

CHAPTER 15

The January wind shrieked and howled, chilling both the ears and bones of those unlucky enough to be out-of-doors.

One of the Stockman clan, a shaggy member of the canine persuasion, was especially happy to be allowed to sleep before a banked fire in the kitchen. Stretched out his full length, as close to the smoldering ashes as he dared without igniting his silky black fur, he was in doggy Heaven.

The rest of the family also slept in the blissful warmth of their home/fortress, grateful to be entrenched against such an evil night.

One of the dog's ears twitched. Then the other. In one swift movement, all his senses came alive and he stood, as did the hair along his spine. Emitting a low growl from deep in his chest, he stiff-legged towards the door.

Henry, who slept in a small room off the pantry, heard Furface's growl and did not think twice before leaping to his feet and grabbing his gun. Creeping to a peep-hole in the wall of the house, he removed the plug and, at first, saw nothing. The dog's continuing rumbles convinced Henry to go onto the roof for a better look, even though every bone in his body protested the anticipated cold.

Taking a ladder from the pantry, Henry locked it in place and slowly raised the heavy hatch in the ceiling. A gust caught the hatch and hurled it open with a crash.

"Dammit," he growled, causing Furface to dog-grumble in agreement.

Crawling low on the roof, protected by the four-foot parapet, Henry peeked through a gun port and saw four or five riders moving slowly towards the house, their backs to the frightful wind. The single file, direct approach of the group relieved Henry's anxiety somewhat. It was his experience that those of bad intent didn't arrive in a straight line.

Henry watched one of the riders dismount and walk towards the house until he lost sight of him under the roof of the breezeway. The intruder knocked loudly on the wooden door. "Señor Estocoman, it is I, Felipe de la Garza."

"Hold on a minute, *Comandante*, I'll be right there," Henry heard Frederick yell.

Crouching on the roof, Henry sighted his gun on the other riders. He would take no chances until he knew for certain there was no threat.

"Felipe," Stockman snarled, opening the door, "what in God's name are you doin' out here in the middle of the night? Come on in before you freeze."

"It is an urgent matter, Frederico, a special request from His Excellency, Governor Salcedo. A matter of much importance. I am not alone, so with your permission I will get the others. You may inform Enrique that it is safe for him to descend from that cold roof."

Katherine, frightened by the nocturnal disturbance, asked from behind her husband, "Frederick, what's happening? Can we light a lamp?"

"Not until everyone's inside," Frederick whispered, then he yelled, "Henry, come on down. Open the kitchen door, and call off that hound."

When Henry opened the door, de la Garza, a woman, a small girl, and three soldiers trooped in, followed by Frederick and Katherine. After a whispered conference with the commandant, Frederick announced, "Seems we got us some mighty important visitors, Katrin. How's about some coffee to take the chill off?"

"Henry, you make the coffee. I'm going to get this child into a nice warm bed," Katherine said, leading the girl back out the door towards the sleeping rooms on the other side of the dog run. The woman followed.

"Señora, what are you doing out on such a night?" Katherine asked in Spanish.

"I speak English, Señora Estocoman. Please allow me to introduce myself. I am María Salcedo and this is my daughter, Marquita. I am afraid we have come for a very big favor. I will, of course, understand if you find it too much to ask—it's just that my husband, the Governor, met you and thought perhaps. . . ." María's voice broke and tears filled her eyes.

"Now, now. It's all right Señora Salcedo, you're safe here. I can pretty much guess what's going on—even out here we're aware of the problems in San Antonio."

Katherine patted the bed. "Why don't you rest and I'll go heat some stew for you and your daughter. I'll be right back."

Katherine crossed the breezeway to the kitchen, and when she entered, the men stopped talking.

Frederick cast a worried look in her direction.

"Uh, Red," he said, "we've been talking about the situation in San Antonio, and in Texas in general. The Governor's sending his family to Louisiana, but he's afraid to send them with a regular escort 'cause someone might figger out who they are. They're asking George here to pass them off as his wife and daughter."

"With your permission, of course, Señora Estocoman," Felipe de la Garza said with a slight cavaliers' bow. "It is, we realize, a great deal to ask."

"George is a grown man. What he decides, we'll abide by. But are things that bad? Should we be worried?" Katherine asked.

"Señora, these are indeed dangerous times, but mostly for us—the Spaniards. It seems we have enemies on all sides. We hesitated to ask your family to become involved, but the Governor could think of no other way to get his family safely out of Texas. As I said, he will understand completely if. . . ."

"I'll do it," George said, "but my way. No soldiers. Just me and the lady and the girl. I'll get them to friends in Nacogdoches who'll see to it Señora Salcedo gets to the border. Folks are used to seeing me on the road—they just haven't ever met my wife and little girl."

Governor Salcedo did not hear of his family's safe delivery to Louisiana for many weeks, as he was arrested in a military coup just hours after his wife and daughter escaped from San Antonio.

His captors, members of the Army of the North, sent a message to Father Hidalgo, the George Washington of the

Mexican uprising: *We have taken Béjar in the name of the Revolution!*

In February, Governor Salcedo was taken south to Monclava, inside Mexico, where his legendary charm influenced his jailers to join him in a counter-coup. He then arrested Father Hidalgo, along with most of his Army of America, and tried them for treason. To nobody's surprise Hidalgo was found guilty and executed.

But the Revolution did not die with the father of the movement. And even though by December, 1811, Governor Salcedo was back in control of Texas, he dared not send for his family. Trouble still loomed.

The Texican settlers, unsettled by the winds of revolution and gravely concerned for their futures, fled in droves.

The Stockmans decided to stick it out, leaving their fate to Governor Salcedo and the Spanish government.

A year later, Destiny intervened.

CHAPTER 16

"Señor Estocoman—Frederico—I will not beat around the tree. It is with deep regret that I must tell you to leave Texas at once. You and your family are being deported and must be out of this country within ten days, or my Uncle Nemesio, the Supreme Commander of Texas, will bring charges against you."

Frederick, summoned to San Antonio by the governor in January 1812, had anticipated a kind word for his family's part in getting María Salcedo and her daughter to safety the year before. He was stunned by the dictum being handed down by Governor Salcedo.

"Frederico, it is not my wish that you be forced to depart, but the matter has been taken from my hands. My uncle claims he has irrefutable proof that your family has passed military information to Mexican rebels here in Texas and in the Zone."

He paused, searching Frederick's stone face for a sign of guilt. Seeing nothing more than tightened jaws, he continued. "As you, and all settlers know, aiding sworn enemies of the Crown is an act of treason. Uncle Nemesio actually ordered me to put you to the sword, or hang you, but I convinced him that the trial necessary to do so would only further damage relationships with other settlers. In prosecuting your family, he would create—what is the word in English?"

"Heroes?" Frederick said with just a touch of irony.

"Martyrs, most likely. At any rate, he reluctantly saw my point and after all, when our own family was in danger, yours rendered assistance at risk to themselves."

Salcedo paced as he talked, obviously distressed.

"I am embarrassed to deport a man such as yourself, when there are others far more deserving. And because I am at odds with my uncle concerning your deportation, I am sending an army escort to help you safely gain the border. Yesterday I sent word to *Comandante* Felipe de la Garza at the Trinidad garrison to ride to your ranch and lend assistance to your family. By the time you return, they should be ready to leave."

Frederick, despite his inward shock and anger, stifled a smile and thought, *Oh, what I would give to be a fly on the wall when that slick son of a bitch, de la Garza, tells that copperhead I'm married to that she has to leave her home. Better him than me.*

Salcedo stopped pacing and looked at Frederick.

"One more thing—no circumstances should you linger in the Neutral Zone. Go immediately on to the United States. Very soon, the Zone will be burned to the ground by the joined forces of the United States and Spain. If found there, you will be jailed or hanged as a criminal."

"I could. . . ." Governor Salcedo's voice faltered and his face softened. After taking a moment to regain his composure, he continued. "I *will* be hanged if anyone finds out I have told you of this proposed invasion of the Zone, but I trust you to use the information carefully. It is the least I can do.

"Now, Frederico, you have much to do so I will let you do it. Please relay my sincerest apologies to la Señora Estocoman. *Vaya con Dios.*"

Twelve days later, Governor Manual María de la Concepciòn José Augustín Eloy de Salcedo y Quiroga, of Texas, sat alone in front of his fireplace at Casa Reales in San Antonio. Mesmerized by the dancing colors of a cedar log fire, warmed by flames and his last bottle of Spanish brandy, he fell into a trance-like state.

The visions that fandangoed in the fire before him were not pleasant ones. He had no false illusions concerning the horrors he and his loyal officers faced when the rebels came. The expectation of what was to come was so terrifying he snapped out of his reverie to find his heart pounding and his face bathed in sweat.

Fear? Surely not. Fear is not a word to be mentioned in the same breath with the Salcedo name. Salcedos are cavaliers, not cowards.

And yet, for just a moment, he allowed himself to entertain thoughts of riding to the safety of New Orleans. In a few days he could be with his wife and child. He and Maria could, once again, host exquisite dinners boasting fine wines, and dance until dawn to the strains of splendidly performed music.

It would be so easy. But, of course, impossible.

Pulling his gaze from the fire, he slowly surveyed his surroundings, elegant by territory standards. The ballroom, converted to a war room soon after his wife's departure, boasted heavy imported silk draperies hanging from cedar-beamed ceilings.

Woolen rugs, hand-woven in Mexico City, warmed the rough-hewn flagstone floor. His eyes came to rest on a painting of María that still graced his mantelpiece. The flickering incandescence of firelight gave the portrait life, and for a time he stared longingly at the luminous image of his beautiful wife.

Shaking off his senseless self-pity, Salcedo breathed a ragged sigh and focused his attention on the message in his hand. It told of the culmination of his uncle's decision which, while not ruinous on its own, would add more kindling to the revolutionary flame. Leaning closer to his lamp to capture its light, the Governor reread the missive:

January 13, 1812

To: Sir Lieutenant Colonel Governor Don Manual Salcedo

Yesterday Frederico Estocoman was deported to the United States with his family, who lived here, through the post at Nacogdoches, in compliance with the Superior order communicated from the Superior Government. I performed this expulsion which I report to your Lordship for your information.

God preserve Your Lordship many years
Felipe de la Garza

Reading Felipe's formal, but standard, closing to the memo, Governor Salcedo laughed, raised his glass in a toast to the empty room and growled, "Not very damned likely, de la Garza. I fear God has other plans for his Lordship."

CHAPTER 17

"Pa, do you think Mama will ever speak to us again?" Henry asked as he rode next to his father on the King's Highway.

Henry and Frederick rode point, a quarter-mile in front of the Stockman wagons. The rear was guarded by four extremely nervous Royalist soldiers.

"Somebody said that Texas is grand for men and dogs, and hell on horses and women, but Red is tougher than the average gal. Truth is, Henry, she ain't so much mad as scared."

Henry nodded and scanned the horizon.

"Right now, son, even though your mama appears madder'n an ole wet hen, she's pert'near scared to death. You know, she grew up hearin' about how her Pa saw renegade redskins kill *his* Ma and Pa, so she's more afraid of Indians than most. Hell, I ain't exactly what you would call real comfortable right now, myself."

"I know what you mean, Pa. We picked one heck of a time to hit the road. With them murderin' Comanches on the warpath there ain't a Texican, Mexican, or Spaniard safe in Texas. I just don't know what I'd do if they took our girls—there's some things worse'n death. Why do you think the Comanches are so danged mean?"

Frederick shrugged. "I suppose to an Indian's way of thinking, us settlers are out to steal their land and buffalo. 'Course, they're right. We've run 'em out of everywhere we go. I fought Indians back East, but those were *normal* Indians. There ain't too much normal about a Comanche, far as I can tell."

"Pa, I heard somewhere they think they get magical powers by torturing their enemies, which is what they seem to consider just about every living, breathing human being in Texas." Henry shifted uneasily in his saddle.

The two men rode in silence for a few minutes, then Frederick said, "We couldn't let Comanches take us alive, you know. You and George know what to do in case they got me first."

Henry nodded, shuddering at the thought of shooting his mother, brothers and sisters in the head.

"Dang, Pa, can't we could move a little faster?"

"Not with the wagons." Frederick glancing backwards again saw the soldiers were riding in a huddle. He chuckled.

"I think those soldier boys are even more scared of Indians than your Ma is. But that ain't their only problem. We'll be out of Indian territory soon, but there's some white scoundrels about that'd surely love to get hold of some Royalist hides. 'Course, I'm acquainted with most of the scoundrels from here to the Mississippi, which is why your Ma says we got told to leave this paradise."

Henry gulped.

"Pa, I think it was me that got us kicked out. I told Miguel a couple of things about the garrison strength at Trinidad."

"Hell, Henry, we all did. But I don't think ole Uncle Nemisio really knew that. I got a feeling the Spaniards are trying to hedge their bets by gittin' rid of as many of us foreigners as they can. And who knows, they might have done us a favor."

Henry was startled. "A favor?"

"Maybe. Things are about to get real rough here, and we would've got caught up in it one way or t'other. Now we don't have to make any big decisions that might get our butts kicked."

"Could be, Pa, but I'm pretty damned mad about the way we were treated. I just haven't decided what to do about it."

Henry's tone of voice caused Frederick to look at his son closely. He suddenly realized Henry wasn't a boy anymore, and that he meant to wreak revenge on the Spaniards. The old man thought about discouraging such vengeful thoughts, but decided against it. *A little retribution once in a while keeps a man's blood moving.*

"Henry, we'll drop back with the others after a spell, but meantime keep your eyes and ears open. Not that you ever see or hear the murderin' red s.o.b.'s before they're all over you. I think the only way to lick 'em is to join 'em."

"Join them? What you mean?"

"What I mean, boy, is if we're gonna rid ourselves of Comanches, we'll have to fight fire with fire. Fight 'em just like we were Indians ourselves. Use their heathenish tactics."

"You mean scalp and torture them? Cut off their privates and then burn them alive? I don't think I could do those things to another human being, even a Comanche," Henry said and then fell silent. After a while he added, "But then again, Pa, they ain't never done nothin' personal to me or mine."

The two rode quietly, scanning for trouble.

"Pa, you know that alligator me and George killed? We wasn't even sure it was the one that got our David, but we killed it anyhow, 'cause it was a gator."

Frederick nodded. "That's what's gonna happen here with the Indians. When men get it in their heads that a group of folks are bad, it don't matter to them that maybe they kill a few who never harmed anyone. Mark my words, those damned Comanches'll get every Indian in Texas killed or run out, even the peaceful ones like we met at Orcoquisac.

"Enough Indian talk, son—makes me twitch in my saddle."

"Pa, I think it's that prickly heat rash on your ass doing that."

As soon as they passed Indian country, Henry and Frederick galloped back to join the wagons bouncing slowly along El Camino Real.

Nearing the Sabine River, the Stockman clan grew more relaxed while the Spanish soldiers became downright paranoid. One fidgety Royalist called Henry aside and asked him how much further it was to the border.

"I guess maybe we'll make it to the Zone late this afternoon, Pedro. We've been lucky so far, what with the trail being dry and the weather so nice. You can turn back anytime now. I don't imagine you'll be wanting to meet with any Mexican rebels."

Henry grinned at the young soldier and added, "They're a might techy where you boys are concerned."

"Señor Enrique, perhaps you can help me," the soldier said, looking about nervously. "My *compadres* and I have heard you have. . .friends. . .in the Zone. Perhaps former friends of ours who have, uh, left Texas."

"Maybe. Maybe not. Anyone in particular, Pablo?" Henry asked carefully.

"There is a man I did not know personally, but I have heard of. His name is Miguel Gonzales. Do you know him?"

Henry stopped his horse and studied the soldier. There was a large reward on Miguel's head, causing him to be both outlaw and rebel folk hero.

Henry wondered which of these Pablo sought "You thinking to arrest him? I hear he's mighty mean. I think you'd have yourself a bobcat by the tail."

"*Momento por favor,*" Pablo said and rode back for a whispered conference with his fellow soldiers. Returning to Henry's side, he announced, "We wish to join him."

"I kinda figgered that's what you had in mind," Henry said solemnly. It was all he could do not to laugh—Felipe de la Garza going to have a fit of apoplexy when he found out he had lost his escort of hand-picked soldiers to the despised Miguel Gonzales.

The Stockman procession rolled into the village in the Neutral Zone with some fanfare.

Henry and George rode in front guarding their Spanish "prisoners," followed by the wagons carrying Katherine and the children. Frederick and Peter rode rear guard.

Some unruly types in the village wanted to string up the soldiers for entertainment, but the Stockmans held them off. And once they reached Miguel's cabin, the deserters were heartily welcomed by their Mexican compatriots.

Heeding Governor Salcedo's warning, Frederick did not tarry long in the Zone and, after a couple of days, prepared to move eastward. Without Henry.

"Mama, I ain't going with you," Henry told Katherine, who remained cool towards her men folk. "Me and Miguel are going back to kick those *gachupín* son's'a bitches out of Texas, and off our ranch."

Katherine, who had been gazing west, fiercely grasped Henry's arm. "You do that, son. You go get my ranch back. But be careful, you hear? I've given enough to Texas."

Henry hugged his mother and sisters, shook hands with his father and brothers, and watched them leave for Louisiana. He was twenty-one, and mature beyond his years, but as he watched his mother roll away, tears stung his eyes like a five-year-old. He wondered when, or if, he would see her again.

A few days later he was wiping smoke tears away, smearing soot on his face in the process.

Smoke still hung over what was left of the village and Miguel's cabin, but a fine drizzle was trying to put out the forest fire.

"You look very much like a raccoon, Enrique," James Gaines, Miguel's rebel friend, told Henry.

"You don't look too good yourself, Gaines. Dang, that Magee is a mean little bastard, ain't he?"

As Governor Salcedo had warned, a United States Army troop, led by Lieutenant Augustus Magee, descended upon the Neutral Zone like avenging angels—or devils.

Sent on a moral mission by a president and a king, Magee sought to banish the blackguards who were causing so much trouble for God and Spain. He arrested some, whipped some, and hanged some. Then he burned every building to the ground, set torches to the forest, and rode back to Louisiana, satisfied that the criminal element in the Zone had been dealt with properly.

The buildings still smoldered when Henry, Miguel and James Gaines emerged from hiding.

"Yep, he's an ornery cuss all right," James said, surveying the devastation while agreeing with Henry's assessment of Augustus Magee.

He kicked a smoking ember. "But I'll say one thing for him, Henry, he didn't hang no one that didn't need hangin'. He just saved us the trouble."

Poking around in the incinerated rubble, hoping to find a few salvageable items, Miguel sighed, "I just wish he'd a left us more horses."

"Looks like we'll have to go into Texas and borrow a few," Henry grinned, looking forward to a good old mustang round-up.

Miguel shook his head. "Enrique, sometimes I think you like the danger. Our old friend, Felipe de la Garza, would give his very soul to catch us in Texas, stealing the King's horses."

"Naw, I don't cotton to danger any more than the next man. I just sorta feel my roundin' up a few head of His Majesty's mustangs helps make up for them treating us so mean. I'm a very sensitive fellow."

Henry's wit drew guffaws, and they went to work rebuilding their cabins. Then they'd go help themselves to a few horses.

"Would you look at that!" someone shouted when they rode back into the village two weeks later.

"Henry Stockman's done hisself proud this time. Where'd you get that splendiferous piece of horse flesh, Henry? And how in hell is it you're ridin' him so soon?"

Henry dismounted and patted the horse's big head.

"It was the dangdest thing," he told them. "Here I was chasing after the herd when I noticed one mare kept tryin' to circle back, which they don't do unless they got a colt somewhere. Anyhow, I let her go and followed her to this ole boy,"

"That ain't no colt, boy."

"Sure isn't. But he was in big trouble when that mare led me to him—clean up to his neck in quicksand and pretty much a goner."

A crowd was gathering, eager to hear of Henry's conquest.

"Anyhow, I managed to halter him, tied my rope to a tree and started pulling him out with my horse. He let me—didn't even struggle. It was almost like he knew I was saving him."

One of the men sneered, "Horses don't know nothin' except who's boss. They'll turn on you in a minute if you let 'em. I keep mine right where I want him."

"That's why he don't like you," James Gaines said. "I see him try to bite you every chance he gets. Go on, Henry, tell 'em, how you climbed on this horse soon as he was out of that quicksand."

"I believe, James, that you just did," Miguel quipped, and Gaines swiped at him with his hat.

Henry smirked and continued his story.

"I sure did. Didn't even wipe the mud off him, just jumped up and off we went. Dangdest thing I ever did see. From now on, that's how I'll break my horses—lead 'em into a shallow bog and let 'em fight the mud instead of me."

While Henry was out bar-o-ing mustangs, Katherine was doing her best to make the run down shack they moved into in Louisiana habitable. And worrying about Henry.

As the wagons had rolled east, and she looked back at her son that day in the Zone, she instantly regretted encouraging him to get back her ranch in Texas. Six weeks later, she was still fretting. And when Frederick entered the house with that bad news look on his face, her heart almost stopped.

Frederick quickly held up his hand. "Whoa, Red. I know that look. . .nuthin' real bad's happened."

"But something has happened."

"Yep. Henry and Miguel are fine, I'm told, but some troops from the United States burned the Zone clean to the ground and kilt a few nesters."

"Why?"

"That's a damned good question. According to what Salcedo told me, it politics."

"Politics?"

"The way I see it, the United States is two-faced when it comes to Texas. I don't think they like the Spaniards any more'n the Mexicans do, but they got bigger fish to fry because the British are still a threat and the Spaniards are against anything British, making them allies."

"So this attack on the Zone was to keep the *gachupín* happy."

"That's the way I see it. But it didn't mean anything. There's talk that a lot of money is bein' raised in the United States to fund that Mexican Army of the North, in hopes they'll take Texas."

"I hope our Henry doesn't have any ideas of joining them."

"I wouldn't count on it, Red. Him'n Miguel are pretty riled up and they're young. . . ." he shrugged, recalling the young men he fought with when he was Henry's age. Katherine would never understand, even if he could find the words to explain.

Katherine stared at Frederick for a few seconds, blew an exasperated breath, and huffed, "Men! Politics! I'm sick of both." Frederick watched helplessly as she stormed from the room. He too, hoped Henry would be sensible and not join the pending invasion, but he doubted it.

The Zone, after Magee's attack, quickly returned to normal: filthy, dangerous, iniquitous.

The Republican Army of the North, founded by Mexican rebel Bernardo Gutierrez de Lara and surreptitiously funded by the United States Government, flourished.

The American government, feigning friendship with Spain, turned a blind eye to the activities of the invasion force building strength in the Zone.

The Spanish Royal Army, hounded on all sides by Mexican rebels, had no choice but to leave the snakes' nest on their border to its own designs.

It was the summer of 1813 when the snakes struck.

CHAPTER 18

"Miguelito, it's hotter'n the hinges of Hell out here. Oh, forgive me, sir."

Private Henry Stockman, newly hired as scout and translator for the first formal offensive—dubbed the Magee-Gutierrez Expedition—of the Republican Army of the North, gave Miguel a sloppy salute. "*Permiso* to speak, sir."

"Permission granted, you lowly cannon fodder," Lieutenant Miguel Gonzales retorted.

Henry dug a battered piece of paper from his pocket. "I want to read you this brochure our fearless leader wrote right before we left the Zone."

"You mean Colonel Magee?"

"Nope. None other than your very own head Mexican, Gutierrez. Ain't he the one in charge of getting Texas and Mexico free from Spain?"

"He is."

"Well then, this is what he wrote." Henry straightened in his saddle, adopted a deep, heavily accented baritone and began to read:

"Soldiers and citizens of San Antonio de Béjar. It is more than a year since I left my country, during which time I have labored indefatigably for our good. I have overcome many difficulties, have made friends and have obtained means to aid us in throwing off the insulting yoke of the insolent despotism. Rise en masse soldiers and citizens; unite in the holy cause of our country!"

Miguel and Henry exchanged grins at the flowery style of the author.

"I am now marching with a respectable. . . ." Henry threw back his shoulders to give his impression of what respectable looked like, *"force of American volunteers who have left their homes and families to take up our cause to drive the tyrannous Europeans beyond the Atlantic."*

Miguel chuckled at his friend's antics.

"Henry, he fails to mention that our army consists mainly of the criminal element. Or that Colonel Magee, who, as I recall, we called a 'mean little bastard' not long ago, is now one of us. And that same Magee, newly appointed to lead our Army of the North, has recruited, and is leading into battle, the very men he tried to shoot as 'undesirables' a short while back."

"Hell, Miguelito, Magee still is a mean little bastard, but now he's *our* mean little bastard. And we're still undesirables, it's just that now we're *his* undesirables."

They rode for a while in silence, then Henry blurted, "Perhaps you can tell me, *Teniente* Gonzales, why Gutierrez writes, *I am now marching*—when he ain't? I personally haven't seen a sign of Colonel Gutierrez?"

Miguel refused to look at Henry, and remained stonily silent.

Henry grinned and prodded. "And why we're riding into Texas, in the name of Mexican independence, led by an American officer? Where, pray tell, *is* our dauntless leader?"

Miguel's jaw worked, then he shot Henry an annoyed look. "Enrique, it is not up to us, the soldiers, to question the actions of our commanding officers," he scolded.

"No? Says who? How come Gutierrez ain't here with his troops? The *norteamericano* volunteers keep asking me that question, and I don't have an answer—other than the obvious one," Henry said, folding his arms with his hands under his armpits, waggling his elbows and squawking loudly.

Miguel glowered. "I am certain that Colonel Gutierrez has good reasons for his actions. And what *you* think, Private, is of little importance to the world," Miguel huffed, spurring his horse forward and away from Henry's taunts. Despite himself, Miguel, too, wondered if it was cowardice keeping Gutierrez far behind the front of the invasion force.

Nacogdoches, the incursion's first objective, fell easily into rebel control when the Spanish garrison, out-armed and out-manned, retreated. To Miguel's dismay, Lt. Colonel Bernardo Gutierrez de Lara arrived only after the Stone Fort was secured.

At least the Mexican commander brought a printing press and issued the first newspaper in Texas.

La Graceta churned out anti-royalist propaganda designed to recruit and inflame even the least rebellious among the military and civilian populations in Texas and Mexico.

Henry didn't need inflaming or recruiting, but the paper spurred his enthusiasm for their invasion to new heights.

"Here it is, Miguel," he announced, waving a copy of *The Gazette*. "History in the making, amigo, and we're flat smack dab in the middle of it. If I was one of them old soldier buddies of yours in San Antonio de Béjar, I'd have the pure piss scared out of me after reading this stuff."

"They will lose more than water if they are caught reading it. Salcedo will hang them without a blink of a tear in his filthy *gachupín* eyes." Miguel took the paper and read the first few lines.

"Just think, Miguelito, when Pa whipped the Redcoats back in the American Revolution, a whole new country was founded. And it started with men like us, some guns, and a paper or two."

"Enrique, what has brought about this sudden burst of patriotism?" Miguel teased his friend.

"I guess I just realized that it won't be long before we'll head for the Trinity River. When Pa was kicked out, I never thought I'd see it again. I don't know. . .it's like. . .coming home. That's it. Texas is home. And always will be."

"Mine too, amigo. We will live here, or die trying."

Miguel and Henry shook on it, experiencing the euphoric bond of fellow crusaders since man began such missions.

Henry was secretly relieved to find the garrison at Villa Trinidad deserted. He had mixed feelings about a showdown with Felipe de la Garza, although he knew the Spaniard would not have the same reservations. While perfectly willing to fight the faceless army of Spain, Henry had qualms about shooting at someone he knew.

He'd soon get over that.

Splitting off from the main force, Henry and Miguel rode south along the Trinity to the old Stockman ranch and found Juan and Lupe keeping the home fires burning.

"*Madre de Dios*," Lupe cried when she saw them. "Juan, look, our boy has returned."

After a joyous reunion, the two old Mexicans told Henry of a man who petitioned to buy the place, but nothing came of it because the Spaniards were to busy fighting rebels and Indians to do the paperwork. The *gachupín,* they said, did not ask them to leave, so they stayed, hoping for a reprieve for Frederick.

Later that night when they were bedded down, Miguel whispered to Henry, "Enrique, I think it is best for Juan and Lupe to move to Louisiana, and the safety of your family, until we have won Texas. It is dangerous for them to stay here alone."

"You heard me practically begging, Miguel. They flat refuse to budge. They say they're too danged old to be moving to another country where they don't speak the lingo. They just hope we'll win our fight. If that's what you could call what we're doin'."

Miguel asked, "What do you mean?"

"Well, for one thing our Army hasn't fired a single shot. The only Royals we see are the deserters who wait to join us. At this rate, we could ride all the way to Mexico and never see the enemy," Henry said with a slight air of disappointment.

"Do not bet your horse on it, amigo. Remember, I was once one of them, and I can assure you the Spaniards will stand and fight when they feel they can win. They are well armed and organized south of the Rio Bravo. I fear the *norteamericanos* in the Army of the North, and particularly Colonel Magee, underestimate the enemy.

Mark my words, Enrique, the Crown will not surrender without a fight, and we will soon be up to your armpits in Spanish and Mexican Royalists."

Miguel was right.

CHAPTER

19

"Lieutenant Gonzales, it occurs to me that the Spaniards let us chase 'em until they caught us."

Miguel just grinned and gave Henry an I-told-you-so look.

"Here I thought we were right clever, taking this fort at La Bahia and all, what with the place being full of food and powder. But now, here we sit, with plenty of everything, surrounded by the whole danged Spanish Army." Henry was not adjusting well to confinement *or* army life.

Miguel looked resigned. "I would estimate that a good percentage of the Spanish troops in Texas are indeed just outside these walls. Now, if you wish to quit whining for a moment, I will explain how war works. It is so simple that, if you listen, even *you* might comprehend."

"I'm listening," Henry grumbled.

"Good. It is your duty as a soldier to follow orders and rush to attack the enemy. Then, if you live, you are allowed to wait until the enemy tries to kill you. We wait for the Royals to attack because it is their turn. *Comprende?*" Miguel asked with a sardonic smile.

"I'll tell you what I *comprende.* I understand we're stuck inside these cold stone walls with a crazed, overconfident Mexican Colonel and a demented American Colonel who detest each other, surrounded by Spanish Colonels who want to kill us. Colonel Magee gets more addled by the day, and Colonel Gutierrez—well, you know what I think of him." Henry spat on the floor, bringing a dangerous glint to Miguel's eyes.

Seeing he had angered his friend, Henry tried making amends.

"Well, what I mean is, he ain't the kind of man I want to die for. I don't trust him. Your Colonel," Henry couldn't resist emphasizing the *your*, "seems to think that little parley Colonel Magee had with Governor Salcedo the other day was some kind of conspiracy. Like he thinks that Magee is gonna kill him off and turn La Bahia over to the Spaniards. That just ain't so—hell, I was *there*, translating."

"Exactly what was said?"

"Well, Governor Salcedo offered Magee exactly what he told Gutierrez: The Army of the North—well, he didn't call us that, 'cause he refuses to acknowledge we're a real army—could leave Texas safely if we surrendered and promised not to come back. I thought it was a right generous offer, considering Salcedo's boys have our butts surrounded."

"Enrique, I think Salcedo meant you *norteamericanos* could leave Bahia and go home, not the Mexican rebels. He would hang us," Miguel said quietly.

"I've gotta admit that's what Governor Salcedo wanted, but Colonel Magee wouldn't stand for it. He said all of us get safe passage, or no deal. I heard him, amigo. Why won't Gutierrez believe him?"

"Colonel Gutierrez is a peasant, Enrique."

"Spoken like a true *gachupín*, Miguelito," Henry said with a snort of laughter. The tension eased with his teasing.

Miguel looked sheepish. "What I meant is, Colonel Gutierrez has suffered many indignities at the hands of the Spaniards. We—they—have taught Mexicans to trust no one. Especially northern foreigners."

"I guess," Henry said, standing and touching La Bahia's stone walls as if wishing them to disappear.

"Miguel, if you and your buddies want to rot in here, that's fine by me, but I, for one, would just as soon charge out for a showdown. It's gettin' more dangerous inside than out."

Miguel leaned forward and whispered, "I have heard rumors that Magee is even more *loco* than you think. Some say he cries at night, whether from pain or fear we do not know. Something bad is going to happen."

On February 6, 1813, six months after leading the Army of the North into Texas, Colonel Augustus Magee was dead.

"What killed him?" Henry asked Miguel.

"There is a rumor. A very sinister one," Miguel said. "They say Magee committed self-murder."

"I can't rightly believe that, Miguel. Augustus was a little on the peculiar side, but hell, who isn't by now? I hear there's gonna be some kind of burial ceremony this afternoon."

Strutting in full regalia before his troops, Colonel Bernardo Gutierrez pulled a sad face.

"It is," he said, "never good to lose a fellow soldier and military leader. But we must not let this loss deter our valiant mission to free our enslaved fellow Mexicans."

He continued his flowery rhetoric for some time, then dropped a verbal bomb.

"Before he took his own life, Colonel Magee confessed he had agreed to accept fifteen thousand pesos, and a position in the Royal Army, in exchange for surrendering this Army, his very own men, to the Spanish mongrel, Salcedo."

Gutierrez paused for effect. When the buzz died down he said, "The traitor, Magee, poisoned himself rather than face a firing squad. We shall now, without this betrayer in our midst, continue our perseverance towards our noble goal to be free. *¡Viva Mexico! ¡Viva la Revolution!*"

Henry glared at Gutierrez, then turned to Miguel and James Gaines, and hissed, "That's the biggest pile of horse shit I ever heard."

Two weeks following Magee's so-called self-murder, when Henry felt he could not survive another day holed up at La Bahia, Governor Salcedo's army mysteriously disappeared.

Fearing a trap, the Army of the North stayed behind the fortress walls until some Royalist Army deserters outside convinced them that the Governor's forces had indeed retreated to San Antonio.

"I don't give a damn why they left, Miguel, so long as they're gone. I'm so glad to be shut of that cussed presidio, I'd kiss ole Quicksand smack on the lips if he had better breath. Look at this horse smile. He don't even care if we're riding into a Royalist trap," Henry yelled, urging Quicksand to a full gallop.

A cool breeze wafted steam from the horse as man and beast rejoiced in racing across Texas in pursuit of the retreating Royalist troops.

The battle at Salado Creek, just outside San Antonio, lasted a furious twenty minutes. Neither Henry, Miguel nor James Gaines fired a shot, but were instead engaged in chasing down and rounding up Royalist deserters who were all too happy to throw down their arms. The Royalists had seen, in the first few minutes of pitched battle, three hundred of their fellow soldiers fall, while only six men of the Republican Army of the North lost their lives.

When the dust cleared, Henry surveyed the carnage and decided Frederick Stockman was right—this revolution business wasn't all it was cracked up to be. Even when you won the battle.

Governor Salcedo ordered his army to retreat to San Antonio and, in an effort to negotiate a fair surrender, invited his enemies to dinner at Casa Reales. Henry went as translator and when he returned to camp, Miguel and others waited anxiously.

"What happened in there?" Miguel asked as he and others gathered around Henry.

James Gaines, who had also attended the dinner, prompted, "Go ahead Stockman—tell 'em. You talk the best Mexican and understood more than most of us. I was too busy drinking up His Excellency Salcedo's wine to pay much attention. I'll say this, though, those Spanish gentlemen have got some manners on 'em. They're slicker'n a New Orleans card player, and almost as fancy in their dressing habits."

"Enrique, did they surrender?" Miguel demanded impatiently."

"Naw, they didn't even talk much about the war, or surrendering. It ain't considered polite at a social function. My Mama taught me that." Henry thought for a minute, and then said, "It was all real civilized. Salcedo even congratulated us on our victory, and then we ate pretty good. Too bad Colonel Gutierrez refused to attend, because. . . ."

James Gaines interrupted. "That's *General* Gutierrez, *Private* Stockman. He gave himself a promotion today."

"Well, pardon me," Henry rolled his eyes. "Anyhow, *General* Gutierrez wasn't missed much, but maybe if he'd a gone this stand-off could'a been fixed. I always found that if you sit down face to face with a man across a dinner table, it's easier to understand his side of the story. I kinda got the idea the col—uh—the general, is uncomfortable rubbing elbows with highborn types, him being a *mestizo* and all. He don't have very good manners, you know."

Henry had the full attention of his fellow rebels. They loved a good story and he knew how to draw one out.

"And I suppose you do, *General* Stockman," one of the men yelled.

Henry, feigning indignity, shot the soldier an arrogant look.

"I sure as hell do, Bob. I don't always act proper, but I know how, thanks to my dear Mama. Too bad you didn't have one."

Bob blushed and the men laughed. One of the troop quipped, "Ole Bob had a mother, it was his pappy what was a fence-jumper. Get on with the derned story. And what exactly is a '*mestizo*?'"

"A *mestizo*," Henry explained, "is part-Spanish and part-Indian. Gutierrez' Pa was probably a Spanish soldier, but no one knows for sure."

"I thought a Mexican was a Mexican and an Indian was an Indian. What the hell does that make you, Miguel?" the soldier asked.

Miguel fondled the smooth bone handle of his fighting knife. "That makes me a lieutenant, private."

Henry, sensing trouble, stepped in. "Permit me, Lieutenant Gonzales, to try to educate this oaf who obviously knows nothing of Mexican culture.

"Miguelito here is a *criollo:* a Spaniard born in Mexico. That's why he's got all that beautiful blonde hair and purty blue eyes. Hell, if he was a girl I'd marry him." Henry batting his eyelashes at Miguel, earning him a frown, then a grin.

Henry continued. "And then there's *peninsulares* like Governor Salcedo, who are home-grown Spaniards sent here to govern us lowlifes. And then there's. . . ."

James Gaines cut Henry off, yelling "Goddammit, Henry, sometimes you can get to sounding like a teacher or a preacher. Get on with the damned story."

"Well heck, Jaime, they asked. Now where was I? Oh, the dinner last night.

"Like I said, nothing much came of it. Tomorrow, the Spaniards will ask for terms, and surrender when the particulars are worked out. Salcedo might be trying to buy time, thinking he'll get help from somewhere, but our scouts tell us that's not likely. The Royalist have more men than rattlersnakes across the Rio Bravo, but lucky for us they aren't close enough to grieve us anytime soon."

Governor Salcedo and his officers surrendered the next day, requesting only humane treatment for the civilians of San Antonio and safe passage from Texas for their men.

In a melodramatic gesture, the Governor offered his sword to the American officers. When they diplomatically indicated he should surrender to General Gutierrez, Salcedo haughtily thrust the tip into the ground.

"Oh, Lord," Henry whispered, "he shouldn't have done that."

But Gutierrez, either not understanding the subtlety of the insult, or ignoring it, pulled the sword from the sand and waved it, shouting "*¡Viva Mexico!*"—and named himself Governor of Texas.

A quick trial found Salcedo guilty of treasonous behavior and sentenced him to death. Governor-General Gutierrez, at the insistence of his American officers, reluctantly overrode the death sentence, agreeing to safe passage for all the Spaniards to the United States border. Henry and James Gaines stood by as the party prepared to leave for Louisiana.

Governor Salcedo, his arms tied, gave Henry a slight bow and said, "Please give my regards to your family, Señor Estocoman. I want you to know it was not of my wish to deport your family from Texas. Your family's kindness to my wife and daughter was most appreciated. I should look forward to going to New Orleans, but since the fever claimed my wife. . . ." Salcedo's voice faltered.

"I heard of your loss, Your Excellency, and I'm real sorry. Doña María was a real nice lady. *Vaya con Dios*, sir," Henry said as he returned the bow.

"Gentlemen, just one more thing," Salcedo said to the Americans before he was led away. "I want you to know I appreciate what you have tried to do. Anything that happens from here forward will not be on your conscience. *Adios*."

Henry, Miguel, and James Gaines exchanged puzzled looks, but didn't have to puzzle long over the Governor's ominous parting words.

"Those lyin', murderin', sons-a-bitches have killed him," a Texican soldier wailed the next morning, capturing the attention of all who heard him.

"Who?" Henry asked.

"The Mexicans. They're out in the plaza braggin' about how they took 'em to the creek, slit their throats and left 'em for buzzard bait."

Henry grabbed the soldier by the arm. "Who, dammit? Who got their throats slit?"

"The Governor. Salcedo. And all his men. The Mexicans butchered 'em like hawgs. The murderin' sons-a-bitches. I knew you couldn't trust no Meskins." The man ran off to tell others.

Henry turned to James Gaines and Miguel, who were as nonplussed as he was. "That does it for me, boys. I'm headin' home to see Pappy Stockman. I can't take no more of this horse shit."

Gaines put his hand on Henry's shoulder and said, "Me too, Henry. This ain't right."

"How about you, Miguel? You comin' with us?" Henry asked.

"No, Enrique, I must stay. I do not approve of this treachery, but Salcedo *was* condemned to death by the Mexican people, and they wished satisfaction," Miguel said, a bit sadly.

"Satisfaction? More like murder. Out and out. Your *people* need to learn the rules of war," Henry snarled, then stomped off to get his saddle. Over his shoulder he called back, "Let's go, Jaime, and leave this pack of cowardly coyotes to do their own dirty work."

Miguel, wounded to the quick, spun on his heel and stormed away. Henry was too furious to care.

"Henry, sometimes you're just a little too damned self-righteous for your own good," James Gaines said quietly. "Miguel's like a brother to you, and this wasn't his fault."

Henry didn't answer.

"Stubborn cuss, ain't you Henry?

"Sometimes. I don't want to spend another day with that bastard Gutierrez. Let's get a burial party together and attend to Governor Salcedo on our way out."

CHAPTER 20

"Well James, I'm guess this is where we part company up if I'm going to go down and talk Lupe and Juan into going to Louisiana with me. You heading to the Norris place?"

"Yep. There's a young lady I have a hankerin' to see. I'll wait for you there, but don't take too long—I got a feeling all Hades is about to bust loose in Texas."

"That's what I've got to convince Juan and Lupe of. Say hello to the Norris bunch for me. *Hasta la vista.*"

Henry watched as James Gaines rode east along El Camino Real, then he turned Quicksand south along the Trinity River. As he rode, he mentally listed all his arguments to coax Lupe and Juan away from the ranch and out of Texas. Pronto.

A mile from Ganado Stockman he sniffed the air and picked up his pace. A few minutes later, he saw smoke.

"Oh m' God, Quickie, looks like trouble up ahead!"

A scene straight from Hell brought Henry and Quicksand up short when they entered the clearing near what had been the barn. In the yard, he found Lupe, Juan, and Furface, their mutilated and burned bodies nearly unrecognizable. Everything and everyone still smoldered.

Henry carefully reconnoitered the area, then dismounted, hot anger and profound sorrow churning in his gut.

"Oh, Quickie, whoever did this ain't even human," Henry whispered in his horse's ear. Quicksand, smelling death and danger, nervously snuffled Henry's chest.

"And there's only one bunch of bastards I know of mean enough to do something like this. Comanches." The horse nodded his big head and pawed the ground, seeming to agree.

Tears streaming down his face, Henry spent the rest of the afternoon burying Juan, Lupe and Furface. Exhausted, he pitched camp in the woods behind the rubble that was once his home. Before falling into a troubled sleep, he told Quicksand, "Now you wake me up if anyone comes, you hear?"

Just before dawn his horse nuzzled Henry awake. Stroking Quicksand's velvety nose he whispered, "I hope to hell you're just lonely. What is it, boy?"

Crouched in the inky darkness, Henry heard a wolf howl. Quicksand shivered, then his ears twitched and they heard the distinct sound of a horse's hooves shuffling over soft earth.

Peering into the darkness, Henry's eyes detected a shadow, just a little darker than the gloom. Then he saw a horse and rider and was slightly relieved to see that the horseman wore a hat. Not a Comanche. He hoped.

The shadow stopped to get his bearings, and Henry growled, "Just hold it right there, friend. Dismount real slow and put your hands on your hat."

"Enrique, is that you?"

"Miguelito! Oh, man, am I ever glad to see you."

Henry filled Miguel in while they drank coffee, and after sunup they searched the area for clues to identify the murderers.

"Enrique, it was most certainly the Comanches who did this terrible thing. I know their work from when I was in the army—the Royal Army, that is. It seems I am once again a deserter," Miguel said as he knelt by a trail of dried blood.

Standing, he added, "I think one of the Indians is wounded, unless this blood is from the scalps of your friends. Let us track them for awhile, amigo, what do you say?"

"I say tracking down Comanches is like pissin' into a strong wind—you get the job done, but the result can be a might messy," Henry said grimly. "But, if the odds are anywhere near in our favor, I want to go after the bastards."

After following the blood trail for an hour, they stopped to sum up their findings.

"Miguel, I make out twelve horses—ten with riders. Most likely they have Juan's gun, and Pa's musket, Old Bessie. Mama left Bess with Lupe, for what good it did her. If the Indians had another gun when they got to Ganado Stockman, there wasn't any evidence of it. They did their dirty work with knives and arrows. I think at least one Indian is wounded, so maybe we can dog his trail."

"So," Miguel held up nine fingers "to be on the side of safety, let us assume there are ten of them," he pushed one finger down, "nine healthy. With at least two guns."

"I reckon that makes us about even then, right?" Henry asked with a roguish grin.

"You are an arrogant man, Enrique. Perhaps that is what I like about you. In this case, it just so happens I agree with you. Let us go and bring them to justice."

“Texas justice, Miguel, Texican style. We'll track down the godless bastards and give 'em a little of their own evil medicine.”

It took them five days to close in on the Comanches.

Luck was with them, for the raiding party, instead of heading west to open range as Henry and Miguel had expected they would, turned south.

The Indians, not expecting to be followed, continued their rampage, leaving a wake of destruction and death through the East Texas thicket. Henry and Miguel found several unfortunate victims from other tribes, and one lone trapper, who had been savagely slaughtered.

“I sure hope they didn't get more'n one gun off that poor old trapper, Miguel. I doubt those mission Indians they killed had any.”

Miguel was deep in thought as he surveyed what was left of the ransacked camp.

“Enrique, I think the Comanches stole some kids from this tribe—I see children's things, but no bodies.”

Henry picked up a smooth wooden ball—a toy—and rolled between his palms.

“I'll bet you a peso to a cow patty those Comanches are on their way to sell the stolen children to the Karankawas down on the Gulf,” he said.

They remounted and continued to stalk their prey. Henry, who had been very quiet, suddenly threw the ball angrily into the woods.

“Bastards. Miguel, just last year Pa and me were talkin' about Comanches, and how to deal with them. I said I wasn't sure I could fight 'em with their own means, but now I know I can. When we catch those heathen bastards I plan to take me a scalp or two.”

If Miguel was shocked by Henry's announcement, he didn't show it. He understood the practicality of his friend's reasoning.

More and more white men were taking an eye for an eye, giving the Comanches a touch of their own terrorist medicine. Maybe the *norteamericanos* would finally come to see the necessity of what they seemed to think was cruel behavior on the part of the Mexicans and Spaniards when it came to dealing with their enemies.

And perhaps one day the Comanches would think twice before they butchered another grandmother.

As if reading Miguel's thoughts, Henry turned to him and said, "Miguelito, I'm real sorry for what I said back at San Antonio. I was angry about Salcedo being killed the way he was, especially after we told him he was going to New Orleans. I suppose if the tables were turned, he would have had us all shot. Maybe your way is the only way to be sure your enemy don't come back at you."

"Enrique, you were right to be upset. After you, Jaime, and most of the American officers left, things became very bad. The trash who stayed preyed upon the innocent villagers of San Antonio. They stole from them, raped the women—disgraced our cause."

"What was Gutierrez doing all this time?" Henry asked.

"Exactly what you thought in the beginning, my friend," Miguel said, then mimicked the chicken imitation Henry had used to express his disdain for Gutierrez at the onset of the Magee-Gutierrez Expedition many months before. "Strutting around in his General's uniform like a rooster, doing little to protect the good Mexicans of Béjar."

They laughed, then Miguel became serious again. "I am very ashamed that I could do nothing to stop him."

“Miguel, it ain't your fault Gutierrez is a coward and a glory-seeker. It's just a danged shame most folks will look at him and think all Mexicans are like him.”

“Enrique, you are a good man—for a *norteamericano*, that is,” Miguel grinned.

“I think we've kissed and made up enough. Let's go get us some Comanches. Do you know how a body goes about scalping another human being?” Henry asked.

“Yes, we Mexicans have learned from the Comanches.”

“Good. It don't seem like something I want to learn the hard way.”

Henry and Miguel vowed never to speak of their raid on the stunned Comanche camp.

When it was over they had washed away the Indian blood covering them, then returned the two captive children they rescued to the grateful Indians at Orcoquisac.

Returning to what was left of the Stockman ranch, Henry buried ten Comanche scalps near the graves of Lupe and Juan. He knew that Lupe, a devout Catholic, would not approve of such pagan offerings, but he could almost hear Juan say, “*Gracias*, Enrique, now go in peace.”

“Hello the house,” Henry yelled as he and Miguel entered the gated fence surrounding the main house at Naconichi, the Norrises ranch near Nachogdoches. Susannah Norris flew from the house, made a beeline for Henry, and nearly knocked him over.

Henry looked sheepishly at Miguel. “Me and Miz Susie have been sweethearts since we were little. She don't act like this with just anybody.”

"And she'd better not be actin' that way with you much longer, Stockman," James Gaines shouted with mock scorn as he walked from the barn, "seein' as how we're gonna get hitched."

"Jaime! Good to see you, amigo. I thought you would be in Louisiana by now."

"Probably should be—word just arrived that the entire Royalist Army, led by Colonel Arredondo, is about to cross the Rio Bravo, headed for San Antonio. The *gachupín* are a might perturbed over Salcedo's murder and this General Arredondo sent word he plans to kill every Mexican rebel and *norteamericano* he finds in Texas."

Miguel paled and said, "General Arredondo is a man of his word."

CHAPTER 21

"Those *norteamericanos* are a cowardly pack of dogs," the young Royalist sub-lieutenant sniffed, a look of disdain on his handsome face. "I would have expected a more. . .worthy. . .enemy."

He took a sip of wine.

"It eludes me how professional soldiers such as Governor Salcedo and Colonel Herrera lost their army, and their lives, to such pusillanimous mongrels."

He sat down on what was left of the murdered Governor's chair and gave the room a once-over. Nothing, save a half-burned portrait of María Salcedo, remained to suggest the former opulence of the ballroom. Gone were the silk curtains, wool rugs and intricately carved tables and chairs she had so lovingly collected.

On the other side of the room, General Arredondo poured himself more wine, then said, "I would remind you Antonio, my young friend, that it was not the *norteamericano* insurgents who murdered Salcedo, but Mexican rebels. Our very own people. Traitors, of course, but ours nonetheless. I am convinced we did not encounter the same army that Governor Salcedo's troops confronted at Salado Creek."

"I agree with you, General," another officer interjected, "and I do not think we will witness another invasion by *norteamericanos* soon. I believe our retaliations over the past weeks have captured their attention. Word of our punishment of those who would challenge the Crown will spread quickly. I would wager those *norteños* who have not already fled Texas will soon do so."

Antonio nodded. "I, too, am sure the pitiful curs have decamped for the safety of their American masters. They run and die like coyotes, yelping and crying. I do not find them worthy adversaries," the haughty nineteen-year-old lieutenant insisted.

General Arredondo did not comment further, preferring to let the arrogance of youth have its head. Young Antonio had fought bravely and ruthlessly, inflicting cruel revenge upon both *norteamericano* and Mexican rebel alike.

Perhaps, General Arredondo thought, *this Lieutenant Antonio Lopez de Santa Anna bears watching, lest his cruel zealousness becomes a danger to the Crown. Or myself.*

CHAPTER
22

"Riders comin' in, Mama," John Stockman yelled as he streaked past the open kitchen window of their Louisiana farmhouse. "Maybe it's Papa and George."

Katherine dusted flour from her hands as she ran to get her rifle, then walked out on the porch cradling the gun confidently in the crook of her elbow.

"John," she yelled, "come back here by me until we see who it is. You just never know these days. . .oh, my God!" She put down the gun and bolted towards the two men riding into the clearing between the house and the barn.

The smaller children, hiding behind Katherine's skirts, were left dumbfounded their mother's hasty departure, only following after John, Peter and Margaret ran after her. When Katherine threw her arms around one of the men, little Mary Sarah started to wail. After over a year, she held no memory of her brother, Henry.

"It's all right, sweetheart," Katherine said, scooping up the little girl, "don't be afraid. This is your big brother, Henry, home from the war in Texas. And our very best friend, Miguel."

The toddler smiled shyly, still hiccuping little sobs.

After more hugging and crying, Katherine pushed the two men towards the cabin. "My, you two look so, so. . .grown up. But too thin. And plumb wore out. Well, we'll fix that soon enough. John, why don't you take care of their horses, while I put something on the stove."

Henry and Miguel were soon happily seated at the kitchen table, surrounded by adoring family members.

Surveying the house, Henry said, "Looks like you could use some help around here, Mama."

"That's the truth. We just moved in a month or so ago, and haven't had time to do many repairs. You should have seen the first place we found after we left you. Compared to that, this is a palace," Katherine told them as she ladled thick squirrel stew into crockery bowls. "Here, boys, there's plenty more if you want it, so eat up. When you're ready, though, I want to hear all about your adventures. We got word you took Béjar—listen to me babbling. Go ahead and eat, and I'll simmer down."

"Mama, I've got an awful lot to tell you, but right now I just want to eat about a million of your biscuits. With all due respect to Miguel's people, I'm sick and tired of tortillas and beans."

Henry was talking with his mouth full of food, a great source of amazement to the younger children. Mama would *never* allow *them* to get away with such a breach of manners.

Henry swallowed half of a biscuit, waved his fork, and said, "The Spaniards are dead set on taking San Antonio back, from what we hear. I could be wrong, but I'd be willing to bet there won't be a settler left in Texas within a few weeks."

Taking another bite he smiled. "Mama, these biscuits are Heaven sent."

Katherine, overjoyed to have her son back home, nevertheless sensed a falseness behind his jocularity. She knew Henry would eventually tell her what was bothering him, but for now she was just happy he was safe.

"Dang, Ma," Henry mumbled through crumbs as he finished off his fifth biscuit and washed it down with buttermilk, "I think I've lost my appetite. When'll Pa and George be home?"

"Any day. They went over to the Mississippi to trade some hides, then they plan to stop in Natchitoches for building supplies. Like you said, this place could use a bit of fixing. Now that you're back things'll get done, too." She patted Henry's hand.

"Your Pa's been real busy trying to get us back on our feet. I plan do a little farming and ranching here, but it's sure not Ganado Stockman," Katherine said, somewhat wistfully. "Lordy, how I miss that house."

A shadowy glance passed between Henry and Miguel, and Katherine's heart skipped a beat. They had something dreadful to tell her.

"Maggie, take José Antonio and Mary Sarah out to play—John, Peter, go tend to your chores. I want to talk to Henry and Miguel in private," she said quietly.

"Why can't I stay?" Maggie whined. She had, at first, been uncharacteristically shy, but now she stayed glued to Miguel's side.

"I don't need any sass, young lady. Now skedaddle," Katherine sternly ordered, reaching for a peach twig switch she kept near the fireplace.

Margaret flounced out of the house and Katherine turned to Henry. "Son, what's happened?"

Katherine sat alone on the porch, rocking and watching the sun sink. Unlike some evenings, the sunset wasn't particularly pretty, for there were no clouds for the lowering sun to paint pink and orange. *Such an ordinary sunset, on such an extraordinary day*, she thought.

Supper over, the dishes washed, and tomorrow's bread on the rise, she had time to grieve. A warm tear rolled down her cheek as she pictured Lupe as she wanted to remember her: round, warm and cheerful.

Lupe and Juan, who came to them as employees and stayed to become family, were like parents to her— grandparents to the Stockman children. Now she would never see them again, and for the same reason she had never met her paternal grandparents—Indians.

A surge of loathing and hate for Indians suddenly displaced her grief, taking Katherine by surprise.

She had always feared and mistrusted Indians, but never hated them. And she knew, on an intellectual level, it was not logical to hate a group of people just because of their color.

Emotionally however, Katherine was engulfed with a deep malevolence towards the red-skinned people who had brought misery to generations of her family.

She wanted revenge. She wanted, at that moment, to murder, with her bare hands, every single Comanche—man, woman and child.

That last thought brought her up short. *I couldn't do it. Not the children. But I'm glad Henry got the men who killed Lupe and Juan. Thank you, Henry, for not telling me the details of the deaths. . .any of them. Some things are better not known. Please God, tell me you didn't let those kind old people suffer. I couldn't bear it.*

Katherine was sobbing softly when Henry returned from his chores in the barn. "Mama, do you want company?" he asked.

She wiped her eyes and patted the porch next to her. "Yes, son. I was just thinking about Lupe and Juan. I can't quite picture them dead, or the house as ashes. Perhaps that's best—but doesn't stop the hurt. And I can't stop thinking that if we had been there, would the Comanches have attacked? And if so, would we all have died? Could it have been God's will, through Governor Salcedo—rest his soul—to deliver us from this evil?"

"I don't know, Ma. Maybe the governor did save our lives by deporting us. It's just too bad he didn't leave and save himself, but I guess it wasn't his way."

Mother and son fell silent, then Henry said, "I wonder what it would be like to live where there wasn't someone out to kill you, or something trying to eat you? Is that what its like back East? Is it safe there?" He looked very much like a small boy with a perplexing problem. Katherine took his hand in hers.

"Well, son, I guess there are places like that, but you wouldn't like them. You'd feel all cooped up. Folks there judge you by your clothes, your manners, and the way you talk. No, Henry, it's not for us."

They fell silent again, then Katherine said, "I'm so glad you're home safe, Henry. That's all I really want anymore, for us to be together."

Henry took her hand and they watched fireflies and stars come out to blink at them.

CHAPTER 23

LOUISIANA 1814

"Ma, you'll never guess who we saw in Natchitoches! And you'll never guess what I did!"

George had ridden straight to the house, tied his horse out front and run into the house with his news.

Katherine smiled at his enthusiasm and cocked her head to hear what had him so excited.

"I met Andy Jackson himself. And I've joined up with him. We're marchin' for New Orleans in two days. Ain't that grand?"

Katherine blanched and fought to catch her breath as George jabbered on.

"The General says we'll be in New Orleans by Mardi Gras time. He says taking on the British will be as easy as shootin' ducks in a mill pond, what with them wearing bright red jackets with nice white X's acrost their chests."

Henry, hearing voices, walked into the great room to find his mother pale and speechless, his brother flushed with excitement. "You're gonna do *what?*" he asked.

"Enrique, you're back! Man, am I glad to see you," George exclaimed, hugging Henry. "I've volunteered under General

Jackson and we're goin' to New Orleans to kick some British bee-hind."

Frederick joined them and gave Henry a bear hug.

"I saw your horse in the barn, son—glad you're home." Turning to face his wife, he added, "Red, I tried to talk George out of this Jackson thing, but those boys in Natchitoches did a better job of talking."

Katherine found her voice—a raspy, quavering one. "In which brothel, Frederick, did you two find your good friend Andrew Jackson?"

All three men stared at Katherine, stunned by the bitterness in her question.

Frederick held out his hand in a defensive gesture. "Now Katrin, I. . . ."

"You know I've never liked that man, and now I can truly say I hate him. He's been nothing but trouble for this family ever since you two traded horses and slaves back in Bayou Pierre. He was trash then, and he's trash now—General or no. How could you entrust your oldest son's life to that whiskey-swigging, whore-mongering rapscallion?"

George's enthusiasm vanished. His mother, though not easily angered, had an atrocious temper when she let go. Even so, he thought he owed his father some defense. "Aw, Mama, Pa didn't have nothin' to do with it. I was talking with some of the General's men and they sorta recruited me. You wasn't riled when Henry took off to fight them Spaniards. And now they say if the British take Louisiana we'll all be run out and lose our home again. Dern it, Mama, I'm near thirty and I've never really done anything on my own. I won't be gone long, I promise."

Katherine's stare didn't waver, but her vicious attack on Frederick stopped. "I made a mistake back then. I should have never encouraged Henry to go back into to Texas. I was wrong."

Henry put a protective arm around her. "George, you'd best listen to Mama and rethink this thing. Army life ain't one bit glorious. I'm sure old Jackson is a damned sight better man than that Gutierrez I got mixed up with, and at least you'd be fightin' with the United States Army, but believe me, you really ought'a ponder on it some. After you've talked with me and Miguel."

George jumped at the chance to divert his mother's fury. "Miguel's here? Great. All right, little brother, I'll think about it, but I doubt I *can* change my mind, Mama. I already signed up."

Katherine shrugged off Henry's arm, whirled, ran out the door, mounted George's still-saddled horse, and rode away, leaving the men openmouthed.

Half an hour later, while George's horse contentedly munched sweet green grass, Katherine anguished.

She sat on a sun-warmed rock at the edge of a spring-fed pond, clenching and unclenching her fists and occasionally swiping tears of despair from her cheeks.

Standing abruptly, she whipped off her clothing and jumped into the chilly water, as if to baptismally remove her pain. Whether or not her soul was cleansed, the cold water lifted her spirits.

Stretched out on the bank after her plunge, a more serene Katherine cherished the soothing tinkle of water over stones, the trees' sighs—and the absence of posturing male voices.

Remembering Henry's question the day before, she looked to the sky and asked, "Well, is there, God? Is there a place where no one is trying to harm you? Or take your loved-ones from you? If there is, I sure would like to know where it is."

While Katherine was gone, the Stockman males and Miguel—an honorary Stockman—held a confab in the conference/smoking-room (also known as the barn). They sat on sweet smelling bales of hay and tried not to ignite their podiums.

Outside, Margaret and Mary Sarah secreted themselves near a knothole. Margaret, ear literally to the wall, quieted her three-year-old sister with sugar cane cubes while she eavesdropped.

Frederick waved his pipe and said, "Boys, looks like we're in hot water again. Red's real steamed up this time. George, let me ride back to Natchitoches and have a talk with Jackson. I think I can get you out of this deal. Hell, boy, let someone else take care of them redcoats."

"Pa, I *want* to go to New Orleans with Jackson," George insisted. "They say I'll be real valuable as a scout, 'cause I know the territory so well. And they're gonna pay me."

"Yep, that's what they told me, too, Jorge," Henry said ruefully, "but it turned out my value as a Hero of Mexico consisted of trying to stay alive while Colonels on both sides did their level best to get my brave ass shot."

Henry looked at Miguel. "You tell him Miguelito—have we ever been paid a single peso for our efforts?"

Miguel shook his head and Henry added, "Of course, we did desert, but they can't do nothin' to us. If you was to change your mind once you're in the United States Army, they'd shoot you for desertion. . . ." Henry stopped when James Gaines entered the barn.

"Jaime, I'm surprised to see you over this way so soon. How's everything at Gaines Landing? And what's the news from Texas?"

"Things are real busy at the landing. Me and the boys have been running that ferry acrost the Sabine day and night getting folks over to this side. All hell's broke loose in Texas. General Arredondo and the biggest damned army you ever saw swooped into San Antonio and wiped out what was left of our outfit. Word is, they didn't take no prisoners."

"Did they get Gutierrez?" Henry asked hopefully.

"Naw, the lucky son of a bitch left right before they came. But," Gaines drawled, "they did get the skunks that murdered Salcedo."

Henry shook his head in disgust. "So, we spent all that time fighting for nothing. The Spaniards, except for poor Salcedo, are right where they started. See what I mean about this war business, George?"

"Ain't the same, Henry. The United States is being threatened by England. It ain't like a bunch of outlaws, farmers, and such goin' up against the whole danged Spanish Army."

Henry laughed and winked at Jaime and Miguel. "We must be the *such*."

George blushed, saying, "Sorry, I didn't mean any offense to you boys. You've made us proud. I just hope I can."

"We're proud of you already, George. We're proud of all our boys," Frederick said as he sidled along the wall, leaned over to the knothole, and bellowed, "and girls."

Laughter followed the scampering of little feet.

James Gaines pulled Henry and Miguel aside on their way out of the barn.

"I know you're wondering why I left the ferry landing when we're so busy, but it's real important that I meet with a fellow in Natchitoches who's recruiting Mexican patriots."

Miguel's face lit up as he listened to Gaines.

"This Hero of Mexico," James told them, "is gonna sail from New Orleans for the Yucatan to fight the Spaniards. I want to talk to him about their plans. Wanna come?"

"I do," Miguel beamed. "It has been far too long since I have done injury to a Spaniard. And to do it on my own soil would be a pleasure."

"How about you, Enrique?" James asked.

"Naw, I've had just about all the revoltin' I can stomach for the time being. Anyhow, Ma would kill me if I left so soon, what with George taking off. I figure I'll hang around here a while, then I'm planning on going back to Texas when things settle down a bit. But don't tell Ma."

"I can't go to the Yucatan neither," Gaines said, "but some of us plan to run raids into Texas and maybe even settle along the border. That way we can squat in Texas territory, but run for the border if the Spaniards come looking for us. I want the support of the Yucatan bunch so's when we do take Texas—and we will—they'll recognize us for our efforts. But first and foremost, I'm getting married."

"You and Suzie are really gonna do it, huh? That's grand," Henry grinned. "I see Ma's back, so let's go tell her. She needs some good news today."

Katherine, still fuming, slammed bowls of fried chicken, cornbread, black-eyed peas, potatoes, gravy, and fried fruit pies on the table. She was so mad she hadn't bothered to cook much.

Between swallows of buttermilk, James Gaines said, "Miz Stockman, that's the best danged fried chicken I ever ate. If you can come to Gaines Ferry for me and Susannah's wedding in a couple of months, will you please teach my Suzy to fry chicken like this?"

The compliment drew a half-smile. "I'm glad you like it, James. We'll see about coming to your wedding. Maybe a trip would do us a bit of good. Right now I'm afraid I'm not very good company, what with George leaving. Thank God Henry's had his fill of playing soldier."

Katherine saw a look of hurt pass George's face and quickly added, "I'm sorry, Jorge, I don't mean to make light of you. I just wish there was some way I could change your mind."

"I know, Ma. But I got my heart set on it."

Katherine pursed her lips, then bit back a sour reply. She turned to Miguel. "Will you come back here before you go off to fight Spaniards?"

Miguel chose to ignore the disapproval in her voice and smiled. "Doña Katrina, I shall be back in time for more of your wonderful cooking tomorrow night."

Margaret fluttered her lashes and cooed, "Oh, that's wonderful, Miguel. I'll make a Mexican flan for you, just like Lupe taught me. I know you love it."

"*Gracias*, Margarita. I will look forward to it. Now, we must go."

Walking towards the barn, Henry said, "Miguel, I think little Maggie is sweet on you."

"She is a child, Enrique. Much too young for such thoughts."

"I don't know about that, Miguelito. When Mama was just a couple of years older than Margaret, she married my Pa," Henry warned.

James Gaines grinned and added, "I'd be real careful of those butterfly eyelashes, deep green eyes, and special-made flan, if I was you."

Miguel stopped, dramatically clamped his hands over his heart and intoned, "My temptress is the Revolution and, until she is won, I cannot embrace another."

Henry stared at Miguel, turned to Gaines and said, "James, don't you just love the way he talks?"

Back in the house, Margaret was effervescent.

"Mama, whatever shall I wear to the wedding? Something new, for sure. How far is it to Gaines Ferry? Oh, Mama, this is so grand," she gushed, bringing a smile to Katherine's lips.

"Maggie, we're not even sure we're going. Your father and I have to talk it over," Katherine told her rambunctious daughter.

"Can we Papa? Please, please, say yes. If you say no, I shall simply perish."

Frederick looked at Katherine, who was barely speaking to him. *Seems I can't do anything to please that woman no more,* he thought.

Aloud he said, "I guess we can't have Maggie perishin' on us. Get Henry to take you. I'll stay here and keep an eye on things. I never was much on weddings and such."

"Well, then, that settles it," Katherine said without looking at her husband, "I guess I'd best start looking around for cloth for a dress or two. It'll give me something to think about besides George leaving. Margaret, go get some peaches for a pie. We'll have that *and* flan tomorrow night."

Margaret rushed out the door for the storage cellar, Mary Sarah toddling after her.

"Is there anything you want me to do, Katrin?" Frederick asked.

"You can get my son back from that whore-mongering friend of yours, Frederick. That's what you can do."

CHAPTER 24

"Dammit Pa, I can't believe Ma thinks we'll be needing all this stuff for a one month trip," Henry groused as he made his tenth trip from the house to the wagons. "I mean to give James Gaines a swift kick for getting' married. And inviting us."

"Son, your Ma and me's been travelin' since before you were born and we put a passel of miles under us. We've learned a lot. Your Mama's learned that if you even think you'll need it, you will and I learned not to argue with her," Frederick said as he secured a barrel of flour to the sideboard.

Henry looked at the other barrels already piled in the wagon and shook his head in disgust.

Frederick smiled. "Besides, all this packin's given your Mama something to do besides pine for George. And mark my words, once you get on the road you'll be glad she packed everything except the barn."

"Have you checked on the barn lately, Pa?" Henry grumbled.

The Norris clan and several other families were already encamped by the Sabine River when the Stockmans reached Gaines Ferry landing. Henry and his brothers pitched camp, then helped with the common facilities.

Those families with slaves put them to work building a pavilion for dancing and visiting, while the young male guests hunted, fished and drank.

Old men whittled, spat, drank and talked of wars past and present while roasting meat, fish, and fowl over low-burning mesquite fires.

Young women fawned over the bride-to-be, while Katherine and her lady friends griped about the men's drinking and spent hours reminiscing about Texas, trading recipes, gossiping, and cooking hundreds of pounds of beans, cornbread, pies, and cakes. And mentally matching up their young for later marriages.

In the evenings, musical instruments—fiddles, a violin, and even a cow bell—were unpacked, and the dancing began.

Virginia reels, transformed by Mexican influence into uniquely Tejano-fandangoes, were performed with great gusto. Some older revelers enjoyed polkas and waltzes, but frowned upon the rowdy Texican-style cavorts.

Baptists and Methodists castigated all revelers, prophesying damnation for the lot—and each other.

Katherine, catching her breath between dances, saw that Henry shied away from dancing and vowed to teach him soon. Peter, on the other hand, was frolicking with anyone whose toes had a high threshold of pain. *Another candidate for dancing lessons*, she thought.

Margaret, very popular, but haughtily unimpressed with her youthful suitors, oscillated between being a rambunctious twelve-year-old and playing the coquette.

After a week of setting up camp and ten days of festivities, the wedding was almost anti-climactic, but the Susannah glowed and James was almost sober, so all went well.

Margaret sobbed throughout the ceremony, embarrassing her brothers even more than the kissing part.

Katherine shed a tear as well, and wondered if it was for the occasion, or herself.

After the wedding Katherine decided they would stay another week to help with the clean-up. She was inside her tent packing to leave when she heard Margaret shriek, "Mama would you just look at your sons?"

Katherine, happy to hear that the boys were back from what they told her was a hunting trip, hurried out just in time to witness Henry, John, and Peter swimming a herd of frantic mustangs across the Sabine.

Henry, in the lead on Quicksand—the Judas horse— guided the herd helter-skelter through camp and into a makeshift corral. Cheers arose, but Katherine was not amused.

Henry shut the gate, then walked back to face his disgruntled mother, a sheepish grin on his dusty face.

"Henry Stockman," Katherine fumed, hands on hips, "I cannot believe you took your little brothers into Texas." The crowd gathering to congratulate Henry dispersed quickly.

"Heck Mama, we didn't go that far and there ain't no Spaniards this close to the border. Besides, we got us enough horse flesh here to pay for a whole heap of house fixin'," Henry beamed.

Katherine harrumped and went to her tent, but Henry knew he was redeemed when she later brought apple pie to him as he was preparing to brand his new herd.

"Thanks, Mama," Henry said, devouring the piece of pie in three chomps, then sitting on his haunches to twirl the branding iron in the fire. "We're 'bout ready."

"Henry, is that a new iron? You're not using the Ganado Stockman brand anymore?" Katherine asked.

Mischief twinkled in Henry's eyes. "Mama, me and the boys made this one up not long ago. We think it's a right fittin' brand for borrowed Spanish mustangs."

Katherine watched her son take the branding iron from the fire and thrust the red-hot end against a tree trunk. Henry stepped back so she could admire his handiwork. Burned into the tree, Katherine saw:

Giggling with delight, Katherine slapped her son on the shoulder. "Henry, you know danged well that you don't just 'Bar-O' His Majesty's mustangs. You steal 'em fair and square."

All visited out and homesick, the Stockmans started for home. After four weeks Henry missed his dog, Maggie missed her friends, and Katherine missed her home. But more than anything, they all missed Frederick.

Katherine rode in front of the wagons, pondering Margaret's volatile mood swings.

The girl had fallen into a dismal slump after Miguel left, but a few days later she was back to her impetuous self, preparing for the Gaines wedding. At Gaines Ferry she was as unpredictable as the weather, shining one minute and clouding up the next.

Katherine suspected her daughter's unrequited crush on Miguel to be the culprit. *Not surprising,* she thought. *Miguel is strikingly handsome and cuts a romantic figure when he charges onto the scene, twangs a few heart strings, and disappears in a cloud of dust, leaving the people who love him a little breathless. Just like Frederick.*

She suddenly realized how *much* she missed Frederick. *Why do I always blame him when things go to hell? He does the best he can under the circumstances.*

Maybe all the years of trials and tribulations in their marriage had wounded the love between them, but there was a big difference between somewhat-worse-for-the-wear love and no love at all. *I do love him, and when we get back today I'll tell him so. And ask him to forgive me for being so hard on him.*

Feeling an urgent need to see her husband of thirty years, she spurred her horse and yelled back, "Henry, I'm going on ahead. See you at home."

What put a bee in her bonnet? Henry thought. *Women can be mighty peculiar.*

Frederick heard a horse approaching and was waiting on the front porch when his wife rode in at full gallop, jumped from her horse and threw herself into his arms. He held her tightly for a few minutes, then, taking a deep breath, he looked into her eyes and started to say something, but she put her hand over his mouth to stop him.

"Shhh, Frederick," she whispered. "In a while you can tell me, but first I want to ask you to forgive me. I've been wrong to blame you for our son's decision, and whatever's happens we'll face it together. Our children have their own lives, but we only have each other."

Frederick held her even tighter, and she felt tears on his face, the first she knew to be there.

"George never even made it to New Orleans, Red," he sobbed into her hair. "He was killed outside of town before they got there."

CHAPTER 25

On February 6, 1815, ghostly clouds of war-smoke and ghosts of war-dead haunted the skies over New Orleans. On this day, Miguel began his search for George Stockman.

Although well acquainted with the quirks of war, Miguel still puzzled over how he, a Mexican revolutionary, ended up fighting the British.

He had left Natchitoches, bound for Mexico with a Mexican patriot named Peter Ellis Bean, and next thing he knew he was in someone else's war.

During the ride from Natchitoches to southern Louisiana, Bean had told Miguel how, after he'd joined a group of filibusters lead by a man named Phillip Nolan, he'd ended up in a Mexico City prison.

Peter Bean snorted in derision. "Now that I look back on it I should have knowed better than to hitch up with a fella who wanted to crown himself King Nolan of Texas."

As Miguel listened to Bean make light of losing fourteen years of his life because he had followed another man's delusional dream, he silently vowed not to do the same.

"Pedro, please explain to me why we are going to this place called Barataria. I know it is in the river delta south of New Orleans, but who, or what, is there for us?" Miguel asked.

"Truth is, Miguelito, a bunch of pirates."

"Pirates?" Miguel asked in astonishment. "Real pirates? Not *filibusteros*?

"Genuine, cutlass-totin', rum-sluggin', throat-cuttin' articles. They sail the Gulf on their faster'n-brush-fire ships and waylay just about anyone who's out there. They consider themselves American patriots, in their own fashion, but give the British, Spaniards and just about everyone else hell."

"How is it you know these pirates?"

"Well, after what seemed like about a million years in the *gachupín* prisons, and after every last man I'd been captured with in Texas was dead, I decided I'd better come up with a plan."

Miguel resisted asking the man what took him so long and continued listening to the tale.

"I got myself out by convincing the Royalist they needed me—a *norteamericano* who knew how Americans think. 'Course, the minute I was free, I found me some Mexican patriots, 'cause after all those years in their tender care, there ain't nothing I hate more'n a Spaniard. Anyhow, the Mexicans gave me money for a ship so I could come here to recruit men like you. I got the ship all right, but the crew was pretty green and I didn't know much about sailing. Still don't."

Bean spit and stretched in his saddle, then continued. "We were taking on victuals off Vera Cruz when I saw this ship come out of nowhere and attack a British vessel nearby. There was a hell of a battle, but the English lost their ship, their cargo, and then their lives. The whole thing didn't take more'n three hours.

"A couple of days later we were sailing north when we spotted that British ship sittin' aground where those French pirates, drunk as skunks on British grog, had put her. High and dry." Peter Bean smiled, recalling the scene.

"What did you do?" Miguel asked. "Were you not afraid the pirates would attack you?"

"Naw, they already had their chance and besides, we were flying Mexican revolutionary standard. Anyhow, we pulled 'em off the beach and they helped us sail to New Orleans. We been thick as thieves, you should pardon the expression, ever since. You gotta meet 'em."

"Why, Pedro, would I want to meet these bloodthirsty Frenchmen, when I do not even like the *francés*?" Miguel sniffed.

"Because, my friend, they're gonna help us fight the Spaniards."

"Perhaps, but it has been my long experience not to trust a Frenchman. What are their names?" Miguel asked.

"Jean and Pierre Lafitte."

One week after their arrival in the Lafitte stronghold at Barataria, the United States Navy, concerned that British sympathizers lurked there, attacked.

Miguel and Peter Bean ended up taking refuge with the Lafitte brothers in New Orleans.

Then the British attacked New Orleans and Colonel Miguel Gonzales, would-be Hero of Mexico, found himself with Bean and a bunch of pirates fighting for the preservation of the liberation of the United States. Although exhilarated to end up—for once in his life—on the winning side of a war, the sweet taste of victory soured when he learned of the death of George Stockman.

He sent a note to the newly proclaimed "Hero of New Orleans," General Andrew Jackson, requesting an audience. He signed it *Frederick Stockman,* hoping that would get him in the door. It did.

"Say there, Frederick, whatever you've been eatin' and drinkin', I want some," Jackson said wryly when he saw Miguel Gonzales enter his office.

"Please forgive me, General, for my subterfuge, but I am in need of your assistance to find the grave of George Stockman. My name is Miguel Gonzales, and Jorge Stockman was like a brother to me. I feel I owe it to his family to make certain the grave is marked."

"Stockman's boy is dead? Damn, I hadn't heard," Jackson sighed, shaking his head sadly. "Death is a fact of war, but never impersonal."

Taking a closer look at Miguel, Jackson said, "I like a man with initiative, Gonzales. Are you in my army?"

"No, General. I am a Mexican patriot—a colonel in the service of the Republic of Mexico. But I fought in your battle against the British."

"Ah, the Gutierrez patriots?" Jackson asked.

"I was not with Gutierrez in this battle. I do not consider him a patriot," Miguel growled.

"Now I know who you are. You and the other Stockman boy and James Gaines were on that Magee-Gutierrez campaign into Texas. I wish you Mexicans all the luck, but you can't tell anyone I said that, since my government still officially recognizes Spain's claim to Mexico.

"Let me guess, Colonel Gonzales—you fought in New Orleans with the brothers LaFitte, didn't you?"

Miguel nodded uncertainly, not sure if he should own up to being in cahoots with a passel of pirates.

Jackson winked. "Don't worry, son. Whatever troubles those Lafittes have had with the law here in the past, they've earned my gratitude and respect. Tell them that.

"And," he scribbled a note, and handed it to Miguel, "give this to my aide. He'll help you find out what became of George Stockman. When you see George's Ma and Pa you tell 'em I'm sorry as hell this happened."

"*Gracias,* General. I am very grateful for your help. And I shall pass on your condolences to Señor and Señora Stockman," Miguel said, saluting the famous Indian fighter and American hero. He did not say that if Señora Stockman ever crossed the General's path, he was certain to be a dead American hero.

"And I am grateful to you, Colonel Gonzales. You and those Lafittes helped save our butts. Next time you need to talk to me, use your own name," Jackson said, smiling and shaking Miguel's hand.

Andrew Jackson returned to his desk and wrote a note reminding himself to look into this Texas thing. With men like Gonzales, the Mexicans just might pull off their revolution. Then with Mexico in turmoil, the General's men could possibly get a foothold on Texas soil.

Unofficially, of course.

Miguel marked George's grave with a slab of carved wood, paid a stonemason to replace it with something that would last, then sat nearby to look through George's personal effects. He found a half-finished letter that he read though blurring eyes.

Dear Mama and Pa and the others,

We are getting close to New Orleans, and I figger we'll whip the Brits and I'll be home real soon. I miss your cooking, Mama, and can't wait to have some of your biscuits and gravy if I can beat Henry to the table.

Henry you was right about this fighting not being much fun. We mostly just march and wait to march some more, but we'll be seeing some action soon.

We're leaving now, so I'll finish this after we get to New Orleans.

Miguel arranged to send George's letter and his gun to the Stockmans, then went to find Peter Bean. He had a revolution to fight.

CHAPTER 26

Peter Bean, along with his Mexican patriot recruits, had already sailed when Miguel reached Barataria.

Using his legendary charm, a cache of personal funds, and his Lafitte connections, Miguel secured passage on a small trader bound for Vera Cruz.

Although the *Molly* was of American registry, Miguel suspected the swift little vessel guilty of one or two international maritime infractions. The fact that she had wafted in from Galveston Island, off Texas, was evidence enough—legitimate vessels gave that pirate-infested island a wide berth.

On their third afternoon out of port, the humidity rose to an unpleasant level and the wind died. Without a breeze the ship turned sideways to the waves and wallowed between building troughs.

"Captain, what do you make of this?" Miguel asked, struggling to keep his mind from his roiling stomach.

"Lieutenant, if I tell you what I think, you're liable to turn a might greener than you are now," the Captain growled.

"How much worse can it *get?*" Miguel asked through clenched teeth.

"A lot. I've sailed these waters many a year, boy, and I'd wager we're about to get a blow that don't normally happen this early. I can usually halfway out-guess the weather, but anyone who thinks they can get one up on old King Neptune usually ends up meeting with the gentleman. I think I'd best get all hands on deck."

A freshening breeze two hours later allowed the crew to raise sails and change course, so the captain decided to make a run for Cuba.

Miguel, exhausted by seasickness, was grateful for the change in course—even if it was in the wrong direction—but the ride became a heart stopper, with the little ship slamming through huge cresting waves.

Miguel wedged himself into a relatively dry spot under an oiled tarp and fell asleep as the sun set.

"*Madre de Dios*," he cursed, jarred awake by the sickening sound of cracking wood followed by a loud crash. Peering out from under his tarp he was greeted by a dawn whipped up by the angry gods of the sea.

Held only by lines and shredded sails, the ship's main mast had broken off and was trailing overboard

The crew worked frantically on the heaving deck to cut the lines before the sails filled with thousands of pounds of water and dragged the entire ship under. The Herculean efforts of the crew paid off, but once the mast was free there was little more they could do but heave to.

The entire crew lashed themselves in below decks, resigned to riding out the storm.

Days and nights of Caribbean fury followed, but the little ship held her own. Then as suddenly as it hit, the storm stopped.

Miguel, daring to untie himself and escape the foulness below, stumbled on deck and reveled in a fresh, salt-tinged breeze. Unfortunately, the pristine air allowed him to get a whiff of himself and his fellow seamen.

"*Jesús y María*, Captain, we stink," Miguel said, surveying his surroundings. Sailors bustled about, carrying lines, canvas and all manner of wooden objects unknown to him. "What are they doing?"

"Tryin' to get up enough sail to get us there," the Captain said, pointing over the bow. The ship still rolled in a confused sea, making it hard for Miguel to focus, but on the crest of a wave he caught a glimpse of land.

"Cuba!" a sailor yelled. A cheer arose from the crew and they redoubled their efforts to rig a makeshift sail.

Finally underway after days of being dashed about by the will of the storm, all onboard were overjoyed with the promise of safety and civilization. But, in his haste to deliver his ship and crew to safe harbor, the Captain made the worst, and last, navigational error of his long life.

He had mistaken Haiti for Cuba.

The seas outside Port-au-Prince harbor were choppy, but the water inside was placid. After *Molly's* anchor was dropped, Miguel took a refreshing salt water bath and lay down on the sunny deck to dry. He was almost dozing off when, with a roar, gale force gusts hit suddenly and furiously.

With unbelievable swiftness, large incoming waves built in the suddenly treacherous harbor, crashing onto the decks of the moored vessel.

In minutes, *Molly's* anchor was in danger of dislodging and, with no way to safely sail out of harbor, Miguel could only pray their anchor held. Using launches, the crew bravely battled to set a second anchor, only to have it foul the first one.

"She's a goin' in!" Miguel heard a sailor yell as the *Molly*, without an anchor to hold her nose into the wind, turned broadside to the gale and swell and started blowing rapidly towards shore.

Confusion reigned on deck and before Miguel could decide whether to hold on or jump, the ship hit a rock jetty with a bone-jarring crash.

The next wave washed him overboard where huge rollers pulled him down, then spit him out. He gasped a little air before being towed under again.

During one of these dizzying tumbles Miguel grabbed a piece of ship's timber, which kept him afloat long enough to spot a slice of white beach near the jetty. Although the waves were pounding the little beach as maniacally as they were the jetty, Miguel figured that landing on sand would be far less dangerous than being dashed into the rocks.

Clinging to his timber, he paddled his feet as fast as he could, trying to propel himself away from the jetty. Each time he crested another of the frightful waves he tried to spot his little beach and swim towards it. Although the Caribbean water was warm, Miguel was losing strength and body heat. He knew he would die if something didn't happen soon. And it did.

A granddaddy wave lifted him and his timber onto its crest and carried them all the way to shore.

A few Haitians on the beach watched as Miguel was thrown about, not expecting him to live through the ordeal. Not that it mattered; they were after whatever booty the sea regurgitated from the all the ships breaking up in the harbor.

Seeing the big wave pick up Miguel, they oohed and ahhed in awe as he was carried for what seemed forever on its crest. As the roller, nearly twelve feet high, crashed onto shore, the spectators scrambled for the safety of higher ground in the edge of the jungle. The water subsided, leaving Miguel's still form beached on the sand. The Haitians moved in to see if he had jewelry or money on him.

Miguel, nearly naked and shivering with cold, opened one eye, then the other. His skin burned, as if on fire. *How can I be cold and burning up at the same time?* he asked himself.

He sat up—no small feat—and a self-inspection revealed bloody scratches, sand burns, and jelly fish stings covering most of his body. Hundreds of small, blue Portuguese men-of-war lay dead and dying around him, their lapis lazuli-colored air sacks glowing like jewels.

Never did care for the Portuguese, Miguel thought. His stomach lurched and what seemed like gallons of foul-tasting salt water launched itself from him. He crawled to the jungle's edge and collapsed again.

Giggles wakened him. Through swollen eyelids he saw little brightly dressed black dolls surrounding him. He moved and the dolls shrieked, scattered, and then stood at a distance, tittering.

"*Agua*? Water?" Miguel asked, hardly recognizing his own gravelly voice. Wetting his tongue with what little saliva remained in his dehydrated mouth, he tried again—this time in French. "*Eau*?"

One of the little girls, bolder than the others, handed Miguel a hollow gourd filled with the sweetest tasting water he would ever consume. He drank too much, vomited, and drank more.

"*Monsieur, vous et malade?*" the little girl asked. Miguel, though not fluent in Creole, had picked up quite a bit of the guttural French during his days with the brothers Lafitte.

"*Oui," he rasped, "malade. Por favor,* uh, *si'l vous plaît, un docteur?*" he rasped, hoping there *was* a doctor about. His doll and her friends scampered away, leaving him greatly disheartened.

Miguel feared death from exposure, but was too weak to help himself to safety. Despair enveloped him, but lifted an hour later when a white man returned with the little girl.

"Please help me," he said in English, because he couldn't remember how to say *help* in French. Then he pleaded, "*Ayudame, por favor.*"

"Of course, Señor," the man answered in Castilian Spanish.

Dear God, Miguel thought, *I have survived drowning only to fall into the hands of the gachupín. I am a dead man.*

But Miguel's incredible good luck held. His rescuer was a Spanish dissident named Don Francisco Xavier Mina.

Mina, in Port-au-Prince seeking support from the president of Haiti, Alexandre Pètion, for an expedition against the Royals in Mexico, was delighted to find a fellow patriot.

"How are you feeling today, Miguel?" the Spaniard asked when he returned to their quarters after surveying the damage to his ship. Unlike Miguel's, she was damaged, but afloat.

"Much better, Don Francisco. In a day or two I shall be ready to sail for Mexico."

"I, too. Unfortunately, our ship will not. Dictator Pètion, as sympathetic to the Mexican freedom fighters as a despot can be, has agreed to basic repairs. Probably to get rid of us. But most of my crew has deserted. When you feel well enough, would you help me recruit enough men to get us to Galveston Island."

Galveston? Madre mia, Miguel thought, *will I never get to Mexico?"*

At last, in April of 1817, Mina's fleet sailed from Galveston to invade Mexico.

After encountering headwinds and heavy seas, the expedition anchored at the mouth of the Santander River where they debarked and "liberated" the sleepy little village of Marina de Soto.

"Miguel, we are on Mexican soil, we have liberated the oppressed peasants, and they love us. We must celebrate our victory," Mina gushed.

Victory over what? Miguel thought. They had seized a deserted village and only when they shouted to the hidden villagers that they brought wine did the people return. Not exactly a triumph for the Heroes of Mexico.

Mina refused to understand the precariousness of his small conquest, even when Miguel relayed the villagers' news that a troop of Spanish soldiers had left Marina de Soto only when they saw the size of Mina's invading force. It was, he told the Spaniard, only a matter of time until Felipe de la Garza, the officer in charge of that troop, returned with General Arredondo. And the entire Royalist Army.

Colonel Henry Perry, a rebel who had fought against— and lost to—Arredondo, shared Miguel's concern.

"Colonel Gonzales, we must talk," he whispered, pulling Miguel away from camp one evening. The two men walked along the dry riverbed while Perry talked in hushed tones.

"I'm worried. Arredondo's sure to be here soon. We've got to get Mina moving. He wants to stay here and start a newspaper, for christ's sake."

"I know, Colonel Perry. And he thinks we should go south, recruit more men, and march on Mexico City. He is an idealist who, bolstered by the praise of a few drunken villagers, thinks taking Mexico will be easy. He knows nothing of this part of the world, and his plan is not sound," Miguel said.

Then added, "In my opinion."

"My opinion is the same as yours. If we don't move north to San Antonio, and strike full force, we're in big trouble. Do you think Mina'll listen to two old Texas veterans?" Perry asked.

Mina did listen to Miguel and Perry, but—not heeding their warnings—took most of his officers south, leaving only a token force to march with Perry into Texas. And, to Miguel's dismay, right back to La Bahia—the now-deserted fortress where he and Henry had spent so many months a few years before.

"Colonel Perry, I cannot say I am delighted at the sight of La Bahia after my time penned inside those stone walls with the Magee-Gutierrez Expedition. I do not embrace the idea of being in there again," Miguel crossed himself and mock-shivered.

"If I didn't know better, Miguel, I'd think you were superstitious. You don't really believe the story about Magee's ghost haunting the fort, do you?" Perry asked him.

"No, I just have a feeling there are Spaniards near."

"Me too. You ride on ahead as scout, Miguel. I'll keep the rest here until you return."

Miguel had ridden only a few miles towards San Antonio when he spotted a dust cloud. Then, his worst fears confirmed, he saw what appeared to him the entire Spanish Army advancing towards La Bahia.

"Colonel Perry, they are coming," Miguel shouted as he galloped back to camp as if pursued by a thousand devils. "They are many, and they have artillery."

Perry quickly assembled those men who had not already fled and calmly ordered, "Fellow patriots, save yourselves. Use any means necessary to survive in order to fight another day for Texas. God Bless and preserve you."

Miguel joined Perry in retreat, Royalist troops closing on their heels. Once again, Perry gave the order to split up and Miguel never looked back as he headed along the Opelousas Trail for the sanctuary of the familiar piney woods along the Trinity River.

Colonel Felipe de la Garza reined in his exhausted mount and watched in frustration as Miguel disappeared from view. Turning to his Corporal, he growled, "That Gonzales has the luck of Lucifer, but we shall meet with this traitorous devil another day."

Miguel, not knowing that his antagonists had given up the chase, plunged through the trees, mindless of the dangers there. Then his horse stepped in a hole and everything went black.

CHAPTER 27

Margaret and Joseph Anthony Stockman basked in the Louisiana spring's soft warmth, lazily analyzing fluffy white travelers adrift overhead.

Miss Maggie, her girlish imagination full of mushy ole romantic ideas, was not Joseph Anthony's favorite cloud-picture partner, nor he hers. Today, though, everybody else had something to do so they were stuck with each other.

"It's your turn, Maggie. What do you see?" Joseph Anthony asked.

"I see a white knight on a charger. A cavalier. He's riding like the wind, carrying a banner."

"Where? What's a charger?"

"Right there, José," Margaret pointed, "see the horse? That's his charger. They called them chargers back in the old days 'cause they used them to charge at dragons threatening beautiful princesses and slay those oversized horny toads with their magic swords. Then the knight scoops up the princess and rides away to his golden castle where they will live happily forevermore. Oh, and he lavishes on her lots of gowns and jewels from his overflowing coffers."

"Coffins?"

"No, you dolt, coffers. . .money and jewels—treasure he's been hoarding just in case he finds a princess."

"I wouldn't spend my money on some ole girl. I'd buy a gun," the practical boy told her, then settled back to study the clouds again. "Hey, I think I can see that charg. . .horse, now. Yep, I sure do."

They lay watching the knight and his mount dissolve.

"All right, José, your turn. What do you see?"

"Indian."

"Indian? Where?" Margaret asked lazily.

"In the tree!"

Margaret let out a bloodcurdling scream, jumped to her feet, covered her eyes with her hands as if to make the Indian disappear, and continued to shriek.

Katherine, hearing the screams, ran from the house with her gun. As she neared the children, she saw Joseph Anthony menacing something or someone in the tree with his knife.

A terrified Indian boy clung to a tree branch and stared wide-eyed at the howling red-haired banshee and her knife wielding brother below.

"Stop that caterwauling, Margaret Stockman. Right this minute," Katherine yelled, taking aim at the Indian.

"José Antonio, put your knife away. And you," Katherine gestured at the Indian with her gun, "you come down out of that tree."

The Indian boy did not budge.

Katherine, sensing he was too petrified to move, lowered the gun and her voice. "Come on down, boy, we won't hurt you."

The boy reached for a deerskin pouch slung around his neck, causing Katherine to raise the gun again for fear he had a weapon. But, quaking with fright, he dug out a small piece of hide and threw it to the ground.

Katherine relaxed. "Maggie, pick it up."

Margaret warily retrieved the hide and gasped. "Mama, it's a note. From Miguel. He needs help."

Katherine read the note and motioned for the boy to come down, sighing, "Oh, dear God, what now?"

Coaxed from his perch, the wary boy kept pointing to the message, then towards the horizon, but only grunted unintelligible sounds. Through clever pantomime he conveyed an urgent need to be away from these strange white people.

"Mama, maybe he doesn't speak English. Try Spanish," Margaret implored.

"*¿Habla Español?*" Katherine asked.

The young man pointed to his mouth and shook his head from side to side.

Katherine studied his face, then asked, "Do you *understand* Spanish?"

The boy nodded. Then he opened his mouth to reveal a jagged mass of scar tissue where his tongue should be.

Katherine, expecting Maggie to faint, was surprised when her normally squeamish fourteen-year-old gently took the boy's hand.

"Who did this to you?" Maggie asked softly.

The kind gesture broke through the boy's fear and, after a series of false starts, they began to communicate. Hand gestures, ink drawings, mime, and a few written words unfolded why Jesús had traveled so far to deliver Miguel's message.

"Mama, what are we going to do? Daddy and Henry might not be back for weeks. We have to help Miguel."

"I'll think of something, Maggie. Who would have imagined that a young boy Henry and Miguel saved from the Comanches four years ago would end up risking his life to save Miguel? It just shows you, one act of kindness begets another."

"What if Miguel's dying?" Maggie cried, her voice high and wavering.

"Calm down Maggie. It doesn't seem that Miguel's in danger of dying from whatever is wrong with his legs, but he can't travel without help. Evidently more help than Jesús here could give him. My guess is that his urgency has more to do with our Hero of Mexico getting out of Texas, away from Spaniards."

"But Mama, what if he *is* dying? What if we wait until it's too late? We have to *do* something," Margaret insisted, verging on hysteria.

"All right, Maggie, just calm down. Here's what we'll do. When Peter and John come in from hunting I'll send them to fetch your father and Henry from New Orleans. You can write to Miguel and tell him Henry will come for him as soon as he can. Then, after Jesús has a good night's sleep, he can leave to deliver the message to Miguel."

Margaret, not at all mollified, nonetheless nodded and sat down to compose a note to Miguel. She was still writing when Katherine made her turn out her lantern.

"Rise and shine, Sunshine," Katherine called early the next morning. No Answer.

"Maggie, move those lazy bones. I've sent José to the barn for Jesús, since no amount of coaxing would get that little Indian to stay in the house last night. Breakfast is almost ready, girl, so get your. . . ."

"Mama!" Joseph Anthony crashed through the door, interrupting his mother. "Jesús is gone, and the scoundrel took two of our best horses. You should have let me stab him."

Katherine gasped, dropped the knife she was using to slice smoked ham, and ran to the girls' bedroom chanting, "Oh, no. Please, no."

Tossing a mound of blankets from Margaret's empty bed, she whirled—bowling over small children too slow to get out of her way—and ran to the barn faster than she thought her forty-six-year-old legs would carry her.

Skidding to a halt at the grooming stall, she gasped, "Oh, dear God."

Margaret's saddle was gone.

When Frederick Stockman saw his sons, Peter and John, waiting on the porch of the New Orleans boarding house where he and Henry were staying, his heart skipped a beat. Without a greeting, he asked, "What's wrong?"

Peter blurted out the story and Henry shook his head. "I just can't believe Maggie would do something so stupid," he ranted. "My god, two fourteen-year-olds in Texas with Comanches and Spaniards thicker n' flies. I thought she was smarter'n that."

"You know she's got a soft spot where Miguel's concerned," Frederick said with a calm he did not feel.

"And that's another thing, Pa. Miguelito must be pretty danged desperate to send that Indian boy for help. Ma must be having fits."

Henry paced, thinking on his feet.

"The way I figure it, they ain't to Orcoquisac yet. If Jesús didn't have Princess Maggie in tow he'd probably be there, but she's gonna slow him down good. If I leave right now I can take the Opelousas Trail and be there in a few days. I wonder how they got acrost the Sabine? Well, never mind, look's like they did. I'd better get going, pronto."

"Henry, maybe we ought'a see about grabbing a boat," Frederick suggested.

"Pa, a ship would be faster, but I don't want to lose time trying to locate one. Tell you what, why don't you and Peter go see about finding a boat, and John can ride back to let Ma know what we're doing. If you can get to Galveston, we'll rendezvous at Orcoquisac. That way we've got more'n one party headed for Maggie and Miguel, just in case one of us gets fouled up."

"That's that, then. Henry, you take care, and I'll see you at Orcoquisac. Whoever gets there first waits for the other, all right? We can use Galveston Island as a fall back meetin' place."

"Sounds good to me. *¡Hasta luego!*, boys. See you in Texas, Pa."

Margaret and Jesús easily swam their horses across the Sabine, which, due to a dry spell, was running low. Maggie considered this a stroke of luck, for there was no way on God's-green-earth she and Jesús would have been allowed to board a ferry. Certainly not Gaines Ferry. Or any other. A young white girl traveling with an Indian would be cause for great suspicion.

Taking a cue from the often-repeated story of her mother's defensive camouflage years ago when they first came to Texas, Margaret dulled her copper hair with ashes and smudged her pale complexion with clay.

She wore her brothers' clothes, as did Jesús, just in case they were seen. From a distance they might pass for a couple of short cowboys, but their plan was to avoid contact with another living soul.

Jesús, although he had been surprised by Margaret's nocturnal visit to the barn, had not questioned her plan to leave under the cover of darkness. Miguel had once saved his life, and if the pale-haired man wanted Jesús to bring this strange white girl to Orcoquisac he would ride through Hell to do so.

Jesús well remembered the first time he saw Miguel and his friend.

Ten years old and in terrible pain, he had watched helplessly as his tormenters turned their knives toward his little sister. One of the Comanches had grabbed the tiny girl by the hair when, out of the woods, rode two terrifying apparitions he would never forget .

One ghost warrior had hair the color of gold, the other the red of clay. Their naked white bodies, adorned with stripes of black and red war paint, shimmered in the sunlight and their screams ripped through the forest.

Jesús had been more frightened by his rescuers than he was of the Comanches who had been torturing him.

The story, retold among the peaceful Indians along the Trinity River, had made legends of Miguel and Henry.

There were times when Jesús almost wished he had died at the hands of the filthy Comanches who killed his parents and cut out his tongue. It was difficult living as a mute, even among the kind elders of his tribe. A Spanish priest had taught him to write, but mostly he mimed his way through life.

Traveling by night was a hazardous, slow, and exhausting way to go for the boy and Maggie. And to make matters worse, Jesús sensed they were being stalked. He hoped it wasn't a panther.

The man stopped his horse and smiled at the signs left along the trail by the children.

He could tell that the Indian boy was skilled at covering his path, but, with the girl in tow, not clever enough to outfox a veteran tracker. It soon became obvious that his quarry traveled by night and hid by day—a good plan, but one which led to leaving small signs of their presence. Strands of red hair, snagged by low hanging branches, shone like banners among the gray-green leaves.

His preys' horses were shod, and though Jesús covered the horse's hooves with pieces of leather, left their mark in patches of soft earth.

The man smiled and whispered to himself, "Lead on, my little Judas goats."

"Have you lost your mind, Margarita?" Miguel railed. "And you, Jesús—I gave you a message to take to Enrique and you bring me this child. *¡Madre de Dios!* What have I done?"

Margaret, stung by Miguel's anger, reacted in kind. Unlike poor Jesús, who was hurt, she let go a fit of pique.

"Miguel, you ungrateful wretch! How *dare* you holler at us. Jesús risked life and limb to go to Louisiana, and we've traveled for what seems like an eternity with hardly any sleep or food to come here and save your sorry hide. And in case you haven't noticed, I am not a child."

Miguel, although surprised by Margaret's fierceness, furiously countered. "If you are not a child, then why have you behaved as one? Your family must be sick with worry. And no, you do not look like a little girl, you look like a little boy."

"Well, I'm not, Miguel Gonzales, and right now I'm the best bet you've got to get out of Texas alive. Can you ride?"

Sullen, he answered, "If I could ride I would have left long ago. Every day I stay increases my chances of arrest by the Royalists. Twice they have been near, but the Indians hid me. I must leave Texas, but I will not put you in danger. Jesús will take you home immediately."

"No, he won't, and that's that. The only way I leave here is with you. We could hide and wait for Henry, but it might be weeks." Margaret's lower lip began to tremble and tears welled up in her eyes. She was tired, dirty, and hungry. She wanted her Mama.

The long trip and tiff with Miguel suddenly took its toll and all the fight left Margaret as quickly as a bird takes flight.

She fainted.

The tracker knew he was close, so he and the others paced themselves. Their goal was not to overtake the children, but to follow them to the man they sought.

Frederick and Peter were surrounded by pirates.

Using the elder Stockman's black-market trade connections, along with Miguel's name, they gained swift entry to the Lafitte lair at Barataria where, with a snap of his fingers, Jean Lafitte conjured a ship.

Ironically, the very wrongdoings that Katherine objected to—smuggling and slave-trading—could very well lead to a connection that saved her daughter.

Frederick, who had never met Jean Lafitte personally, knew the man had an odd sense of loyalty where friendships were concerned. He also knew that same man could easily slit their throats. It was a chance they would have to take. Or rather, Frederick would have to take.

"I know how you feel, Peter. Believe it or not, I was once young myself. But son, this time it's best you stay in Louisiana. These Lafittes seem decent enough, but I don't think they can be trusted one-hundred percent, if you know what I mean. With you waiting in New Orleans, at least someone on this earth will know I left on the tide with a passel of pirates. If I disappear you can tell your Ma not to set my place for supper like she still does for David and George."

Patting his disappointed son on the back, he added, "I don't want you waiting here in Barataria son, that's for damned sure. Go on back to New Orleans—stay at that boarding house where me'n Henry always bunk. I'll make a deal with one of these pirate fellas, pay him half now, and if the ship returns without me, he can get the other half when he lets you know. If I ain't on that ship, head on home, 'cause we could be coming back overland."

"All right, Pa," Peter said reluctantly, "but I sure wish you'd let me come along. I ain't never been on a big ship. What's its name?"

"She's called the *Tiburon,* and for what it's worth she's flyin' the Stars and Stripes. At least until she leaves port. I've heard a thing or two about this *Shark*, and I can't say it was all flatterin', but she's all I got right now. I better go get some travelin' grub, because they may not be prepared to feed another mouth. On these ships, every bit of space is taken up with powder barrels and weapons, so they don't carry extra victuals. Makes a man a little nervous sitting on all that powder, but I got no choice.

"You get on the road now. Barataria ain't safe in broad daylight and I'll wager it gets downright ugly after dark. I'd sure as hell hate to get back here with Miss Maggie and find out you were pressed into service. I hope to see you soon, Pedro, but if not, you take care of your Mama."

Frederick turned to walk away, then turned back and added, "And my horse."

"What happened?" Margaret asked when her eyes fluttered open from her swoon. The soft buffalo skin cushioning her evoked memories of her own bed at home, but she knew where she was when she saw Miguel on his littler next to her. His handsome face was strained with pain and worry.

"Margarita, you scared the. . .what is that word Enrique uses?. . .beJesús, out of me." Miguel pronounced the word *bee-hay-soos,* eliciting a giggle from Margaret and a look of expectation from Jesús.

Miguel grumped, "You might find all of this amusing, but I was truly alarmed when you faded."

"Fainted, not faded. I did faint, didn't I? Imagine that. I've read that ladies swoon, but I never thought it would happen to me. Wait until I tell my friends."

"Unless your friends live in an Indian village in the piney woods of Texas, I doubt you will be telling them of this nonsense soon," Miguel growled.

"Don't be so mean to me, Miguel. I came here because I love y—uh. . .because. . .you're my brother's friend," Margaret blurted. Blushing, she abruptly changed the subject to cover her embarrassment. "Is there anything to eat around here? I'm hungry."

Three hundred miles east, Frederick was being rowed out to the schooner *Tiburon.*

The *Shark* looked every bit like the beast she was named for—sleek, dark and deadly. Her masts were raked back stylishly, giving her an illusion of movement, even at anchor in Barataria Bay.

Frederick estimated a crew of seventy or so men and counted eight cannon and six swivel-mounted guns. With sixty-five feet of length and a very narrow beam, she was capable, he was told, of picking up eleven knots in a stiff breeze.

Swift and shallow drafted, the *Shark* could lurk in bayous and rivers, then viciously attack and devour her prey.

Frederick was relieved to find one of the Lafitte brothers, Pierre, was making the voyage to Galveston, giving him a modicum of protection from the motley and multihued crew.

Miguel sucked in his breath and stared.

A beautiful young woman entered camp from the same direction where the grimy child had left to bathe.

Dressed in a clean shirt, hair glowing like fire, Margarita looked like her mother, but, if possible, more beautiful.

It is true. Margarita is no longer a child. But, Miguel reminded himself with difficulty, *neither is she a woman. And she is practically my sister.*

Margaret gave Miguel the shy coquette's smile she had practiced in the mirror so many times, and was pleased it had the proper effect.

Henry was making excellent time, aided by dry weather and low-running rivers. If he and Quicksand were lucky and their strength held, they would make it to Orcoquisac in a few days.

Covering sixty miles a day—riding eight hours, resting only four, then pushing on—Henry was concerned that he was driving his horse too hard, but as much as he loved Quicksand, he loved Margaret and Miguel more.

Maggie—clean, fed and rested—was beginning to see the folly of her actions.

Here I am in Texas with a bunch of Indians and a man I can't help or move. Maybe Mama was right. Maybe we should have waited for Henry—he'd know what to do. The only good thing is that Miguel can feel his legs again. She frowned. *Maybe that's not so good.*

Miguel, euphoric when his legs began to tingle, soon despaired when the prickle turned to throbbing, white-hot pain.

Jesús and Margaret took turns rubbing his feet and applying warm poultices made of leaves and warmed clay, but the treatments did little to alleviate Miguel's suffering.

The men following Jesús and Maggie were very near, and when the Indians at Atascosito sensed the impending danger, they took to the woods. All except Jesús.

"Jesús, listen to me," Miguel hissed between his teeth. "You take Maggie and go into hiding. There's no sense in me going with you."

It was true. Miguel's pain was such that he could only control his screams when he was conscious. Once it became too much, he passed out and while unconscious he moaned loud enough to be heard for some distance.

Jesús stubbornly shook his head. Pointing at Maggie, he let Miguel know he would hide her, then he'd be back. But Maggie refused to leave as well. Neither would abandon their Mexican folk hero.

An old woman hidden in the forest watched with increasing apprehension as her grandson stayed by the Mexican and the girl. She had no intention of allowing Jesús to sacrifice himself for Miguel, even if the man had once saved his life.

Returning to her cave, she rummaged into a leather bag she kept buried under a rock and removed bits of dried leaves, roots, and cactus.

Grinding the ingredients to a powder, she added boiling water to steep an ancestral soporific forbidden by the white mans' religion. Even though she was supposedly converted, she had never really warmed up to all of those bell ringing priests and their ways.

Miguel protested weakly as the old crone poured warm, bitter liquid down his throat, but within seconds he felt better. Minutes after swallowing the draught, he lost consciousness.

The old woman watched Miguel sleep. She had made the potion very strong and sincerely hoped her medicine would not kill the Mexican, but either way, he would be silent.

They pulled his litter to her cave.

Campfires still smoldered in the abandoned camp when the men stalking Jesús and Margaret arrived. Cleverly laid clues, left by the Indians to draw the searchers into dead ends, left the men frustrated after a day or to, and they gave up.

Cursing their failure loudly, they made a great show of defeated departure, then later crept back to set an ambush.

We shall see just how clever these Indians are, the leader thought. *We shall just see.*

Margaret was tired, frightened, filthy, hungry, and worried. Whatever the old woman had given Miguel stopped his pain, but he had been out cold for two days.

The ancient insisted that Miguel be turned over every hour and his arms and legs moved about to keep his blood flowing and his lungs clear. The schedule was exhausting, but imperative if he were to survive.

Concealed in an underground cave, the fugitives suffered from dampness and cold. No fires were permitted and food was scarce. Two of the men left each day to scavenge for food, usually returning with a rabbit, a coon, some fish, or even a snake.

Margaret at first refused to eat the meat raw, but on the second day was forced by hunger pangs to try some rabbit. She gagged. The old woman, taking pity on her, rubbed salt into the thin strips the meat, making it barely palatable.

Just when Margaret thought she would go mad in that cave, the scouts returned with good news. The soldiers were gone.

Frederick watched as a crew member repeatedly dropped a plumb line into the murky waters off Galveston Island. The sailor shouted, "Two fathoms and holding." They seemed to be inching into port.

"What's taking so long, Lafitte?" Frederick asked with a touch of impatience.

"Monsieur, *Tiburon* draws much less than two fathoms, but we must take care. If we run aground our arrival will be much delayed. It would be most unkind if, after our little ship made such a swift voyage from Barataria, we were to scrape her beautiful *derrière* on the sands of the bar," Pierre explained reasonably.

Then he graced Frederick with a Gallic shrug and added, "*Mais*, you could swim."

Frederick peered into the brown water and imagined fins on patrol.

"No thanks. I can barely tread water. It's just a little frustrating to stand here and, with a hearty imagination, see the tree tops at Orcoquisac.

"*Quelle imagination, monsieur*. It is at least twenty miles to your Orcoquisac. Take heart, I have a small sailing vessel on

Galveston Island that can cover those few miles in short order," Pierre said patting Frederick on the shoulder.

"*Mais Monsieur* Stockman, we cannot take horses on this small boat, so we will have to walk part of the way for my swift little boat does not have the flat bottom." Then he added with a leering grin, "I do not care for flat bottoms."

"We? You plan to come with me?" Frederick asked with grateful surprise.

"But of course, *monsieur*. A fair *mademoiselle* in distress is always a grave matter to me. It is my honor to accompany you. We will take some of my men, as well, in case we encounter a problem."

Frederick, appreciative as he was for Pierre's generous offer of accompaniment, had some concerns.

"Pierre, my daughter is quite beautiful, but very young. Still a child, really. Will her presence in Galveston, with so many men of various, uh, characters, pose a problem?"

"Not when she is under the protection of *les freres Lafitte*. No man will dare to *look* at her in such a way that would cost him his eyes. We shall tell everyone she is the intended bride of Miguel Gonzales, a man we hold in high regard. Ah, we are across the bar, Frederick, but now we must keep a sharp lookout for sunken ships in our path. They have, of course, perished of natural causes."

Frederick looked into Pierre's grinning face and thought, *I'll just bet they did.*

When Miguel regained consciousness, he hoped he was having a bad dream. His throbbing head, fuzzy vision and searing legs were all but eclipsed by the shock of finding himself staring into the malevolent smile of Felipe de la Garza.

"So, we finally meet again, Gonzales. I have looked forward to this day for many years, as you have caused me many moments of vexation."

Miguel said nothing as he watched his enemy strut and crow.

"I was especially disappointed when you deserted your friend, Colonel Perry at La Bahia. But then, what could one expect? Once a deserter, always a deserter, no? The late Colonel Perry surrendered like a true gentleman."

Despite himself, Miguel winced. The *late* Colonel Perry? "What did you do to him, you *gachupín* bastard?" he hissed.

Ignoring the insult, de la Garza's smile widened.

"He escorted himself into Hell, Miguel, just as you will be given an opportunity to do. I only need your head to redeem myself, therefore I must insist that you despatch yourself without damaging that handsome face."

Miguel felt a moment of panic, but not for himself. Death seemed an almost welcome alternative to his suffering, but he was afraid for Margarita. Twisting his body around as best he could, he frantically tried to find her.

"You are perhaps concerned over a certain young lady? We have no wish to harm Señorita Estocoman. After all, I have known her since she was a small girl. She will be escorted to San Antonio, where her brother, Henry, may claim her. Then he, too, will be given a chance to redeem himself to the Crown. Would you prefer to shoot yourself, or shall I do it for you?"

From beyond Miguel's vision he heard Maggie scream, "No!"

"Please, Colonel de la Garza, take Margarita away. Then we can settle the matter," Miguel pleaded.

"Why not? There is no need for her to witness your death. After all, she is merely a child. Of course, if Henry should choose not to come to her rescue, we can always sell her to the

Comanches. They love girl children, and will cherish that lovely red hair."

De la Garza turned to see if his soldiers were enjoying this moment as much as he was, but found their faces frozen into masks of fear. Following their horrified stares, his bowels fluttered. They were surrounded by pirates.

Miguel, unable to see anyone except his tormentor, yelled to Margaret, "Go with them, Margarita. If you resist they may hurt you. Henry will come for you. And," he added, "I want you to remember that I loved you."

"Well, now, ain't that touchin'?" Frederick said, walking into Miguel's line of sight. "I leave my happy home to do a little tradin', and the next thing I know my daughter runs off with some Mexican. And now I hear that same Mexican vowing his ever-lastin' love for that same daughter. I guess I'm gonna have to hang up my damned saddle and sit guard on my front step."

Miguel grinned and passed out.

Felipe de la Garza stared at Frederick, then Lafitte. He wondered if it was true that pirates were inclined to cut off Spaniards' ears for souvenirs.

Jesús, watching from the woods, wondered if it was safe to come out. The pirates were meaner looking than the soldiers.

Margaret was in a daze. Miguel had said he loved her.

Frederick glared at his daughter and said, "Let's go home, Sister. I imagine your Ma has a few things to say to you."

When Henry arrived at Orcoquisac, almost everyone was gone.

De la Garza, minus horses, weapons, boots—and a few soldiers who deserted and joined the pirates—was walking back to San Antonio. Frederick and Lafitte had taken Maggie and Miguel to Galveston.

Jesús handed Henry a note from his father, instructing him to get to Galveston, pronto, because the pirate ship would leave in a few days for New Orleans. *Pirate ship?*

Henry shook his head and handed Quicksand's reins to Jesús. "I guess you'd best paddle me over to Galveston Island, boy, so I can catch that ship. But one of these days I want my damned horse back."

Five weeks from the night she had disappeared with Jesús, Margaret snuggled happily into her very own bed.

Things have worked out quite well, she thought. *Miguel is mending nicely, and Mama was so glad to see me that she didn't even yell too much. Shoot, Henry isn't even mad at me anymore, thanks to that sweet Jesús, who beat us back here with Quicksand. Jesús says he's staying.*

And she was in love.

I can't wait to tell my friends.

CHAPTER 28

"What do you *mean* you're going to Mexico?" Maggie wailed. "I thought you loved me."

Months of Katherine's benevolent but bullying care and Maggie's attentive coddling had restored Miguel. The only evidence of his accident was a quickly diminishing limp.

It was evident to everyone in the family, except the self-centered Margaret, that Miguel was restless and ready to return to his cause.

"Margarita, I do care for you, as I do all your family. But I must continue to fight for my country. I cannot rest until Mexicans are free," Miguel patiently explained.

"You mean I rode into hell and saved your sorry bee-hind so you could go right back out and get it shot off? How can you do this to me? What will my friends say?" Margaret sniveled.

Miguel wondered if what her friends thought wasn't the real root of her distress. He bit his tongue in order not to remind her that, technically, she had not saved his life, but had actually endangered a few more by her rash dash into Texas.

Seeking a way to let the high-strung girl down easily, he said, "You can tell them I was called to fight tyranny and that I shall return when the battle is won."

Maggie let the thought rattle around in her vacuous head for a minute and was somewhat mollified. From her fifteen-year-old point of view, she was rescued from ridicule and transformed into a tragic heroine, patiently (but woefully) awaiting the return of her derring-do knight.

When Maggie bustled off to tell her friends of her plight, Henry rounded the corner of the house grinning.

"You handled that real smooth, Miguelito. Hell, you didn't even tarnish your armor," he quipped.

"Enrique! I did not know you were listening. I am certain our dear girl will soon forget all about me. I owe you all so much, I do not wish to cause your family pain."

"I ain't all that pained, *hermano*. Now I can have my room to myself. When are you leaving?"

"Soon. I have been deterred from my patriotic duty to my country far too long. When I heard that poor Don Mina was executed by the *gachupín* it strengthened my resolve to rid my country of the European tyrants. I wish you would come with me."

"Naw, not this time, but I'll miss you, Miguel. I kinda like bein' around a man who talks like he was constantly recitin' poetry. And if it's any consolation, I'm planning to move back to Texas permanently real soon, so I'll be making life a little harder for the Spaniards myself. If you need to find me ask any Caddo Indian near the Sabine. They all know me, because I'm the one with the firewater."

"You make light, Enrique, but I know you do more than sell whiskey to Indians. Your raids into Texas already vex the *gachupín* enough to gladden the hearts of the Mexican people. I have heard that the Spanish government grows weary of their problems in the New World, and since they have already stolen all the gold and pearls, will soon leave. And when they do, we will have another problem: *insurgentes norteamericanos.*

"Hell, Miguel, I *am* a North American insurgent."

"Yes, Enrique, but you are *our* North American insurgent."

They laughed, then Miguel grew somber.

"We jest, amigo, but mark my words, there will come a day when we will have to fight an invasion by the United States if Texas is to become and remain a free state of the Republic of Mexico."

Henry sighed. "Let's take one war at a time, Miguel—first we gotta get rid of Spain, and I hope you're right and they just pack up and go home. But I sincerely doubt it."

near the Sabine. They all know me, because I'm the one with the firewater."

"You make light, Enrique, but I know you do more than sell whiskey to Indians. Your raids into Texas already vex the gachupines enough to gladden the hearts of the Mexican people. I have heard that the Spanish government grows weary of their problems in the New World and since they have already stolen all the gold and pearls, will soon leave. And when they do, we will have another problem: *insurgentes norteamericanos*."

"Hell, Miguel, I'm a North American insurgent."

"Yes, Enrique, but you are *our* North American insurgent."

They laughed, then Miguel grew somber.

"We jest, amigo, but mark my words, there will come a day when we will have to fight an invasion by the United States if Texas is to become and remain a free state of the Republic of Mexico."

Henry replied, "Let's take one war at a time, Miguel. First we gotta get rid of Spain, and I hope you're right and they just pack up and go home. But I sincerely doubt it."

CHAPTER 29

I *should've known better,* Henry thought as he rode Quicksand along his much-traveled route between Louisiana and his cabin in Caddo Indian Territory in the Neutral Zone.

The Caddos had accepted him and his Indian sidekick, Jesús—whom they had dubbed "the speechless one"—as neighbors. They'd even sold Henry a parcel of land.

Jesús tended the farm while Henry was on the trail buying goods from Louisiana merchants to trade to the Caddos and nesters in Texas. Together they pulled raids far into Texas, *bar-o-ing* a fair number of mustangs.

Dried beef and venison, horses, herbs and furs—just about anything the frontier offered—was quickly snapped up by New Orleans merchants.

Despite the inherent dangers of his chosen line of work, Henry was prospering through a combination of hard work, long hours, quick wits and good luck.

He often stopped in to see his family in Louisiana. This time, in a moment of weakness, he'd made what he considered to be a dimwitted mistake.

"I don't see why we have to ride so fast, Henry," Maggie whined from the wagon she was driving alongside him. "It's such a beautiful day, and it's not like we have to be anywhere on time."

Henry stared ahead, trying to ignore his irritation.

Margaret was driving him nuts.

After pestering and pleading until he agreed she could come with him, his sister had been complaining about one thing or another ever since they left the Stockman farm.

No longer able to contain his chagrin, he stopped. "Look, little sister, I told you you could come only if you wouldn't drag me down. And for your information, I think we *do* have a time problem. See those dark clouds on the horizon?"

Maggie looked where he pointed and nodded.

"Well, just because it's sunny here don't mean it ain't raining up north. One dry wash we've got to cross can be a real son of a bitch when it's raining uphill," he said, rising in his stirrups to peer ahead.

"Oh, you worry too much," Maggie said, rolling her eyes and flapping a limp wrist in his direction. "We'll be fine. How much further is it?"

"I figure we'll be there tomorrow afternoon. If," he emphasized, "and that's *if*, we keep moving."

"Oh, all right. Anyway, I can't wait to see your cabin. And Jesús. I so enjoy his letters. Do you think Miguel might come looking for you anytime soon? It's been more than a year since he left."

"Ah ha! So *that's* why you were so all-fired anxious to spend time with your—let's see, how did you put it? 'Oh, Enrique, I want to spend time with my very favorite brother in the whole world.'"

Henry, raising his voice a few octaves and mimicking his sister's otherworldly manner, continued. "Oh, Enrique, I shall simply *perish* if you don't take me with you this time. I miss you more than I can *bear* when you're gone." He mock-frowned and added, "I should've known you had more on your mind than sisterly love."

"Don't be such an old grouch, brother dear. I *do* miss you. It's just that I miss Miguel, too.

"Hey, what's going on up there?" she asked, pointing to a woman running towards them and waving her arms.

Henry nudged Quicksand forward, yelling back over his shoulder for Margaret to stop and stay with the wagon.

"Help! Oh, help me!" the woman shrieked as she ran towards Henry. "My wagon washed downstream when the water came out of nowhere. I had no time to get them to safety. You've just got to save them—they're all I have."

Henry galloped past the distraught woman and, rounding a bend in the road, saw the usually dry creek bed gushing with two or three feet of fast moving water. One hundred yards downstream, high-centered and tilting precariously on a clump of bushes in the middle of the creek, sat a wagon. The horse had broken loose from his traces, and was casually chomping green grass at the water's edge. He shied away when Quicksand galloped up, but not too far.

Henry dismounted and tied a length of rope to his saddlehorn, securing the other end around his waist. He waded into the knee-high, dangerously swift water while Quicksand, responding to whistled commands, kept the line taught.

Debris swirled around Henry as he inched his way through the rising water and he hoped a log—or something alive and very angry—didn't use him for a place to land.

He could see no sign of life in the wagon. *If it's children in there,* he thought, *they must be hunkered down. Or fell out.*

The front end of the buckboard was facing upstream, so Henry tied his end of the rope to the wagon's tongue and he worked his way back to the bank holding onto the line.

Once on shore, he coaxed Quicksand to slowly back up, pulling the wagon forward inch by inch. Twice, the rig threatened to tip over, but Henry waded back into the hazardous water to hold it upright until Quicksand could get it back on track.

Margaret and the woman stood nearby .on the bank, screeching in despair each time the wagon tipped.

At least, Henry thought, *my damned horse is calm and doing something to help.*

After an hour of harrowing, dangerous, back-breaking work, the wagon rolled up onto the bank. Henry collapsed in a sodden heap.

Rushing forward, the woman looked into her wagon, flipped back an oilskin and cried, "Thank God they're not wet."

Henry, sitting in a puddle of water, looked at her as if she were demented. "Wet? Hell, I'd say you're damned lucky they ain't drowned."

"Aren't. Or are not. Not ain't." The woman responded. Then added, "Oh, never mind. Thank you, sir, for saving my wagon and books."

"Books?! Books!" Henry bellowed. "Are you tellin' me that I just risked my rear for *books*?"

Margaret giggled, but seeing the shocked look on the woman's face, said, "Now Henry, don't be talking crude in the presence of us ladies. Mama would tan you if she heard what you just said."

"I've a mind to do some tannin' myself. Are you out of your mind?" Henry yelled, pushing himself to his feet and taking a couple of menacing steps towards the woman. She burst into tears.

"Just look what you've done, Enrique Stockman. Shame on you."

Maggie took the sobbing woman into her arms while the dumbfounded Henry stood dripping.

"Now, now," she cooed, patting the woman's hand, "he won't hurt you. He's all bark. Let's get both of you into some nice dry clothes and build a fire for coffee. You'll feel better real soon."

Margaret was right.

Dry clothes and coffee spiked with Henry's trading whiskey lifted his spirits, lightened his mood, and restored his normally cheerful disposition.

"I guess books are worth saving," he admitted, "especially out here where we don't have many. Ma says if we lived somewhere with real schools and lots of books I'd be an educated man, what with the way I pick up lingo n' all. We only have about five real books at home, counting the Bible, but Maggie here manages to get her hands on loaners, so we ain't. . .aren't. . .completely ignorant."

"Henry speaks Spanish like a native, Dorcas. And he can also speak French, Creole and several kinds of Indian talk. Mama says he's very bright," Margaret gushed.

Henry blushed and Margaret blathered on. "I know where your name came from, Dorcas. From the Bible. Mama says Dorcas would have been a Jesus disciple if she was a man, but since she wasn't, she wasn't."

"Maggie, you make a man's head spin when you prattle on so. Slow down so I can follow you," Henry grumbled.

"It's more likely the whiskey that's got your head spinning, brother. However, I shall slow down so your dimmed wits can follow," Maggie sniffed.

"Dorcas was that lady in the Bible who sewed clothes for the poor. When she died, the disciple Peter—Peter was a man so he could be a disciple—brought her back from the dead because the poor and the widows carried on so about her not being around to make them clothes."

To Henry's amazement, Dorcas had no trouble at all following Margaret's meandering verbal path. *Must be a gift only women have,* he thought.

Dorcas nodded, as if reading his mind.

"Dorcas was my paternal grandmother's name. I don't ever recall seeing her, or my father. Daddy took off when I was just a baby to go do what men do. Mama died a year ago, then I got word my daddy passed over. And that's why I'm here."

Henry stared into his cup and shook his head, thinking, *Maybe it's whiskey, maybe I'm tired, but they keep talking circles around me.* He stared at Dorcas. Her dark hair was dry and fluffy and she looked very young.

I wonder how old she is? he thought, but asked, "What do you mean by, that's why you're here? And speaking of which, this ain't no place for a young girl to be traveling alone."

"Double negative, Henry. You can't use two negatives in one sentence. I'm here to claim my land," Dorcas replied primly. Then she added, "And I'm twenty-four, to answer your question."

"I didn't ask," Henry protested.

"No, but you thought it," Dorcas told him.

Henry's mouth dropped open. *She does read minds?*

"What land, Dorcas?" Margaret asked.

"The land my father left me. The best I can figure, it's about twenty miles west of here—in Louisiana." Dorcas pointed across the swollen stream.

"My dear young lady, Louisiana is the other way." Henry smiled smugly and gestured towards the east with his cup.

"My dear young man, Louisiana *used* to be the other way. Now it goes all the way to the Sabine River. Haven't you ever heard of the De Onis treaty?"

"De Onis? That *gachupín cabròn.* What's that filthy Spaniard gone and done?" Henry was no longer smiling nor smug.

"I have a feeling what you just called Señor de Onis was not at all flattering. He signed a treaty between Spain and the United States whereby the Neutral Zone now belongs to Louisiana. I'm not surprised you haven't heard, because it just happened. I was all packed and ready to go as soon as it became official that my land was in the United States. I know de Onis is a Spaniard, but what is a *gachupín cabròn*?" Dorcas inquired matter-of-factly.

Margaret laughed, and Henry had the good grace to blush.

"I'm, sorry Miz Dorcas," he said, "it's just I don't care much for Spaniards. I shouldn't've been talking like that in front of you, even in Spanish. Derned if it ain't just like the sorry. . .uh. . .devils. The Spaniards know they're gonna get kicked out by the Mexicans, so they gave away a chunk of Texas. Dammit, that land rightly belongs to Texas. And me."

"Well, I, for one, am glad it doesn't. Belong to Texas, I mean. Otherwise, I wouldn't own anything on this earth except a cranky old wet horse and a wagonload of books."

"That's a danged sight more than I have, if what you say is so," Henry grumped. "Dammit, I finally get me a little piece of land—legally bought from the Caddos—and the da-derned Spaniards up and give it away. You got the paper with you that says where your land is?"

"I do, but it's all in Spanish so I haven't been able to read it. Even if I could read it, I don't know where the landmarks lie. There's a map."

"Well, Miz Dorcas, today's your lucky day. I can read both maps *and* Spanish."

Dorcas smiled at Henry. "My mother always said that an educated person is one who knows how to act given the situation. I guess that makes you the most educated person in these parts, Henry."

Henry didn't know what to say.

Dorcas tipped her chin up. "I doubt Shakespeare could have saved my wagon and books, nor could he read my map."

"Well, I don't know the gentleman, but I will do my best to help out such a beautiful damsel in distress." Henry performed an exaggerated, Miguelesque bow, bestowing upon Dorcas his most dazzling smile.

Dorcas, sitting in the pink glow of the setting sun, returned the smile with a radiant beam of her own, looking directly into his eyes.

When Henry's green eyes locked with Dorcas' dark ones, he felt a wash of desire like nothing he had ever before experienced.

At the ripe old age of twenty-seven, Henry Stockman was suddenly and hopelessly in love for the first time in his life.

It was mutual.

Margaret, witnessing the airborne exchange of passion, whispered, "Well, I do declare. It's a good thing y'all have a chaperone."

CHAPTER 30

"Folks have come from all over these parts to witness the mighty Henry Stockman join us mortals." James Gaines raised his tankard, as did the other men in Frederick's barn.

"To Dorcas and Henry!"

Henry sipped his drink politely, but was being careful. Katherine had given him a good lecture about staying sober at his own wedding.

"So Henry, what're you and your bride gonna do after the wedding?" one of the men asked.

Henry blushed and Gaines saw his color and laughed.

"Hell, Henry, he didn't mean *right* after—we all know what you got on your mind then. Here, have more whiskey so you won't be so damned skittish."

"What I meant was," the man said with a laugh, "where are you gonna live? And what are you gonna do about that problem you and the Norrises have with your land claims in the old Neutral Zone?"

Henry gratefully took a sip of his newly filled mug. "Well, we have to petition the United States damned Congress to get title, that's what. Sam Norris is doing the paperwork. Even Dorcas' land is tied up in this mess. They say we were nesting on Caddo Indian land and don't have any rights to it, even though we got a bill of sale from the Indians. That damned government Indian agent they sent in. . . .

"What's all the commotion?" someone asked, looking out the barn door towards a noisy crowd gathering by the house.

Henry and James walked in that direction and after a few steps let out a war whoops and broke into a trot.

Miguel, in the full regalia of a Mexican officer, sported enough gold braid, fringe, and buttons to turn a Napoleonic officer green with envy. He strode quickly towards Henry and gave him a rib-cracking hug.

"Enrique, my brother, you look so handsome. . .and so *civilized!* Where is the bride?"

"Miguel! I can't believe you're here. Dorcas," Henry yelled, "where are you? You gotta meet this Mexican pirate."

Dorcas, propelled forward by revelers, gawked at the colorful, handsome Miguel, then, after introductions were made, saw his eyes dart past her. She smiled knowingly.

"I believe, Señor Gonzales, you'll find Margaret in the house. She went to make more lemonade."

"You, lovely lady, may call me Miguel. The rest of these *filibusteros* may call me Colonel Gonzales of the Army of the Republic of Mexico. Please excuse me while I find little Margarita."

Henry grinned as he watched Miguel stride towards the house. "*Little* Margarita? I think he's in for quite a surprise."

Dorcas sighed. "My, your Miguel is quite overwhelming, isn't he? No wonder Maggie is so smitten. I'm happy for you that he could come, but I suspect this is more than a social call."

"What do you mean?"

Dorcas look flustered. "I guess I just. . .uh. . .Henry, you wouldn't leave—go off on a campaign with him, would you?"

"Not a chance, darlin'. The only one I want to leave with is you. Let's stay around here just long enough to get hitched, then leave these fine folks to some serious drinking and dancing. They'll never miss us."

Henry and Dorcas spent their honeymoon, all two days of it, in an isolated cabin in the woods.

They made gentle, then passionate, then gentle love, and cavorted naked in a nearby stream. Katherine had packed enough food for the two days and Frederick made sure they had wine and whiskey.

On the third day, when they reluctantly returned to the Stockman place, Dorcas was a little dismayed to see that Miguel and James Gaines had waited for Henry.

Henry saw the worry in her eyes and said, "Now Dorcas, I told you not to worry. Miguel and James can't talk me into anything—my crusading days are over I promise we'll always be of a mind on all matters. I saw what problems Pa caused by always just making up his mind about stuff without asking Mama's opinion. We won't have that. My word on it."

"Oh Henry, you're the best and most understanding man in the world. How did you get so smart in only twenty-eight years?" Dorcas gushed.

"Books, my dear, books."

"It's time we went back to our fight in Texas," James Gaines said to the group of men sitting in the barn/conference room at the Stockman farm.

"If we get together enough men we'll ride south, driving the Spaniards into the Mexican revolutionary's hands. All the Spaniards need is a final push. You in, Henry?"

"Nope. You go do all the pushing you want, but I just got married and I ain't interested in joining any more expeditions."

"Strangely enough," Miguel said, "I agree with you, Enrique."

Henry gaped at Miguel in disbelief. He had expected a persuasive dissertation with lots of '*vivas*' and revolutionary rhetoric thrown in.

He made an exaggerated sniff of the air. "Do I detect skunk? Since when don't you want me in your revolution? What exactly do you want from me?"

"I am wounded, Enrique," Miguel feigned indignity and clamped his hands over his heart, "that you could distrust me so. But there is one little thing."

"Surprise, surprise. What 'one little thing?'"

"We want you, and your entire families," Miguel gestured to the men sitting around on hay bales, "to move into eastern Texas. Permanently."

Henry opened his mouth to protest, but Miguel held up his hand to fend off his objections.

"Not to fight, Henry, as James proposed. To live. Not squatting, like some of you are now—we wish you to build houses, plow fields. Settle."

Henry eyed Miguel warily, asking, "Before or after you win the war?"

"Well, we thought perhaps now."

"Is there more than *you* behind that *we*?"

"My government, the Republic of Mexico, wishes to assure you, the friends and Heroes of Mexico, that you will be given first consideration of lands when we take power. Especially if you are already there at our request. Those who are trespassing will be dealt with severely. But you will be the first to become Mexican citizens of Texas—official Texicans."

A round of cheers.

Miguel assumed a stance well known to Henry and James. They rolled their eyes, grinned at each other and waited for Miguel to pontificate.

"The Republic of Mexico wants its first president to be like your Jorge Washington, and our country a democracy—with freedom for all." As he took a breath to continue, Henry interrupted.

"My, my, Miguel," he said with a twinkle in his eye, "are you planning on running for President of Mexico yourself?"

"Oh, no. I am a soldier, not a politician. I will leave politics to those who like that sort of thing. I will return to Mexico to finish up with the Spaniards. There is only one particularly troublesome Royalist Army troop near Vera Cruz to be dealt with, led by Antonio Santa Anna."

Henry vaguely remembered hearing that name before. "Santa Anna?"

Miguel nodded.

"He is ruthless—as you, James, and I would have found out had we not had the good sense to desert that dog Gutierrez. Santa Anna was with General Arredondo when they took San Antonio in retaliation for the death of Governor Salcedo. They say he personally executed almost every prisoner they took."

"Sounds like we need this soldier on our side," James said.

Miguel smiled. "If we did, the conflict with Spain would end very quickly, I think."

"The sooner the better."

Henry clamped Miguel on the shoulder. "And, as usual, you've roped me in. If Dorcas agrees, I'm game for Texas. What about you boys?"

Most mumbled assent.

"Wonderful," Miguel grinned. "Now, I must prepare to leave, but I do not relish telling Margarita of my departure. She can be rather. . .difficult."

Frederick chuckled. "I'd say *difficult* was a compliment when describing our Maggie. Katrin says she's high-strung, but I just think she needs a good walloping. She's way too old for me to spank, so I guess we'll have to leave that to her husband."

"Husband?" Miguel blurted, obviously caught off guard. "What husband?"

"Well shoot, Miguel," Frederick said casually, "I'm tired of feeding her. She's getting a might long in the tooth, and unless you plan to take her off my hands pretty soon, I thought we might put her on the market for some eligible bachelor. She's pushin' twenty, you know." Frederick looked solemn, managing to keep a straight face.

Henry watched his father smoothly reel in the catch of the day and decided to add a little bait.

"Pa's right, Miguelito. Do you know anyone who might be willing to take her off our hands? I kinda had one of these Norris boys here in mind, but Maggie's smart enough so she won't have nothing to do with neither of them."

Miguel squared his shoulders, inhaled a chest-puffing breath, and said gallantly, "Señor Estocoman, if your daughter will have me, I would like your permission to ask for her hand in marriage."

"No kidding? Well, sure, you got my permission, but just when do you plan to come and fetch your blushin' bride? When Hell and Texas freeze over?" Frederick asked his trophy.

"I shall discuss it with her immediately and we will decide on the date. Let us say. . .within a year? That is, of course, if she will have me."

"That would be just dandy, Miguelito. Just fine and dandy indeed." Frederick pumped Miguel's hand.

Miguel strode purposefully from the barn, leaving the men who remained in awed silence.

Samuel Norris, a note of admiration in his voice, broke the quiet.

"That was just about the slickest piece of horse trading I ever saw, Frederick Stockman. Remind me to never do any serious business with you."

"Sometimes a man needs to be led to water, Sam. It's just a little easier when he thinks his well's about to run dry," Frederick told him with a sly smile.

"Maybe we should send *you* to Washington to settle our land claims," Norris said. "The United States Congress wouldn't stand a chance against a real horse trader like you."

"Good idea," Henry said. "But I don't think our problem is with those Yankee politicians. It's that Indian agent over in Caddo country who doesn't think we have a legitimate claim. He says we ain't nothin' but squatters and common firewater merchants—the man downright hurt my feelings. I mean, we might do a little whiskey trading, but we sure as hell ain't *common.*"

"What's so funny?" Dorcas asked as she walked in the open barn door.

The laughter stopped and all the men except Henry looked uncomfortable.

"Nothing, Dorcas darlin', they just don't believe I can get my feelings hurt. I'm glad you're here, 'cause I need to ask your opinion on something. Miguel wants us to move to Texas and become Mexican citizens. What do you think?"

Before Dorcas could answer, Frederick said, "Now Henry, your little bride don't need to be worrying her pretty head over such matters. I'm sure she has things to do over at the house." He shot a meaningful look at his son.

"No, Pa, she don't have nothing. . .er. . .anything more important to do than putting in her opinion where her future is concerned. Right, Dorcas?" Henry asked.

Dorcas, embarrassed by the shocked expressions of the men in the barn, was determined not to undermine Henry's groundbreaking behavior.

"Henry, I am certain you would think long and hard before casting our lot, but I appreciate you including me in your decision-making. If you think we should move to Texas, then Texas it is."

She graced the men with a brilliant smile and turned to leave, then stopped.

"And if it's worth anything, Mama Stockman and I have already discussed the possibility at great length, and I'm sure she'll agree that going to Texas is a good idea as well.

"Oh, and supper's ready."

Frederick stared at the spot vacated by Dorcas, then shook his head. "I guess this old dog needs to learn a few new tricks, son. If I had gone in that house and told Katrin we was moving back to Texas she'd have dug in her heels like an old mule. I guess, after seventy-one years on this earth, I've still got a thing to learn about womenfolk."

After supper, Miguel pulled Henry aside.

"I will never understand women, Enrique. Margarita will not give me an answer to my proposal of marriage, and I must depart soon. What should I do?" he asked.

"Oh, I think she's playing you, Miguelito. She knows you don't want to leave without an answer, and she doesn't want you to leave. My sister's a mite troublesome, but she ain't stupid. Just tell her you're going for sure—she'll come around."

Lowering his voice, Henry added, "I shouldn't be tellin' you this, but there ain't any ole boys sniffin' around here after Maggie that she's shown any interest in. Like Pa says, though, she can't be expected to wait forever. What did she say when you proposed?"

"She said I had to choose between her and my revolution. Why does she insist on such a choice? My war is almost won and soon we can be married and live in Texas." Miguel looked genuinely distraught.

"Miguel, Pa would kill me if he heard me ask, but have you ever considered that maybe Maggie isn't the right woman for you? I love my sister, but she has some pretty grand and romantic ideas about life. Maybe you need someone who feels as loyal as you do to Mexico and your cause. Haven't you met some nice *señorita* who shares your dreams?"

"You sound like a man who has found his perfect mate and wants all of us to be as happy as he is. I am very glad for you. But no, I have not met a nice *señorita.* In Mexico the women are so sheltered they have no *fuego*—fire. They have not experienced life."

"And you think Maggie has? Granted, she's been through a couple of adventures, but that doesn't mean she can put that experience to work in everyday life. I'm not sure she'll ever be content to settle down to raising babies and cooking—the regular stuff women do. She thinks life should be like one of them romance books she reads all day. What happens when *real* life settles in? Have you thought about that, my friend?" Henry asked.

"I am aware of Margarita's dreamy nature, but once we are married, that will change. She is still young, and like most young girls she will learn to handle everyday life as it comes. That is, if I can get her to agree to marry me."

"Oh, she'll marry you, all right. I just hope you know what you're getting into, *hermano*," Henry told his friend.

"Margarita, my love, I am leaving tomorrow," Miguel said firmly, "and I need your answer. As a token of my commitment to have you for my wife, I would like you to wear this lavaliere that was my grandmother's. It comes from Spain and is very precious. As precious as my love for you."

Margaret took the heavily bejeweled gold locket and gasped, "Oh, Miguel, this looks like something a princess—no, a queen—would wear. Was your grandmother royalty?"

"My ancestors were highly born, and my grandmother was at court when she was a young girl. When she married my grandfather she disappointed her father and he disowned her. Fortunately for you, my great-grandmother outlived my great-grandfather, so the jewelry, if not the land, was passed down. I cannot offer you a crown, but I do offer my love. What is your answer?"

"I accept," Margaret said, and raised her long red hair for Miguel to fasten the priceless lavaliere's heavy gold chain around her neck.

"It looks lovely on you, *corazòn*." Miguel bowed slightly and kissed her lightly on the lips. "When I return we shall be married. In Texas. I will build you a beautiful house for our many children. I promise to do everything I can to make you very happy."

Maggie, blushing crimson from the kiss—her first—gushed, "You already have, Miguel. No one I know has a piece of jewelry this fine. I shall be the envy of all Louisiana. And Texas."

Before departing New Orleans for the Yucatan, Miguel thanked Jean Lafitte for the lavaliere—pirated from a Spanish vessel—that the Frenchman had given him. The little bauble had certainly come in handy.

CHAPTER 31

"¡*Soldados*! ¡*Soldados*! Many soldiers are coming. Run for your lives," shouted an outpost guard as he rode into Nacogdoches in a full gallop.

Henry ran from his barn and waved down the panicked Mexican.

"¿*A donde*? Where?" he asked, almost choking on the dust raised when the man reigned in hard. "How far away? How many men?"

"*Muchos*. Many men. About two hours back. They are not riding fast, but they will be here soon. There are perhaps two hundred of them, Señor Enrique. I must go to hide my family."

"You go on, Martinez, and *gracias. . .muchas gracias, amigo.*

"Dorcas!" Henry yelled, running towards his own home, "gather up the family, douse the fires, scatter the stock, and head for our hiding place. I'll be there as soon as I ring the church bell to warn the others."

Nacogdoches, Texas, in the spring of 1820, wasn't much, but it was home to the Stockmans and a few other families.

In their first year, the Stockmans added their cabins to the few shacks scattered around the Plaza Principal, planted crops, and settled down to a life only occasionally interrupted by excitement like today's.

Spanish troops seldom ranged as far north as Nacogdoches any more, but when they did send out a few soldiers to rattle their swords, the nesters in Nacogdoches simply went into hiding.

Henry, Dorcas, and their newly born son, Henry Joseph lived in a dog-run next door to a larger home housing Katherine, Frederick, Margaret, John, Peter, Joseph Anthony and Sarah.

Jesús, the tongueless Indian, and his ancient grandmother, steadfastly distrustful of indoor living, had a lean-to off the barn.

Maggie spent most of her time making grandiose plans for her wedding, and fretting impatiently for the elusive Miguel to return from Mexico.

As time passed, and it became obvious that Miguel had been a tad optimistic on how long the Spaniards would hold out, she became increasingly unpleasant to live with. The saving grace, to Katherine's thinking, was that her high-strung daughter spent most of her time next door at Henry's, fawning over little Henry Joseph and reading Dorcas' books.

Joseph Anthony, fifteen, spent his time hunting or adding a little cash to the family coffers by building furniture for the sparse population of the area. And, like all males over thirteen, he served outpost duty, guarding against a surprise invasion from the west.

Spanish retribution was of prime concern to all who lived in Nacogdoches, legal or not. The few legal residents were just as much at risk as the nesters: failure to report interlopers was a serious crime. Hanged if you did or hanged if you didn't they liked to say.

Peter and John, twenty-four and twenty-nine, and both still bachelors, became the traveling-trader branch of the family and were gone most of the time. Frederick went with them at times, but age was slowing him down.

But now the Spaniards *were* coming, and everyone, young and old, legal and illegal, quickly dispersed to their hiding places.

The drill, oft-repeated because of Comanche threat, insured that an arriving raiding party found little to raid save a few abandoned homes and a stray cow or two.

False floors and walls made good hiding places for blankets and clothes not taken with the fugitives. Concealed trap doors led to roofs laden with cookware and furniture. If the intruders were to take the time, booty could be found, but few did. Most looked about nervously and left quickly, sensing, rightly so, that they were being watched.

The Stockman-Norris-Gaines clan's emergency enclave lay two miles from Nacogdoches in a heavily wooded area with underground caves.

The families, although they scattered separately, rendezvoused there quickly after an alert. Babies were given sugar-laced whiskey to put them to sleep, silence fell on the encampment, and the waiting began.

Joseph Anthony and John Norris were posted a quarter-mile west, along the El Camino Real, while others guarded the north, east and south perimeters. Just because the enemy was coming from the west didn't mean others, namely hostile Indians, didn't lurk in other directions.

"Mama," Maggie whined, "I just hate hiding out like some common criminal. When will we ever be able to live like regular human beings?"

"Hush, Maggie. For crying out loud, girl, you're not a baby anymore, so act your age. You aren't the only one being inconvenienced, you know. Do you think we like leaving our home? Perhaps you'd rather stay and face the Spanish soldiers," Katherine scolded.

"I'm sorry, Mama. I guess I'm just scared. I feel as though I'll die before I have a chance to live. Does that make any sense?"

Katherine stroked her daughter's copper hair and said soothingly, "Honey, you read too many books. Besides," she smiled, "God wouldn't take you until he's had a chance to let me get even by giving you a daughter just like yourself. One who's a real pain in the derrière."

Maggie giggled softly behind her hand and picked up Henry Joseph, who was in a deep whiskey slumber.

"Isn't he just the very image of, well, all of us, Mama? Dorcas, you're so lucky to have your two Henrys. Someday I want a little Miguel and Margarita for my very own. I shall dress them like a prince and princess and everyone will be jealous of my precious children and my handsome husband."

"Yes, Maggie dear, you'll have those things, don't worry. For now we'd better be quiet and listen for the all clear," Dorcas told her sister-in-law.

"Are you sure they are here, *Comandante*?" A lieutenant scanned Nachogdoches nervously and could see nothing but a dog.

"Yes, they are, and we will not leave until they are found. Tomorrow we will divide forces and scour the area. These are very elusive people who have lived long by their wits, but now the time has come for them to reveal themselves. Tell the men to be very careful, and under no circumstances are they to fire their weapons. That is an order that will have dire consequences if ignored. Am I clear?"

The officers saluted. Then his sergeant asked, "Colonel, where shall we set up your headquarters?"

The Colonel surveyed the area, saw what he was looking for, and pointed to Henry's house.

"There. That house. And set the main camp up in the center of the church square. Tell your men to stay out of the other houses. There will be no looting of the villager's belongings. Anyone caught stealing will be shot."

Darkness fell like a wet blanket on the fugitives. Without the warmth of campfires, their hideaway was soon chilly. Katherine, reminded of other nights in hiding, pulled a quilt over her head, sighed, and asked herself, *Will it never end?*

Henry and Frederick used the cover of darkness to creep back and survey the situation in Nacogdoches.

They were surprised to find but one guard posted on El Camino Real. Easily skirting around him to the edge of the village, they were within twenty feet of Henry's cabin when they saw a magnificent horse with fine trappings tied to Henry's personal hitching post. And the glow of a fire in his hearth.

Incensed, Henry started forward, but Frederick grabbed his arm and signaled a retreat.

Henry balked and the old man whispered, "Son, don't do it."

"Pa, some bastard's sitting in my nice warm home, probably eating my nice hot food, while my wife and baby are cold and hungry. Sometimes a man's gotta take a stand."

"This ain't the time, boy. There's probably two hundred soldiers camped around town, and there's only two of us."

"I'd say that makes us about even," Henry said through his teeth. "If we get the owner of that horse—the leader—we cut off the head of the serpent. The others'll scatter to the wind."

"By the looks of that horse, I'd say he was the boss, all right," Frederick agreed.

"Pa, I'd wager most of these soldiers were stolen from their villages and pressed into service without a day's training. You know damned well they can't hit the broad side of a barn, 'cause they ain't been given any ammunition for practice. And even if they could shoot, their hearts ain't in their work. What say let's do a little snake huntin'?"

"I think we should wait. If I let you get killed your Ma and your wife will shoot me."

"Suit yourself, Pa. But I'm going to get me some *gachupín* reptile."

"Oh, hell, I done lived long enough anyhow. I'm in, son. Have you got a plan, or are we just gonna walk in the front door and despatch the bastard?"

"The *jefe* is probably toastin' his toes in front of my fireplace, and there's no guard outside the door—don't know about inside.

"Let's suppose there's at least one man in the backyard. Pa, you take him, and I'll take the house."

Frederick nodded. "I'll go around to the left, and when you see me come 'round right, hit the front door like an ill tempered he-goat."

"All right, Pa. Now, let's send that son of a bitch to Spanish Hades."

Frederick crept forward slowly. Circling the house, he found no guard, and had barely rounded the corner on the way back when he saw Henry begin his run for the front door.

Henry hit the solid pine door of his home full force, hoping the arrogance of the Spaniards had prevented them from bolting it.

The door crashed open and Henry, pistols in both hands, catapulted into the great room. Prepared to start blasting away, he was caught up short when he found himself face-to-face with his future brother-in-law.

"Enrique, what took you so long?" Colonel Miguel Gonzales asked mildly.

Henry let loose a holler of surprise and delight and, pistols still in his hands, fell into Miguel's bear hug.

Frederick rushed through the door and saw what appeared to be a struggle. "Let him go, you Spanish devil, or I'll blow you straight to Hell," he yelled.

"Señor Frederico, you wish to kill your future son-in-law?" Miguel asked, releasing Henry.

Henry grinned and added, "Shut the door Pa, before you let in some soldiers who might shoot first and ask questions later."

Frederick kicked the door shut. "You got some explaining to do boy. What do you mean riding here with all these men, scaring the bejesus out of us all."

Miguel stood tall, opened his arms widely, and announced, "It is my great pleasure, my fellow Texicans, to welcome you to the Republic of Mexico and her free state of Texas."

Frederick sagged into a chair and tears welled in his eyes. After fifteen years of constant turmoil, all he could say was, "What in heck took you so long."

The next evening the residents of Nacogdoches—back in their own homes and in a festive mood—held a fandango to honor their new country and their new, relatively legal, immigrant status.

They danced, drank *aguardiente*, ate *cabrito* (baby goat) slow-roasted over mesquite fires, and shot pistols into the cool night air.

"*¡Viva la Republica! ¡Viva Mexico! ¡Viva Tejas!*" Miguel proclaimed loudly. He held a glass of whisky in one hand and Maggie's shoulder with the other. "I wish to propose a toast to my future bride, Margarita."

"To Margarita!" the crowd chorused.

"To freedom!" he roared.

"To freedom!" they toasted.

"To General Antonio Santa Anna!" Miguel shouted.

"To. . .who?" Henry asked above the noise.

"Santa Anna, the Hero of the Revolution. Without him, the Spaniards would still be in power."

"I thought he was a Royalist, Miguel."

"Oh, he is. Or was. But so were we all at one time. When Santa Anna changed sides, though, it was the very turning point of the revolution. He is a great leader of men and he won our freedom."

"Well, then, to Santa Anna!" Henry shouted, then turned to Dorcas with a wry grin and asked, "I wonder how many of his men had to take themselves prisoner?"

Dorcas looked puzzled. "A little joke, honey, between me and Miguelito," Henry told her. "I'll tell you about it later when there isn't so much noise."

The celebration promised to continue throughout the night, but Henry and Dorcas opted to go home. As they lay in bed listening to sporadic gunfire and singing, Dorcas asked, "Honey, what was that joke between you and Miguel?"

"Well darlin', when we were fighting Spain, folks were changing sides so fast that you could be following some Colonel into battle and damned if he wouldn't up and switch sides. If you didn't jump to the other side quick enough, you could end up arresting yourself for treason."

Dorcas giggled and snuggled closer to Henry.

"You two can find humor in the strangest things, but then I guess you'd have to, considering the way things are in this part of the world."

"The sad part of our little joke is that every single, solitary, General in the Mexican Army got there through treason. And with the exception of a few men like Miguel, we can't trust the bureaucrats in Mexico City any more than we did the Spaniards—'specially since they're the same men who just switched allegiances. It don't bode well for us Texicans, unless we can get home rule."

Henry reached under the covers and patted Dorcas' swollen tummy, adding, "We have to secure Texas as a free state for our future Texicans."

CHAPTER 32

"Henry Joseph, tell your ole Pa—what are the colors on that flag?"

Henry pointed to the flagpole in the Nacogdoches church plaza where a Mexican tricolor—the *trigarantine*—swayed indolently in a light breeze.

Four-year-old Henry Joseph stared at the flag, then looked around the plaza. Also enjoying the warm spring sunshine with them were three Mexican soldiers, a couple of ancient whittlers, a redbone hound, and his little brother, Hardy Francis.

"Red, white, and *verde*," Henry Joseph said confidently.

"Good, son. Now, do you remember what the colors stand for?"

The little boy shuffled his feet and looked at the ground, then pointed to his little brother and said, "Ask Hardy."

Henry laughed and hugged him.

"That's mighty quick thinkin', boy. It's all right if you've forgotten. Listen up now, so you can tell your Ma you learned something today.

"The red represents the blood of the Mexican people, the white for the purity of the church, and the green for independence. I never quite figured that green bit out, but I guess it's like spring, when green means a new beginning. All right, what. . . ."

Henry grinned as the soldiers, who had been lolling against a tree, suddenly snapped to attention. "I'd guess," he said sardonically, "that your Uncle Miguel is headed this way. . .yep, here he comes."

The little boys ran toward their doting uncle, who scooped them both up into his arms. Miguel spoiled his nephews, lavishing on them the affection he would have bestowed on his own children. After three years of marriage, he and Margaret remained childless.

"Dorcas told me I would find you here. She said it was history day," Miguel said, putting down his nephews.

"Yep, she's bound and determined the boys don't grow up ignorant like their Pa. I was just explaining the meaning of the colors on the flag."

"Oh, you mean the watermelon?" Miguel asked, making a face at the children.

"Watermelon? What watermelon, Tio Miguel?" Henry Joseph asked.

"Well, they say when Mexico became a republic the new President of Mexico, Iturbide, held a meeting to discuss our future. We needed a new flag and since they were eating a watermelon at the time. . . ." Miguel stopped talking and looked meaningfully at Henry Joseph.

The boy giggled. "I get it," he said proudly, "the flag is red, white, and green like a watermelon. You're so funny, Tio Miguelito."

"Please be so kind as to tell that to your Tia Margarita. I think she finds me boring," Miguel joked, but Henry sensed some underlying truth in his comment.

"Let your old uncle tell you more about the colors of the flag, then we'll go find something fun to do.

"The flag is called the *trigarantine*—three guarantees in English—because the three colors represent the guarantee of independence, equality, and freedom of religion to all of the citizens of Mexico," Miguel said grandly. "Now let's go cool our feet in the spring."

The boys ran ahead, the men followed slowly. Henry, with a sarcastic drawl, said, "Guaranteed independence, equality and freedom of religion, so long as the religion is Catholic and the citizens ain't independent enough to want a jury trial by their equals."

Miguel fixed Henry with a pained look. "Patience, Enrique. All things in good time. At least the new constitution of 1824 gives we Texicans self-rule, with the right to establish schools, and to elect our own officials. It seems to me we have made great progress in only three years of independence. Have you forgotten what it was like, living under the steel swords of the Spaniards?"

"Naw, I'm pretty happy with the way things are, but some of the new settlers, and even a few of the old, are getting a might restless. The Catholic thing bothers them."

"Why? It isn't like Mexico City forces Catholicism on Texas like the Jesuits did on Mexico. Even though the colonists signed agreements to embrace the Catholic faith in order to immigrate, it is not enforced. The church turns a blind eye on Texas, even through they know about the Protestant services in the Austin Colony. And you should certainly not be concerned—you are Catholic."

"I ain't talking about me—I'm just telling you there are others who are getting a mite fed up with Mexico City. 'Course this new constitution should calm 'em down. For awhile."

"That is why I came looking for you today, Henry. I have good news."

"They named you king?" Henry quipped.

"No, but almost that good: General Santa Anna has taken over the Army of Mexico and has vowed to uphold that new constitution."

"*Bravo,* Miguel. That's great news," Henry said, slapping his brother-in-law on the back. "Finally, we have a man in charge who can get things done. Let's go cool our feet, and then we'll have a fiesta in honor of General Antonio Lopez de Santa Anna and the Constitution of 1824."

CHAPTER 33

Each month more *norteamericanos* poured over the porous border into Texas—legally and otherwise. The Republic of Mexico, not unlike Spain, did not have the resources to stem the flow of illegals.

"Dorcas," Henry said late one afternoon as they sat with Katherine on their porch, "I think we should start looking for a place outside of town. With all these new folks showin' up here in Nacogdoches, maybe we'd better stake us out a league or two before it's all gone. Someone said the other day there's almost five thousand settlers in Texas, and more a'comin'."

Dorcas smiled, thinking everything was relative—five thousand people scattered over Texas didn't exactly constitute overcrowding.

But he had a point.

"It does," she said, "seem as though they're arriving in droves."

Katherine nodded. "And things have changed. The buffalo aren't nearly as plentiful as they were twenty years ago, and the wild mustangs and cattle have pretty much been corralled. Shoot, we have almost forty people here in town—most of them human filth. Things being the way they are, maybe we *should* move."

"I wouldn't mind," Dorcas said. "Seems like someone comes by and raises the dust in the road more and more. I'd like to live someplace where I can throw open the windows without suffocating."

A rider went by and waved, but raised little dust because of a light rain earlier in the day.

"And mud," Katherine commented without taking her eyes from the peas she was shelling.

"What?" Henry asked.

"Mud. Sometimes after a rain a wagon comes by too fast and slings mud clear up on the porch," she made a sweeping gesture with her arms.

"What about Pa, John, Joseph Anthony and Peter? Think they'd want to move?" Henry asked. "And Jesús?"

Katherine chuckled, saying, "I imagine they'd go along. John and José Antonio don't show much inclination to wander too far from my cook pot, and Peter's nursing a broken heart since the Caro girl married someone else. As for your Pa, I'll talk to him about it as soon as he gets back from unloading y'all's Caddo land on that northern land speculator."

Dorcas frowned, picturing the smug northerner who had ridden into town thinking to take advantage of the poor, ignorant Texicans—get deeds to their property before Texas became a state.

It was their first inkling that, back in Washington, folks just naturally assumed that Texas wouldn't remain Mexican for long.

It was a worry. The Stockmans were not only pro-Mexican rule, they were considered Heroes of the Revolution in Mexico City.

Henry's chuckles broke into her thoughts.

"That smarty land speculator," he said, "thinks he's got my old Pa hornswoggled, when the opposite is true. That Caddo territory land dispute ain't never gonna get settled. If Pa gets anything for it, it'll be a miracle."

"Too bad. I have affection for that land. After all, it's the reason we met, Henry," Dorcas said wistfully.

Katherine smiled at her wonderful daughter-in-law and wished more of her children would get married. "I doubt Miguel and Maggie will leave town, what with him working for the government and all."

"And I work for him. But I think I could give it up to move into the country. Not too far though—we still have Comanche problems."

Katherine shuddered and Henry didn't pursue that subject. "If we do move," he said, "Maggie won't be too keen on losing Henry Joseph."

"Speaking of, could you go over to Miguel's and fetch that boy while Mother Stockman and I get supper on the table? Henry Joseph spends all his time over there. Maggie's got him reading some of her easier books on his own," Dorcas said proudly.

"I'll round him up. I'm not at all surprised he can already read. When Maggie isn't reading to him, you are. And then there's the fact that his Pa's so smart," Henry teased.

"Smart?" Katherine said. "Humph. Smart folks don't go around sticking their noses into politics like you and the Norris boys and James Gaines."

"Now, Ma, we. . . ."

Dorcas cut him off. "She's right. Next thing I know, you'll be running for Alcalde or some other office. Seems to me you've got enough to do working for Miguel."

Henry felt surrounded and opted to escape.

Walking the quarter-mile to the Gonzales' home, he saw Miguel and another man sitting on the front porch. Not wanting to disturb them, he started around to the back door, but Miguel called him over.

"Enrique, come here please. I was just talking about you. Have you met Señor Stephen Austin?" Miguel asked.

"No, but I sure am pleased to have the honor. I've heard a lot of nice things about your colony, Mr. Austin," Henry said, offering his hand to the thin, almost effete-looking young man.

"The pleasure is mine, sir. And please, call me Estèban. Colonel Gonzales tells me your family came in aught-six. Things must have been pretty exciting around here back then."

"Yep, I like it better now. The Spaniards were even more unpredictable than those fellas we've got in Mexico City."

Austin allowed himself a smile, but Miguel shot Henry a warning look. It wasn't a good idea to voice opinion that smacked of criticism about government officials. Austin caught the glance, and nodded. "They do go on, don't they. Well, hopefully, with settlers like my colonists and those such as your family, we can keep Mexico City out of our hair and build a great Texas."

Miguel added, "And that is exactly what we were discussing, Enrique. I have received word from the Saltillo land office that more large grants are being considered to establish more colonies like that of Señor Austin's. It looks like you and I will be flooded with more paperwork."

Henry rolled his eyes in mock-horror.

Austin laughed aloud. "Mr. Stockman, I was wondering if you would consider running for Alcalde?" he asked.

Henry, startled, looked back in the direction of his house. *That wife of mine is part soothsayer.*

Returning his attention to the men on the porch, he said, "I don't get it, Mr. . .er. . .Estèban. Why are you interested in who runs for Alcalde here in Nacogdoches?"

"I am interested in all of Texas. And the safety of her colonists. Each day brings newcomers from the United States who might, shall we say, unwittingly challenge the authority of the Mexican government."

Henry was silent for a moment, then shook his head. "Estèban, I'm not real interested in being Sheriff, Judge and Mayor all rolled into one, and that's what I understand bein' Alcalde is. But I think I know someone who would fit that picture just fine—I think Miguel will agree."

"Who do you have in mind, *hermano*?" Miguel asked.

"Samuel Norris. His family has been here even longer than mine, and he has a better temperament towards things political than I do. I might shoot someone and have to hang myself," Henry grinned.

"Samuel Norris. I think Enrique has a good idea there," Miguel said. "I will discuss it with him."

Henry stood. "I guess I'd better get on home before my wife throws out my supper. Nice to meet you, Estèban. Miguel, is Henry Joseph here?"

"I'll see if Margarita can bear to part with your son. I, for one, am considering charging you for his room and board."

Miguel and Henry cornered Samuel Norris the next day.

"Sam, it was Stephen Austin himself who came to ask about a good candidate. The only other man running for Alcalde is the son-in-law of Haden Edwards, and Edwards is getting on my nerves with his pushy *norteamericano* ways," Miguel told Norris.

Henry nodded. "We have to make sure these newcomers don't get a hold in government here, because they'll bring down the wrath of Mexico City on us one day. The Constitution of 1824, giving us the right to elect our own officials, also gave us just enough rope to hang ourselves."

Samuel Norris looked skeptical. "I don't think I can win an election. Hell, there's more of *them* than *us*."

"True," Miguel said. "That is a problem. And this Edwards, he is a true worry to me. He and his clan do not understand our ways, and ever since he was given a grant by Mexico City he has been annoying some of the old Texican families."

Henry interjected, "Like Señor Navarro. He came to me after Edwards showed up at his place asking to see his deed."

"Deed, indeed," Miguel scoffed. "The Navarros have been in Texas for over one hundred and fifty years. What insolence."

"Be that as it may, Miguel, Sam's got a point," Henry said reasonably. "There are more of *them* than *us*."

"Enrique, please do not be too insulted when I tell you that sometimes you think much too much like a *norteamericano*. I just said these newcomers do not yet understand our ways. Do not ever forget, amigos, this *is* Mexico. And we Texicans *are* Mexican citizens, no?"

The men nodded assent and Miguel asked, "And who is allowed to vote in Mexico?"

"Only citizens," Henry answered, then his face lit up. "And the Edwards Colony hasn't got all their people registered! In fact, their petitions are still here in your office. You know, someone ought to tell ole Edwards how to do bidness in Texas."

Both Miguel and Norris laughed and chorused, "Not me."

But Henry, when Haden Edwards came to the office with a letter to be forwarded to Mexico City, felt he could not, in good conscience, let the man shoot himself in the foot without a warning.

It was one thing not to bother to lead a man by the nose through the morass of local politics, but it was quite another to forward such an inflammatory missive to the Mexican authorities.

"Mr. Edwards, I don't think you want to send this letter to Mexico City with this particular wording in it," Henry advised the would-be impresario.

"Personally Stockman, I don't care what you think. If I have my way, you and your so-called Texicans would be going to Mexico along with the letter. I should think you would spend more time thinking about the future of Texas, and less playing Mexican," the man sniffed.

Henry smiled a dangerous smile.

"You might be right about that, Mr. Edwards. I'd better start bein' real careful with the future of Texas."

Edwards left and Henry carefully put the man's letter in a pouch bound for Mexico City, grinning and thinking, *I sure as hell don't want this honey of a letter to be delayed or get lost, no-sir-ree.*

Miguel came in and threw his hat on a chair.

"Good morning, Enrique. Wasn't that the honorable Mr. Edwards I just saw stomp out of here? And if so, what was his business this time?"

"His bidness," Henry grinned, "seems to be doin' just about everything he can to get himself in hot water with your bosses down south."

"I am very glad to hear that," Miguel said. "Very glad, indeed."

CHAPTER 34

"Henry Stockman, meet Miz Henrietta Stockman," Maggie said, handing Henry his furiously squalling daughter—his third child.

"Lord, I think she takes after her Aunt Maggie," Henry teased. "How's Dorcas doing, Sis?"

"How do you *think* she's doing?" his sister snarled. "If men had to go through this, there wouldn't be any babies."

Henry threw his hands up in mock self-defense, "What'd I do?"

"I'm sorry, Enrique. I'm just tired, I guess. I've been so anxious about Dorcas and the baby. . .but," she brightened, "the doctor says they're both just fine and dandy. He'll be out in a minute to tell you himself."

"Maggie, is everything all right with you? Lately it seems you've been so. . . ."

"Bitchy?" Maggie finished for him. "Oh, don't look so shocked. It isn't as if you never heard the word. And I know for a fact there are some who think I qualify." Tears filled her eyes.

Henry put his arms around her.

"It'll be all right, Sis, whatever it is. Have you talked to Mama about what's botherin' you? I mean, you could tell me, but I don't know as how I'd be much help, me being a man and all."

"Henry, you are most understanding—for a man. And It's just that. . .it's so awful. . . ."

"Maggie, you can tell me anything. I'm your favorite brother, remember?"

Margaret took the baby and said, "Let's take Henrietta back to Dorcas, you kiss your wife, and then the two of us can take a walk down by the spring. Maybe you *can* help me." She smiled crookedly and nuzzled her eyes against the baby's blanket to wipe away her tears.

". . .and then they called me a *filthy Meskin-lover*," Margaret told him. Her cheeks were blazing.

"The old battle-axes didn't know I was in the back of the store looking at some bolts of fabric. I was so humiliated I didn't even have the courage to show myself until they were gone—hid like some criminal.

The storekeeper was real kind and told me not to pay any mind to the mean old hens, but I can't help it—it hurts," she sobbed.

"Who were they, Maggie?" Henry asked quietly.

"I think it was newcomers from the Edwards Colony. It all started when the storekeeper asked them if they were interested in some dried pinto beans he just got in, and they said they would leave the beans to *frijole*-eating Meskins like Gonzales and his filthy-Meskin-lovin' wife."

As Henry listened his jaw began to work.

"I was so stunned, Henry, I just froze. Why are they being so wretched? What have I done to them?"

"Maggie, there's folks coming here that are finding out they can't just take over, and they're gettin' scared. Haden Edwards' grant's been revoked, after he spent his entire fortune to start a new colony here in Texas."

"Really? Good," Margaret huffed.

"Maybe, maybe not," Henry said. "Now, I don't much care for Edwards, but I don't like to see something like this happen to any man, no matter how much he asks for it. They come in here, sign a paper saying they'll be loyal Mexican citizens, and then set about acting like they own the country."

"But what do they have against me?" Maggie asked.

"Maggie, you're married to a Mexican official, your brother-in-law is Alcalde, and even though none of us has a pot to piss in, we do have a little pull with Mexico City." He smiled, wiped a tear from her cheek and added, "And to make matters worse, you're beautiful. You're a sure-fire target for jealously."

"Those old biddies didn't sound jealous. They just sounded like they hated me," Maggie sniffed.

"Jealousy takes on a lot of forms, honey. Our family has been here so long, and so have all our in-laws, that these new folks think we're closing ranks on them. I plan to do some serious closin' when I find out what pesky newcomers hurt my baby sister's feelin's and made her clabber up and blink."

"Oh, Henry, you have such a way of making me feel better. But I wonder, sometimes, if I'm tough enough to live in Texas; if my. . .character. . .is strong enough to withstand disapproval? You know I've never taken well to faultfinding." She smiled, her chin wavering. "I can dish it out, but can't take it, huh?"

"Princess, I think you're a darned sight stronger than you think, I just don't think you've had a chance to. . . ." his voice trailed off.

"Grow up?"

"Maybe."

"Henry, I'm twenty-six-years-old, and scared. I have a wonderful husband that I treat badly, no children, and I've never accomplished a single thing on my own. There must be a name for this. . .blueness, I feel. It's like a blanket, suffocating me."

Seeing that Henry was totally perplexed, she shrugged. "I guess that's why some call it the vapors—like I sometimes can't get enough air."

Maggie knew her brother had no idea what she was talking about, but just talking about her feelings made her feel better. "Come on, big brother, let's go on back and see how Henrietta and Dorcas are doing."

They had walked only a few steps when Henry stopped and grabbed his sister's hand. "Maggie, I wouldn't tell Miguel about those women if I was you. Someone could get more than their feelings hurt."

Maggie nodded.

"Hell, baby sister, it was most likely some of that Edwards bunch talking mean about you, and by this time next month those ole trouble-makin' hens will be scratchin' up their barnyard dirt back in the United States."

"Why can't they stay and let *me* go to the United States?" Maggie said, laughing at her own joke. Henry suspected she was only half-joking.

Henry was wrong about Edwards.

Edwards not only refused to leave and take his would-be colonists with him, he declared war.

Infuriated with the Mexicans' reversal of his grant, he vowed to free Texas from Mexican rule, then rename it Fredonia. Unwilling to listen to Miguel and Stephen Austin's advice to leave quietly, and unable to enlist any old-time settlers in his cause,

Edwards turned to the Cherokee Indians. He promised that, in return for their help in overthrowing the Mexican government, he would restore the Cherokees' land—land taken by settlers—and give the Cherokees full rights as citizens of the new Republic of Fredonia.

When Miguel heard of Edwards' plan, he snorted in derision, then complained, "Enrique, this Edwards *hombre* is giving me a *dolor* in my back side."

"Yep, he's a pain, all right. Why can't the son of a bitch just leave? Before the real trouble starts."

"Amigo, the trouble has already started," Miguel said, waving a piece of paper.

"Mexico City is," he looked at the message, "greatly concerned with the unpatriotic attitude of many of the new *norteamericanos* entering Texas." He threw the letter down.

"I tell you, Henry, a rebellion such as this Edwards proposes could bring the entire Mexican army marching into Texas, and that would be bad for all of us. Estèban Austin thinks we should handle the problem locally—show Mexico City we will not allow such troublemakers in our midst."

"Since Sam Norris is Alcalde, and Edwards' grant's revoked, can't he just tell Edwards to leave?" Henry asked.

"Of course he can, but he's going to need some backup."

"He can count on the Stockmans. And since you appointed your old Spaniard-fightin' friend, Peter Bean, as local Indian Agent, you can tell him to warn off the Cherokees. He'd better make Chief Fields see the danger of getting crosswise with the government. Enough politics, let's talk about lunch. Dorcas is cooking venison."

"I cannot enjoy your wife's cooking today, *hermano.* Margarita has been so. . .restless. . .I promised her a ride in the country. I wish I knew what was wrong with her. Do you think it is because we have no children?" Miguel asked, concern on his handsome face.

"Who knows. Maybe she's got the vapors, whatever in hell that is."

"Perhaps. She is so unhappy, no matter what I do. I hear her crying at night, but when I ask her what's wrong, she says 'nothing.'"

Henry sighed and sat down again.

"Miguel, I'm gonna tell you something, but you gotta promise me you won't go crazy on me. You know how *loco* you can get when you lose that Mexican temper. Promise?"

"Enrique, if it will help my Margarita, I promise."

Henry told Miguel about the incident at the mercantile and how hurt Maggie was by the women's vicious comments. There was no way to soft-soap the language the old gossips had used.

Miguel, at first, looked shocked, but as the story unfolded, his face flushed and he said, calmly—Henry felt too calmly—"I see."

Henry waited for more, but Miguel just stood and walked out, leaving his friend in heartfelt pathos. In the twenty years the men had known each other, he had seen Miguel mad enough to kill, but never had he seen him dejected.

Henry wanted to kill someone for him.

The one skirmish arising from the Fredonian Rebellion did not last long, nor was it particularly notable in a military sense.

The Norrises, Miguel, the Stockman boys, the Caros, and a handful of other Texicans clashed with Edwards' rebels, with no clear victor.

After much posturing and some shooting, Edwards saw that, without allies, he could not win, and gave up his dream of a colony. Or a new country.

But there were casualties.

The Cherokee Chief, Richard Fields, was murdered by his own tribe, sacrificed on the alter of allegiance to the Mexican government, and Joseph Anthony Stockman received a groin wound from which he would never fully recover.

Satisfied by Stephen Austin that the colonists could handle their own rebels, Mexico City called a halt to their proposed invasion and an uneasy peace reigned.

But for the Stockmans, and the rest of the Texicans loyal to Mexico rule, a new, deep line was drawn in the sand. And for the newcomers lusting for some rich Texas soil, the enemy no longer lived in Mexico City. They lived next door.

CHAPTER 35

"José Antonio, how are you feeling today?" Maggie asked with a false brightness she hoped covered her dismay when she saw her brother. After five years of suffering from his Fredonian Rebellion wound, the twenty-eight-year-old looked like a gaunt old man. Maggie thought their father, in his seventies, looked better.

Maggie and the soldier who shadowed her had ridden out to the Stockman grant north of Nacogdoches for a visit with her family. She went there often and wished she could live nearer, but Miguel's work required they reside in town.

Joseph Anthony's sweet smile still lingered in his skeletal face.

"I'm a little better this week, Sis. Jesús has been makin' me up some stuff that his old granny taught him how to brew before she died—tastes like hell and leaves me woozy, but sure lifts the pain."

"I guess, then, it's a good thing you didn't knife Jesús back when we first saw him in that tree," Margaret teased. "My goodness, that seems so long ago."

"It was, Maggie. Pert' near fourteen years."

Margaret could hardly believe it had been that long. She looked at the house. "Where's Mama?"

"Over at Henry's. Sis, I'm a little worried about Mama. I know she ain't no spring chicken, but lately she's plumb frazzled."

"It's no wonder. She thinks she has to take care of the world. She needs to rest, but you know what the chances are of that."

"Aught. She's been over to Henry's a lot lately, what with Dorcas' baby due any day. I guess everyone's real worried about this one."

Margaret nodded and frowned.

"I am. Losing the last baby was a terrible blow for Dorcas, but she's the one who insisted on another try. I'm sure this time will be fine."

"I hope so. Look at the crib I made," Joseph Anthony said, leading his sister to his shop. He was a skilled craftsman, and when well enough, he did cabinetry for wages. He proudly uncovered his latest creation.

"Oh, my," Maggie marveled. The tiny pine cradle was intricately carved and polished to a sheen. "José Antonio, it's magnificent. You have such a way with wood. How about if I commission a piece from you?"

"A crib?" Joseph said hopefully, then wished the words back in his mouth. "I'm sorry, Maggie, I wasn't thinkin'. I'm sure you and Miguel'll have lots of babies some day."

"It's all right, José, I've about decided maybe it's better I don't have a bunch of children to care for. I can spoil everyone else's, then send them home." She looked around, "Where's Daddy?"

"Him and Jesús left early this morning to drop off Mama at Henry's, then take Henry Joseph fishing. If you ride on over you'll probably find all of them."

"I'll do that. Wanna come?"

"Naw, Maggie. All that bouncing might open up this hole in my side again. Why don't you take my wagon and deliver the crib for me? Tell Dorcas I'm thinking about her," Joseph Anthony said as he limped towards the shop.

Maggie watched her brother hobble off to hitch the wagon, and felt a great sadness wash over her. She knew in her heart he would not live a long life, nor would he be making furniture for his own children.

She and her soldier escort loaded the crib, then drove two miles to Henry's. As Maggie waved goodbye to José she wondered, as she did each time they parted, if she would see him again.

Five minutes after Maggie arrived at Henry's, so did the baby.

Henry was inspecting his newest offspring when Henry Joseph, his oldest, returned from fishing.

"Take a quick gander at this, boy, I gotta give him back to his Mama." Henry held out the baby.

The boy hooked a gill-strung mess of catfish over the rock fence, growled a warning to the hounds to keep their noses out of his fish, smiled a greeting to his Aunt Maggie, and went to inspect the baby.

"What is it?" Henry J. wanted to know. "And what's its name?"

"*It* is a boy, and his name is Harry Santanna Stockman."

"Another little brother? Great. I can teach him to fish," Henry J. beamed. Then he added, "And Tio Miguel will be tickled pink you named him after General Santa Anna."

"Now there's picture I'd just as soon not ponder on— your Uncle Miguel being tickled pink. But he will be pleased, won't he? Let's go see your Ma."

Henry J. thought his grandmother looked as tired as his mother, and wondered what went on when babies were born. Since men always went fishing or stayed out in the barn while any birthing went on, it was a mystery to him.

"Henry J., how does it feel to have a new brother?" Maggie asked her favorite nephew.

"Fine, I guess. I'm gonna run back and tell Paw Paw and Jesús. They're still making their way back from the fishin' hole." He turned to leave, spun back and said, "And thanks, Ma. He's a fine little fella," then bounded out of the cabin."

Dorcas smiled weakly. "I wish I had all that energy. Or any, for that matter. I think I could sleep for a year. Hand over Harry Santanna so I can feed him." Holding her son, she thought, *Why don't you cry more?*

Katherine, sitting by Dorcas, fought her own thoughts. *Something isn't right.*

Harry Santanna Stockman lived only five days.

The Stockman clan grieved, each in his own way.

Henry Joseph read. Maggie cried. Dorcas stoically tended house. Henry and Jesús plowed a new field. Frederick painstakingly carved a stone angel for the tiny grave. Katherine fussed over Joseph Anthony's health. Joseph Anthony worked on a pint-sized table and chair set for the next child born into the family.

Life continued.

CHAPTER 36

"Pa, can I ask you a question?"

Henry Stockman and his fourteen-year-old son, Henry Joseph, were securing the barn for the night.

Henry glanced at his son. The boy was already taller than he, had inherited his Grandmother Stockman's green eyes and pale freckled complexion, and his mother's jet-black hair. People were always telling Henry J. he was too pretty to be a boy, irking the boy to no end. He was a studious child who spent hours reading anything he could get his hands on and questioned everything.

"Sure, Enrique José, ask away."

"Pa, that's what I wanted to ask you—would it be all right if I asked folks to stop callin' me Enrique José?"

Henry continued coiling a piece of rope, but frowned. "Why? What happened?"

"Nothing really, Pa. It's just that some of the kids in town. . .well. . .they think we're Mexicans."

Henry worked his jaw, but tried keeping his tone light. "Well, son, we are. And so are they, if they live here legally."

"Yeah, I guess so. But that ain't what I meant—I mean *real* Mexicans."

"You mean like your Tio Miguel?" Henry asked, an edge of anger tinging his voice.

Henry Joseph heard the tone, but forged on. "Naw Pa, you know I don't mean him. Truth is, I don't rightly know what I mean. I told those kids we were Texicans, but they said that was old-fashioned, and if we were on the side of right, we'd be Texians. Way they figure it, white folks are supposed to be Texians and others is Mexicans," Henry Joseph spoke haltingly, trying his best to explain without making his father angry. He failed.

Henry, his fists clenched, no longer controlled his anger. "Don't you mean *Meskins*? Is that what you think your uncle is? Huh, boy?" He was a portrait of disapproval.

Henry Joseph, stymied and frustrated, threw down his currying brush and ran from the barn, leaving his father just as frustrated. He slammed his hat against a post.

Damn those newcomers. Damn that son of a bitch Santa Anna. And damn Texas, he thought, storming from the barn.

Later that night, when he and Dorcas were in bed, Henry told her what happened in the barn, adding, "Honey, I handled it all wrong. Can you talk to Henry Joseph tomorrow? I just fouled everything up by gettin' mad. Truth is, I hardly know what to think anymore. Seems like everything's turning upside down."

"Don't be so hard on yourself. Your son is a good boy and he'll forgive you this one little temper fit," Dorcas said as she reached over and smoothed Henry's salt and paprika hair.

"And Henry, I hate to add to your bad day, but I was over to see Mother Stockman today and Joseph Anthony is in trouble again. Jesús' concoctions can't even stop his pain. I think you'd better ride over early tomorrow and check on them."

Henry, unable to sleep, quit trying by four in the morning, slipped out of bed, saddled his horse and started out for his father's house.

Henry Joseph, also unable to sleep, ran after him. "Pa?"

Henry reined in and walked his horse back to where his son stood. Before Henry J. could say anymore, Henry apologized. "Son, I'm real sorry I blew up last night. I wasn't mad at you, I was mad at the situation."

"I know, Pa. I guess I didn't put things right, anyhow. Where're you going?"

"To check on your Uncle José Antonio—I mean Joseph Anthony." Henry's grin glowed in the waning moonlight.

Henry Joseph looked sheepishly grateful and smiled back. "Can I come?"

"Sure. Go get your horse. And turn your hat around, so I'll think you're comin' back."

The two rode slowly towards Frederick's place and Henry, now devoid of anger, was better able to explain his feelings regarding their tiff the night before.

"The truth is, son, I'm as confused as you are. Things used to be a danged sight simpler. Right was right and wrong was wrong."

"Sure sounds good to me, Pa."

"In a way it was. Your Uncle Miguel and I fought to free Mexico and Texas from Spain and we just *knew* we were doing the right thing. Now we've supported Mexico City and Santa Anna all these years, thinking that's the right thing. Not once have I raised my voice or gun against the Mexican government.

But now? Truthfully, I don't know what to think." He stopped his horse and looked at his son.

"One thing I *do* know, though. I won't call you Enrique José anymore if that's the way you want it. That's a promise."

"Thanks, Pa. I'm real sorry I stormed out of the barn like I did."

"Like I used to say to your Uncle Miguel after we had a row—I think we've kissed and made up enough for one day."

"You and Uncle Miguel fought?"

"Not with our fists, but we have a difference of opinion on occasion. Miguel is an idealist—your Mama taught me that word—and I'm more practical. Sometimes we don't see eye to eye on every little thing, but your uncle Miguel is a good man—don't you ever forget that."

"I know, Pa. But what if he's. . .well. . .wrong? I mean about how Texas should be run. And by who?"

Henry grinned. "Your mama would make you say *whom*," he puckered-up his lips and drew out the *m*.

They laughed, then rode quietly in the silvery dawn light, both glad the blowup was over.

After a few minutes Henry J. said, "I guess Uncle Joseph Anthony is a real Texican, ain't he, Pa? I mean, he was actually *born* in Texas."

"Yep, he is son. But some of the newcomers think your uncle got what was coming to him when we took the Mexican side of things in the Fredonian Rebellion. The Mexicans gave him a land grant for his loyalty, but now nothin' we've done seems to count for much."

Henry spat. "And now Santa Anna's gone and declared himself a damned dictator and has started actin' like one," he growled. "So much for their Jorge Washington crap."

"Pa, I heard Santa Anna's calling himself the 'Napoleon of the West', and wears uniforms with enough silver to buy Texas."

Henry shook his head in disgust. "That *macho* son of a bitch is spoilin' for trouble and will be the ruination of both Mexico and Texas if somebody don't stop him."

"What are we gonna do, Pa, if he comes here? I mean, will we fight *with* him or *against* him?"

"I don't rightly know, son. I just hope like hell we don't have to choose."

"Me too."

Both of them dreaded the thought of a showdown—one that might force family members and friends to take different sides.

Katherine sat in a pine rocker José Antonio made for her, sobbing softly. She looked up when she heard the horses, but made no move to greet Henry and her grandson.

Henry could see something was gravely wrong. "Ma, what's happened?"

"David's dead," she said.

"Stay here with your grandmother, Henry Joseph."

Henry walked indoors and found José Antonio in his bed, finally at peace after years of suffering.

"Dammit José, I'll miss you," Henry whispered softly as he covered his brother with a quilt. He closed the door and returned to the porch where his son sat holding Katherine's cold hands.

"Your Uncle Joseph Anthony has passed, boy." He knelt in front of Katherine. "I'm real sorry, Mama. You did your best. If it wasn't for you, he wouldn't have made it this long."

"If he just hadn't gone fishing, this wouldn't have happened. I told him to be careful, and now he's gone," Katherine sobbed.

Henry Joseph looked at his father, alarm and question on his young face. *What's wrong with Maw Maw? Why is she callin' Uncle Joseph Anthony 'David?'* He was getting scared. "Pa?"

Henry took his son aside and whispered, "Take Maw Maw Stockman indoors and get her to lay down. She's so sorrowful she ain't thinkin' straight. Joseph Anthony was born on the same day we buried your Uncle David—she's got the two mixed up."

"Yes, Pa." Taking Katherine by the arm, Henry Joseph gently led her past the closed door to his uncle's bedroom into her own.

Henry sat heavily into his mother's rocker, his throat aching with unshed tears. As he rocked he saw his father and Jesús riding in from a night hunt.

Spotting Henry on the porch, Frederick said, "José Antonio's passed on, ain't he?"

"Yes, Pa. I know I should be doing something, but I don't rightly know what."

Frederick straightened his back and wiped his face, as if to clear his mind. "Go get Maggie," he said, assuming a take-charge attitude. "I'll send Jesús for the rest of the family." At eighty-five, Frederick had moments of confusion, but was still decisive when the need arose.

Joseph Anthony, known to all as José Antonio Stockman, was born in Spanish Texas in 1808, and died in Mexican Texas in 1834.

The day of the burial, Katherine stood by stoically while Joseph Anthony's coffin, made by his own hand, was lowered. *Lord, I'm tired,* she thought as she plodded, surrounded by concerned children and grandchildren, from the family burial plot to her porch after the burial.

Sinking into her rocker, she sat, smiling wanly as each family member hugged or patted her as they left. When everyone was gone, Frederick said he needed a nap and went to their room.

Katherine thought a siesta sounded real good. She pushed herself up, walked slowly to her nearby ponderin' pond, and stretched out in a patch of wildflowers.

Nothing smells as good as a Texas Bluebonnet, she thought, breathing in their perfume for the last time.

CHAPTER 37

"Miguel, I just heard Steven Austin is under house arrest in Mexico. Is it true?" Henry demanded as he stormed into Miguel's office.

"What? Where did you hear this?" Miguel asked, visibly shaken.

"Some vaquero rode in with the news, and it's causing quite a commotion. He said your Santa Anna ain't the one who jailed him, but neither has he made a move to release him."

"Oh, so now he's *my* Santa Anna?" Miguel quipped, determined to defuse Henry's anger.

With an apologetic smile, Henry said, "I'm sorry, *hermano.* I ain't blamin' you. I guess I'm mad at the whole situation. When word gets out on Estèban's arrest, all hell's gonna bust loose in Texas. He's been the one who's been busting his ass to keep the peace between the Texians, Texicans, and Mexicans. Up 'til now, he's done a good job. I imagine being thrown in jail might sour his disposition towards Mexico City a mite. I know it's not doing much for mine."

Miguel threw out his hand in frustration.

"Enrique, there has to be some misunderstanding. Of all the people in Texas, Austin is the last man my. . .our. . .government should antagonize." He began pacing the room. "Perhaps I should ride to Saltillo and see what I can do."

"Want me to come with you?"

Miguel stopped in mid-pace. "No, I need you to look after Maggie for me."

Henry looked puzzled. "Is she sick?"

"Enrique, I meant to ride out to talk to you today. About Margarita. I am very worried."

"What's up?" Henry asked.

"As you know, she took the deaths of your mother and brother very hard, as expected. But even before their loss, she was. . .sad."

"I know, Miguel. Dorcas has been worried about Maggie's, well, dammit. . .mind. Maybe she should come out to our place while you're gone."

"Yes, that would be better. If what you say is true about Austin, the political situation here in town might turn. . . ."

"Ugly?"

"Yes."

"We'll be careful, Miguel. Now, about Maggie—is there something we should know? Are you two. . . ."

"Actually, Enrique, there was a strange thing. On the way home from your mother's funeral Margarita told me she wished to be called Margaret Stockman instead of Margarita Gonzales. Since it is not unusual in my culture for a wife to use her family name, I naturally told her it would be fine. But then one day when I called her Margarita, instead of Margaret, she flew into a fury."

"Miguelito, sit down for a minute—I think there's something you need to hear."

Henry pulled his chair close to Miguel's. "Maggie's been troubled for a long time, as we all know. She seemed to have gotten over being insulted by those old ladies in the mercantile a while back," he said, watching Miguel's face darken, "but maybe not. And now there's more."

"What?"

"Well, just before Mama and José Antonio died, Henry Joseph asked me not to call him Enrique José any more because he was having trouble with some of the Texians' kids. My guess is he talked to his Aunt Maggie about the problem before he told me, 'cause they're so close. I'd bet my horse that she decided to use Stockman instead of Gonzales to make my kid's lives a little easier when they come into town."

As he talked, Henry realized that what he was saying was a serious affront to Miguel's Hispanic pride, but he didn't know any other way to broach the subject except head-on.

Miguel said nothing, so Henry continued, striving for delicacy. "You know my children love you and consider you more than just an uncle by marriage. And I couldn't love you more if you were blood kin. But times have changed and maybe we have to change with them a little."

When Miguel finally spoke, his voice was gruff with resentment.

"Perhaps I should call myself Mike Stockman? That way my nephew and my wife will not have to be embarrassed by a filthy *Meskin* in the family?"

Henry put up his hand to stop his brother-in-law, but before he could say anything a young Mexican boy pushed open the door and gave Miguel a piece of paper.

"Sir, la Señora Gonzales asked me to deliver this to you at exactly two in the afternoon, and here I am," the boy announced proudly.

Miguel took the note, read it, and paled.

"Do you wish for me to take her a reply, sir? Doña Margarita gave me the paper this morning, but told me to wait to give it to you and I did. Is there an answer?"

"No *muchacho*, there is no answer," Miguel said quietly, handing the boy a coin. "Gracias."

Miguel handed the note to Henry, who read it, sucked in his breath, and leapt to his feet. "Miguel, we can stop her. I can catch her before she reaches the Sabine."

Miguel shook his head, and in a dangerous voice Henry knew all too well, growled, "No, Henry, I have no wish to bring her back. She has no use for Texas, or, it seems, for me."

"What are you going to do?"

Miguel snatched the note, crushing it. "The Stockmans will no longer have to suffer my embarrassing presence, *Henry*. I am leaving for Mexico—where I belong."

"Oh, Miguel, please tell me you'll come back," Henry pleaded.

"I will return, *Henry*, for this is my country. But when I do, it will be to reclaim Mexico's honor. Meanwhile, your family will have to decide whether to live as proud Texicans—Mexican citizens in the country you fought to create—or with this rabble you claim you no longer belong to."

Miguel strode to the door, but before he walked out he told Henry, "My decision is made. I do not wish to live where even my own wife considers me a second-class citizen."

CHAPTER 38

FEBRUARY 1836

General Miguel Gonzales y Duarte, of the Army of the Republic of Mexico, rode as swiftly as was prudently possible into the sharp teeth of a bitterly cold north wind.

The Texas norther nipped painfully at Miguel's ears and nose, slowing him—but not enough so his companions could easily keep his pace. As point man for a Sapper unit, he rode with only an aide-de-camp and a private. Speed and stealth were of utmost importance.

Had either of his *compadres* suspected what their General had in mind, they would have shot him on the spot. Miguel was on his way to commit an act of treason against the country for which he had fought almost his entire life.

For fear of capture by Texians, Miguel avoided El Camino Real. He had volunteered for—and been given—this mission because of his knowledge of the terrain. And he had chosen his young traveling companions for their lack of same.

More seasoned men, or soldiers with knowledge of Miguel's personal life, might have been less trusting of their General's actions, but these two would, Miguel knew, follow orders without question.

Miguel had narrowly escaped having his old nemesis, Felipe de la Garza, accompany him.

Ironically, de la Garza—a man who would have happily executed him as a traitor a few years back—was now his ally and fellow patriot. Miguel knew the old Spaniard still didn't trust him and arranged for a last minute change of orders that kept de la Garza in Mexico. And safe. Miguel meant to let no man stop him from the unsanctioned part of his mission.

Now he just had to get rid of these two soldiers without having their suspicions, and weapons, raised against him.

Miguel grinned to himself. *Oh wouldn't Henry Stockman love this. The Texians are itching to shoot me for being a Meskin, and the Meskins would shoot me for certain if they knew what I am about to do. Maybe I should save everyone the trouble and shoot myself?*

If his plan worked, Miguel's superiors need not ever find out that he had temporarily redirected himself from official duty in order to discharge a personal obligation. With luck, he would accomplish both missions and escape disgrace or death. Or both.

Perhaps Henry will shoot me. Has he joined the Texian rebels? Considering the troubles between the Texas militia and the Mexican military, he could have. Then what?

Miguel's thoughts of Henry brought back a hurtful memory: Margarita.

His heart pained him, as if recalling how his wife had broken it. *What did I do to drive you away, Margarita? I adored you.*

And she had loved him once—of that he was certain. Was it possible she was in Nacogdoches? Hope soared for a moment, then desire, then despair. *If she's there, will she think me the enemy?* He could not bear the thought of his Margarita looking upon him with loathing.

Another depressing thought: *What if Henry has moved and I cannot find him in time?*

The possibility of failure spurred Miguel to spur his horse to a full gallop, leaving his aides and their exhausted mounts in the dust. It was the dust that brought him to his senses. The last thing they needed was to be spotted by Texian outpost guards.

He reigned to a stop and waited for his men.

"My apologies, Corporal. Perhaps a rattlesnake frightened my horse."

The corporal, taken back by an apology from a General, smiled. "General, I share your horse's nervousness. Ever since we crossed the Rio Bravo, I see Texians behind each cactus."

Miguel surveyed the horizon. "If our information is correct, San Antonio de Béjar remains in the hands of the Texians, and we are not far from there."

The young corporal shivered. "These *insurgentes* frighten me, sir."

Miguel laughed loudly. Both young soldiers looked puzzled and he told them, "I find what you said amusing, Capo Rodriguez, because it was not so long ago that *I* was the insurgent. And right here in Texas. Time and politics have a strange way of changing the very meaning of words."

The Corporal, still in his teens, greatly admired the old soldier—the man was in his mid-forties!—who was his *comandante.* Stories of Miguel's unfailing courage and commitment during the Mexican Revolution were legion and legendary. The young man hoped one day, he, too, could find humor under duress. Right now, though, he was scared of death and scared *to* death of being captured by the Texian Devils.

All Mexican soldiers were told of the horrible deaths awaiting them should they fall into the hands of the insurgents—none would surrender in lieu of fighting to their deaths. They were certain their Generals would do the same. It was the Mexican code of honor.

The next day found the men within spyglass range of their destination. Miguel carefully surveyed the village and reported that everything looked normal, with people going about their daily business. Then he turned his focus on the fortress. Even at this distance he recognized one man he knew—and who knew him. He dared not enter the village as planned.

Lowering his glass, he drew an outline in the dirt with his knife. "They have posted sentries here and here," he made X's, "and they seem to be attempting to shore up the north wall, but I doubt they will be successful in repairing so much decay. Those walls were barely defendable when I was garrisoned there—over thirty years ago."

"Are there many men?"

"No. And they do not look like they are expecting an attack. The sentries look to be taking siestas."

"Perhaps they plan to leave soon?" the Corporal said hopefully.

"I do not think so, Rodriguez. I can see *norteamericanos* moving about inside the walls of the fortress. They have chosen a very poor place to take a stand, but they probably do not think anyone in his right mind would move an army across the hostile desert until the weather warms," Miguel commented, handing the Corporal his glass. Smiling, he added, "And in a way they are right. We are not led by sanity."

Rodriguez, trying to decide whether his superior officer had just insulted their Commander-in-Chief, looked a little startled, then raised the spyglass to survey the fortress and its inhabitants.

"There are so few of them, sir. Why are we planning to attack such an. . .insignificant. . .force?"

"Because *El Presidente* Santa Anna is furious with these Texian outlaws who came here for no other purpose than to steal our land. Most of those men," he pointed, "are not colonists, Mexicans or Texicans. They are land pirates," Miguel growled. "*Fibibusteros.*"

"Sir, you think the colonists are not a part of this rebellion?"

Miguel took the glass and refocused, following the man he recognized as he walked through the open courtyard of the fortress. *Travis.* Married to a Mexican woman—the daughter of an official. *Am I wrong? Have things changed so drastically since I left that the colonists are also in revolt?*

"Sir?"

"It does not matter. If our campaign is waged correctly these outlaws—and others like them in Texas—will be repelled or killed, and the legal, loyal, settlers can go about their business of farming and ranching."

He handed the spyglass to the private, an Indian from the Yucatan. Accustomed to balmy tropics, the Indian was stoically suffering the freezing weather because of an almost religious devotion to Santa Anna. Fortunately he spoke little Spanish; if he had understood Miguel's earlier, not-so-subtle remark regarding his President's sanity, he would have slit Miguel's throat on the spot.

Miguel reached for a pouch attached to his saddle. "I will write a report of our findings here for *El Presidente* Santa Anna so you and the private can deliver it to . . . ."

“General! We are found out,” Rodriguez said, pointing the two riders heading directly for them at full gallop.

Miguel carefully took the glass and hid it in his saddle bag. In a low voice he said, “Let me talk. For God’s sake, you two look humble. And never look them in the eye.”

Miguel turned to greet the riders while his aides pulled off their sombreros and assumed the downtrodden demeanor of proper peons.

As the men pulled their horses to a dusty halt, Miguel pushed his hat back to reveal his blue eyes and graying blonde hair. “Howdy,” he called, sounding every bit like Henry Stockman.

“Howdy,” the younger of the two called. “You ridin’ in to the fort?” The older man, his father by the looks of the pair, eyed the two Mexicans standing by their horses with their hats in hand. Although he thought the peasant’s mounts looked a little too fine, he dismissed the men as insignificant.

“Can’t decide. We was out doin’ a little hunting,” Miguel nodded in the direction of some animal skins he and his men had tied behind their saddles, “and I generally stay away from anywhere the Mexicans have any say-so, if you know what I mean.”

“Sure do. Well, Pa, guess we’d best get on into town so’s we can get back home. Good luck with your huntin’, and keep a sharp lookout for Mexican soldiers—we understand there might be some comin’ in to try to take back the fort.”

“We’ll do that. Don’t need no trouble.”

“Amen,” the boy said, and they rode away.

Rodriguiz stood straight, put his straw hat back on his head and grinned. “Was I properly submissive, General?”

“Perfect. But we cannot stay so lucky. As I was starting to say before those men came, now that we have seen San Antonio I think I should ride to Goliad to see how many are there. I will write a report for General Santa Anna of what we found here. You two can take it to him."

"But, sir, are you certain? Should not one of us ride with you?" asked the corporal.

"Are you questioning my orders, Corporal Rodriguez?"

"No sir, never."

"Good." Miguel dashed off a note for headquarters, then said, "Capo, please tell my personal aide to bring my dress uniform when you return with the army. I wish to fight these Texians in proper attire. Now, go. *Hasta la vista, compadres, y ¡Viva la Republica!*"

"*¡Viva Mexico! ¡Viva el General Don Miguel!*" his men replied as they rode away.

Miguel sagged against his horse and blew out a breath he hadn't realized he'd been holding. He took one last look at the fortress called the Alamo and rode east, not south. He hoped his aides had not tarried within visual range—they might wonder why he was going in the wrong direction.

"Mama! Mama! Tio Miguel just rode in," Henry Joseph yelled as he ran by the closed window of Dorcas' kitchen. Wiping flour from her hands, she hurried to the porch.

There was no mistaking Miguel, for even after so many years, he still rode as the Spaniards had trained him— Conquistador style, his horse trained to a *pasa doble* gait.

Yelling children and barking dogs came running from all directions when Miguel entered the yard and, for moment, he was mentally transported to an earlier time and generation, when those children were George, Enrique, David, José Antonio, Pedro, Juan and Maria Celeste. And Margarita. A tingle of expectancy rippled his spine.

He gathered Henry Joseph into a bear hug. "Enrique José, look at you! You are a man."

Dorcas, delighted to see her brother-in-law, trilled, "Miguelito, how wonderful to see you. I had just about given up hope, but Henry kept saying you'd be back. Oh, he'll be so excited. Come on in the house and warm up. Are you hungry? Of course you are, how silly of me. Tell me everything—it's the only way you'll be able to stop me from babbling."

Miguel, giddy with relief and weariness, could barely contain his overwhelmed emotions. He had left Nacogdoches in a fit of hurt and anger, but—judging by the family's warm, boisterous reception—his bridges were not burned.

"Where is Enrique?" he asked, his voice raspy with emotion.

"Nacogdoches."

"Oh. I did not pass through Nacogdoches. I was not certain of the. . .political climate," Miguel said, trying to be delicate.

Dorcas frowned and told the children to go take care of their uncle's horse. As soon as they were alone, she sat down across the table from Miguel.

"Henry's gone to a Ranger's meeting, Miguel. The Comanches have been pulling raids into the very heart of some outlying communities and the Rangers are trying to do something about it, since your. . .uh. . .the army. . . ."

Dorcas' hand flew to her mouth as her cheeks colored. She had just told a general in Santa Anna's Mexican Army that the colonists had formed a militia—an act of treason.

Miguel took her hand in a gesture meant to reassure her that she was talking not to a general, but her brother-in-law.

Regaining her composure, Dorcas asked, "Miguelito, please tell me—just how bad have things gotten? Should I be afraid?"

"Dorcas, my sister, I think you should prepare to leave Texas for the time being. *El Presidente* Santa Anna is very angry with all *norteamericanos* and I do not think he is capable of differentiating between Texicans and Texians. I myself have difficulty telling the difference between a true colonist and an outside troublemaker when they both carry weapons."

He dug into his satchel and pulled out a journal.

"Let me read to you a speech Santa Anna made to our troops. I do not entirely agree with my Commander-in-Chief about what he is preparing to do, but he is not a man who can be reasoned with."

He opened the battered book, and began to read: "*Comrades in arms, our most sacred duties have brought us to these uninhabited lands and demand our engaging in combat against a rabble of wretched adventurers to whom our authorities have unwisely given benefits that even Mexicans did not enjoy, and who have taken possession of this vast and fertile area, convinced that our own unfortunate internal divisions have rendered us incapable of defending our soil. Wretches! Soon they will become aware of their folly! Soldiers, our comrades have been shamefully sacrificed at Anàhuac, Goliad and Béjar, and you are those destined to punish these murderers. My friends: We will march as long as the interests of the nation that we serve demand. The claimants to the acres of Texas land will soon know to their sorrow that their reinforcements from New Orleans, Mobile, Boston, New York, and other points north, whence they should never have come, are insignificant, and that Mexicans, generous by nature, will not leave unpunished affronts resulting in injury or discredit to their country, regardless of who the aggressors may be.*"

Miguel lowered his journal and they stared at each other across the suddenly vast expanse of the table.

Dorcas struggled to find suitable words, but could not. *What do I say to an enemy I love?*

Henry's abrupt entrance into the room broke the impasse, but he sensed the tension and feared he knew the cause.

"Things have gotten a mite rough, huh, Miguel?" Henry asked, slapping his boyhood friend's shoulders, then pulling him into a hug. "Man, oh man, have I missed you."

Dorcas watched the two men, then busied herself putting food on the table. She sensed this to be a momentous turning point in their lives—one that could send them in such diverse directions that when they met again they would collide.

Miguel handed Santa Anna's proclamation to Henry and watched his face as he read.

Henry, pale and sad, looked into Miguel's equally unhappy face. "When is he coming, Miguelito?"

Miguel exhaled loudly. "He is here."

CHAPTER 39

"Miguel, do you remember the day you decided to desert the Spanish Army? And why?" Henry asked Miguel across the table.

Miguel's stomach clenched, for he knew the question held an answer: Henry and his family would stand against Mexico, General Santa Anna—and him.

The Texicans would join the Texians, and brothers would be enemies.

With a heavy heart, but a clear conscience, Miguel left the Stockman enclave to rejoin his army. He had, in an act of treason, warned his family to flee to safety of the United States. He was mournful that they refused to do so, but his duty was to Mexico. His country.

Nevertheless, tears of acute loss stung Miguel's eyes as he rode back to San Antonio. He wiped his face and patted his breast pocket for the tenth time in an hour to ensure the precious packet of letters Henry had given him were there.

The treasured missives, warm against his chest, were like maidens' scarves carried by his crusading ancestors—paper amulets to shield his tattered heart.

He had read only one of the letters. He planned to give himself a written offering each night during the campaign, thus superstitiously ensuring his life for at least ten days.

The first letter, written to Henry just after both he and Margarita fled Texas in different directions, had contained a note for Miguel.

He had opened the perfumed envelope with shaking fingers, then read slowly as Margaret's perfectly penned hand begged him to forgive her her weakness of spirit and reprehensible flight. It was, she wrote, her own flawed character, not any fault on his part, that was the root of her treachery.

Miguel smiled at her melodramatic wording. It was so...Margarita.

Vowing her undying love for him, Maggie begged him to forgive her for selling his grandmother's lavaliere—here Miguel laughed out loud—to support herself in New Orleans.

New Orleans! ¡Madre de Dios! How would such a girl as Margarita survive the evils of that town?

For a moment he was tempted to read her last letter, dated only weeks ago, perhaps to learn the present status of her life—and loves?—after these years.

He fingered the envelope, then returned it to his pocket. As long as he remained ignorant, he could cling to the illusion, a mental legerdemain, that she remained his wife.

He vowed, when this conflict was over, to find Margarita.

If he lived. And *if* he didn't end up fighting his own family, thereby ensuring her permanent disdain.

Five miles from San Antonio de Béjar he smelled the smoke from campfires. Many campfires.

Three miles further and he heard a sound that both chilled and excited him. He halted to listened. Wafting through the cool March air were the eerie, unmistakable strains of the Deguello—Santa Anna's bugle warning, his musical death sentence, to the men of the Alamo. He would give no quarter. As Miguel had predicted to his corporal only days before, the Texians were doomed.

Before he rode nearer Miguel changed into a uniform jacket and pulled his orders from his pack. He had no intention of ending his military career at the hands of some overzealous sixteen-year-old conscript.

As he entered camp, cannon fire erupted, beginning a twenty-four hours barrage that remained unanswered by the Texians holed up in the Alamo. *Saving their ammunition*, he thought. *Smart.* But not that so smart that they hadn't left before they were doomed. At least fourteen hundred Mexican troops surrounded what his corporal estimated to be no more than four hundred Texians. And that included a group of thirty or so Texians who had charged through the Mexican lines to join their friends inside the fort a few days before. *Doomed.*

The cannons stopped and the bugler playing his unrelenting, ominous solo was joined by another, this one echoing an answer to each note. It was enough to set even a seasoned veteran's teeth on edge. Miguel wished he could silence the damned buglers—and if their sinister strains were getting on *his* nerves, what must it be doing to those men inside the Alamo?

Doomed.

Presidente/General Santa Anna had ordered a full attack just before dawn, and as Miguel donned his full dress uniform his stomach sank. *So foolish. They would lose many men, and for what? A crumbling old fortress manned by a few hundred poorly armed men. All so his president could get even with the Texians for embarrassing him.*

Miguel had practically begged Santa Anna to reconsider. They could wait. Starve them out. He thought he was making a little headway when, out of the blue, the Texians had fired a cannonball right into the belfry of the church behind their army's headquarters, almost hitting the president. Santa Anna was livid.

Miguel smiled as he buttoned his jacket. These Texians had some *cojones* on them. Like Henry. He thought of his family—the only family he had left—and wondered what Henry was doing right then. He prayed his best friend and brother-in-law was not, at this moment, riding to join his fellow Texians in their fight against General Santa Anna. It was a battle they could not possibly win. Unless his president became more arrogantly self-confident that he already was.

Miguel needn't have worried about meeting any Stockmans on the field of battle. They were embroiled in a conflict with another enemy.

One much more pressing and dangerous for them than the Mexican Army.

CHAPTER 40

Comanches.

For the second time in his life, Henry Stockman had set out to avenge a wrong done by Comanches. This time the Indians were much luckier.

He and Henry Joseph, trail-weary and disappointed after their Ranger troop failed to find two white children stolen from Fort Parker a day after Miguel's visit, were nevertheless relieved to be nearing home.

During their unsuccessful search for the Parker children, their minds were never far from worrying about what was happening with the Texian conflict back home.

Rounding the corner of his barn, Henry reigned up short when a shot rang out, raising the dust in front of him.

He motioned for his son to dismount, then, when they were preparing to storm the house, they heard Frederick shout, "Come on out and fight like a man, you Mexican scoundrel."

Henry Joseph chuckled and yelled, "Paw Paw, are you gonna shoot us?"

Frederick lowered his gun and squinted through eighty-seven-year-old eyes. "Oh, hell, I thought you was Santy Anny. I been sittin' here on this porch waiting for that yellow-bellied bastard ever since all them damned Texians started runnin' hell-bent-for-leather for the border. I was hopin' you was him, 'cause I'm getting damned tired of sitting out in this infernal rain," he grumbled.

"Where's Dorcas and the children, Pa?" Henry asked, but as he did so the front door flew open and his family spilled out.

Frederick stomped his foot in disgust, yelling, "Dammit, I told y'all not to come out unless I gave the damned signal, and I didn't give it now, did I? No one in this family ever pays me any mind since I got so old. If your Grandma Stockman, God rest her soul, was here, there'd be the Devil to pay."

"We're sorry, Father Stockman, we just got so excited when we heard Henry's voice," Dorcas told the old man as she hugged her husband.

"Well, it could'a been a damned Mexican trap," Frederick groused, somewhat mollified.

"What Mexicans? Is Santa Anna on his way here? Is that why Pa says everyone is running for the border?" Henry asked.

Everyone started to talk at once, but Dorcas prevailed. She told of the fall of the Alamo, the massacre at Goliad of four-hundred Texians, and the frantic flight of settlers to the United States border.

Led by the fleeing widows of the fallen men at the Alamo, the "Runaway Scrape," as it came to be called, had filled Nacogdoches with refugees.

El Camino Real, saturated by heavy rains, was blocked by mired wagons and littered with forsaken household belongings. Those who made it as far as the Sabine found the river in full flood. Only the heroics of the ferry operators allowed a few to cross.

Texas and Texians were in a state of panic.

Henry became increasingly alarmed as he listened. Dorcas concluded her list of horrors by saying, ". . .and General Houston is said to be in full retreat before Santa Anna's army."

Frederick could no longer let Dorcas hog the podium. "*General* Houston! Did you hear that, Henry?"

"Sam Houston?"

"The very one." Frederick spat and slapped his knee. "Andy Jackson's hand-picked drunk, sent to liberate Texas. Don't look like he's doing so good so far, I. . . ."

Dorcas interrupted. "Henry, we have to go. The Mexican Army could arrive here at any time."

Frederick yelled, "I ain't leavin'. Santy Anny better not get in my sights, I'll tell you."

Despite the gravity of the situation, Frederick's outburst struck the family as funny and they began to laugh.

Henry told the family to start packing the wagons, then rode out to inspect El Camino Real for himself. It was worse than he thought.

Soupy mud spiked with all manner of abandoned debris convinced him that there was no way his family would be joining any panic-stricken mob fleeing an enemy that might not even get this far north.

He believed in retreat in the face of danger, but not if that exodus placed them in the path of a hysterical human stampede. He decided to ride into town.

Nachogdoches' central plaza was in the throes of frenzy. Trying to make sense of what was happening, Henry looked for a familiar face and spotted Peter Ellis Bean, Miguel's old filibustering friend.

"Pedro Bean, what in the hell is going on?" Henry asked.

"Enrique! Man, am I glad to see you. I figgered you and the family had taken to the road like the rest of Texas. It's been quite a show, I tell you. I been sittin' here sippin' whiskey for what seems like days, but not a single soul will arrest me. Will you?" Bean slurred.

"Hell, Frijòle, it ain't against the law to drink whiskey in Texas—yet. If it was, we could just build a fence around the whole territory and call it a jail," Henry told him, watching the chaos around them.

Wagons had lost their wheels, women had lost their children, and men seemed to have lost their minds.

"Henry, you fool, I don't mean for bein' drunk. I mean for me bein' a Mexican official. If you throw me in jail, maybe someone won't shoot me."

"I see your point, Peter. Why don't you just go tell whoever is in charge, if anyone is, that you resign your post as Indian Agent?" Henry asked reasonably.

"Well, I thought of that, but then if Santa Anna shows up and finds out I resigned, *he'll* shoot me. What do you think about that?"

"I think you'd better just come on home with me, Pedro, 'cause if you stay here you might have to shoot yourself. What's all the commotion over there?" Henry pointed to a crowd by the church.

"Damned if I know—wasn't there a few minutes ago. Let's go see," Peter Bean grunted, lurching, in a gravity-defying move, toward a man riding wildly around the church square while shooting at the clouds.

"They got him! We won! We're free! We beat 'em and that bastard Santa Anna is ours. General Houston's got him."

"Hurrah for Texas! Remember the Alamo! Long live the Republic of Texas!" a chorus rang out as Bean and Stockman neared the crowd around the rider.

Henry pushed his way towards the man, anxious to hear details, but the messenger spurred his horse and left, intent on spreading his news far and wide. Skeptical of the veracity of this new piece of information, he and Peter decided to wait for more.

They didn't have to wait long, for within hours hundreds of riders arrived, looking for wives and families who had joined the Runaway Scrape. Among the new arrivals were Samuel Norris and James Gaines.

"Enrique!" James Gaines yelled. "Ain't it grand? We won!"

"Is the war really over?" Henry asked.

"Sure as hell is, amigo. Old Sam Houston caught *El Presidente* with his knickers down. The so-called Napoleon of the *West* got caught with his pants *south*. Seems he was takin' a siesta with some high-yeller gal, and before he knowed it, Texians were all over him like flies on buttermilk. Mexicans scattered in every direction and the whole danged war was over in fifteen minutes."

Sam Norris got off his horse and added, "And that isn't the best of the story. Ole Santa Anna ran for his life on a horse he stole from a nearby farm a few days before. *El Presidente* evidently didn't have any idea which way to go, so he let that horse have his head and danged if the ole boy didn't take him right back to his barn. The folks that owned the horse didn't know it was Santa Anna riding him—they just arrested the man for stealing their property. It's a lucky thing for that s.o.b. that he's president of Mexico. If he was just a horse thief we'd a hung him. We ought to hang 'em all."

Peter Bean looked pained by this last piece of information and stared meaningfully at Henry.

"So now General Houston not only has that bastard Santa Anna as a prisoner, he got him to sign over Texas to us Texians," James laughed. "I gotta go see about Susannah and the kids, then I need all the men I can get to go with me. We're gonna ride El Camino Real all the way to the Rio Grande, roundin' up straggler Mexican soldiers and herdin' em to the border. It'll be like our old mustang roundups."

"You can count me in, Jaime," Henry assured James.

Gaines turned to leave, then yelled back. "Oh, by the way I signed a Texas Declaration of Independence the other day, so the whole thing is official. We got ourselves a country, boys."

"Some country, Bean," Henry said with a sardonic grin. "The father of Texas, Stephen F. Austin, is a confirmed bachelor."

"Yep, so what does that make Texas?"

They laughed.

Henry shook his head in wonder and added, "Sam Houston's runnin' around acting like George Washington and James Gaines thinks he's John-damned-Hancock."

CHAPTER 41

The self-proclaimed Napoleon of the West inhaled another whiff of cocaine—generously provided him by Sam Houston's physician—and smiled.

Perhaps, he thought, *these Texians might not shoot me, after all.*

In his state of drug-induced omnipotence, President Santa Anna further convinced himself that not only would he survive this, well, Waterloo, but he might even redirect this disastrous turn of events to his benefit.

It's obvious I'm dealing with idiots. Were the tables turned, and I had not been robbed of certain victory by a ridiculous little mistake, that dog Houston would be standing in front of my firing squad at this very moment.

And, he thought, enjoying a rush of euphoria, *I will not only survive, I will make these so-called Texians rue the day they dared to defy Antonio Lopez de Santa Anna. If, that is, my overzealous Generals heed the orders I sent and do not do anything foolish, like try to rescue me.*

"We have to rescue him," Miguel told General Urrea at their campsite only a few miles from where Santa Anna was being held.

"As long as they hold our president, they hold Texas. We can have him out in the blink of an eye; we have the men, the weapons and the discipline—three things the Texians lack. Houston's bivouac would fall more easily than the Alamo, and with far fewer casualties."

Miguel, still upset with the way the murderous Santa Anna had shamed Mexico at San Antonio and Goliad, added, "Especially with *El President* on the other side of the wall."

Urrea knew exactly what Miguel's last statement meant. He, too, was ashamed of his President. He hoped to hold Santa Anna accountable for his dishonorable and senseless sacrifice of his own men, and the slaughter of helpless Texian prisoners at both the Alamo and Goliad. He looked forward to a tribunal in Mexico City.

Miguel, as if reading Urrea's thoughts, pushed.

"I know the enemy, General. I have fought beside them. They are untrained, under-armed farm boys and vagrants. The only professionals in their army have little control over these Texians. Sam Houston was very fortunate at San Jacinto, but his luck would not hold against an attack now. I know Sam Houston—I used to live next door to him in Nachcogdoches. He is a drunk and a womanizer, not a soldier. Please, let me try something."

"General Gonzales, I am tempted to do as you say. Our men have traveled far and fought hard, gaining victories in each battle. Now we are like trained dogs, told by our President to sit with our tails between our legs. How would you plan an attack if permitted to do so?"

"First, I could easily scout the enemy camp, because with the right clothes I can pass for a *norteamericano*. Then, after I've located General Santa Anna and assessed the enemy's strength, I would return and we could strike. It is our only chance to liberate *El Presidente* and regain Mexico's honor. What do we have to lose?"

General Urrea was about to answer, "not much," when an aide to General Filisola arrived, summoning him to the new supreme commander's tent.

"All right, General Gonzales, let us see what three generals in a defeated army can come up with to regain our honor."

Miguel stormed from the tent a few minutes later, his face a mask of fury. Urrea caught up to him, grabbing his shoulder.

"Miguel, calm down, or you'll be facing a court-martial. We have received an executive order to retreat all the way to the Rio Grande River, and we must comply."

Miguel blinded by rage, tried to shake off Urrea's hand on his shoulder. "Rio *Bravo*, General. I don't care what these Texians call it."

Urrea managed to grab his other shoulder. "We *will* comply, General Gonzales, that is an order."

"How is this possible?" Miguel asked, his voice quaking with emotion. "We were victorious in every battle save one. We have superior forces, in both numbers and armaments. How can this be?"

"I do not know, Miguel," Urrea said, shaking his head sadly. "I only know we have received direct orders from General Filisola to retreat, and we must do so. Only God, and perhaps Santa Anna, knows why. Please call in the other officers and I will break the news to them."

Miguel stalked away, but after a few strides he halted near the bank of the Brazos River.

Looking out over the countryside, he was stuck by the deceptively serene beauty of the land he so loved. The magnitude of his loss overwhelmed him, bringing tears to his eyes.

It is over. I have lost Texas. And all because of the actions of a cowardly mad man. How could Santa Anna give all of this away to save his own despicable hide? Any Mexican of honor would rather be dead.

"Pa, do you think Uncle Miguel's alive?" Henry Joseph asked as he, Henry, and Frederick rode slowly down El Camino Real towards the Mexican border.

Dorcas had protested when her son and father-in-law insisted on joining the sweep to drive the Mexican army stragglers across the Rio Grande, but the men prevailed.

"I'd bet every Bluebonnet in Texas on it, son. And if I'm right, I know just where we'll find him. He'll be waiting on this side of the Rio Grande until the last soldier has crossed."

"He'll wait till Hell and Texas freeze over for Santy Anny if Sam Houston has any balls. He should hang that polecat," Frederick growled.

"I don't much imagine General Houston plans to do that. He needs *El Presidente* to back up his surrender agreement," Henry said.

"Too bad," Frederick insisted. "Some folks just need hangin'."

Miguel sat in the edge of a campfire's glow, watching his captors get drunk.

He could easily have escaped. His guards—Texian volunteers who had ridden in from Georgia after the war was over—were incompetent opportunists. Their only interest in Texas was the promised free land.

Miguel stayed for two reasons: to gather intelligence on Santa Anna's whereabouts and actions, and to say goodbye to Henry.

He had, in hope of orders to reverse the Mexican retreat, eluded capture for almost two weeks, but was finally betrayed by lack of sleep and a noisy chicken.

He had been captured three times. He had not been a model prisoner.

Miguel spotted the Stockmans riding towards the camp and smiled.

Henry Joseph, when he saw Miguel, spurred his horse and rode recklessly into camp. He was in camp and off his horse before Miguel's guards could throw down their whiskey jugs and grab their weapons. He threw his arms around his chained uncle.

"Say, there, sonny, what the hell do you think you're a doin' with my prisoner?" one man growled as he seized Henry Joseph and threw him to the ground.

The boy scrambled to his feet, ready for a fight, but Miguel said, "Enrique José, don't. He isn't worth it."

The Georgian guard didn't like the sound of that. "Enrique José? What are you boy, some kinda half-breed? Or are you just a Meskin lover?"

The guard's buddies hooted approval. They were spoiling for a fight. The ragtag Texian encampment was in an ugly mood—they'd missed the revolution, their promised pay hadn't materialized, rations were sparse, and worse, they'd been stuck with guard duty.

"He is my nephew," Miguel said. "He's only a boy—you have no quarrel with him."

"Maybe not, Meskin, but I sure as hell got one with you. You been spoilin' for a good ass kickin' ever since you was brought here, and I think I'm just the man to do it."

As he spoke, the Texian picked up a bull whip. "Now, boy, you'd best git out of the way or I'll tan you, too."

Henry Joseph head-butted the drunk Texian, bowling him over into his friends. One of them grabbed the boy and kicked Miguel over while another picked up the bullwhip and drew back his arm to strike.

"Hold it right there," Frederick growled, his rifle leveled right at the man's belly button. "Put down the whip. Now."

"Who the hell are you, old man?"

"I'm a Texican, you piece of Georgia trash. And so is that man you've got chained up. Now, one of you take off them chains, right now. And be damned gentle about it."

"An old man and a boy gonna make us do it?"

"An old man, a boy, and me," Henry said, stepping into the light. "Now you do as your elder just told you to."

Unchained, Miguel put his arm around Henry Joseph and grinned.

"Henry, Frederico. I have been waiting for you. Would you do me the honor of escorting me to the river's edge?" he asked, managing to look dignified despite his tattered uniform.

Henry looked at Miguel's Texian guards. "Why wasn't this man released to cross the border? Those were your orders from General Houston."

"Aw hell, he kept comin' back. I wanted to shoot him, but we was told we couldn't shoot no prisoners. Son of a bitch has been nothing but a pain in the ass since we got him."

"That son of a bitch, you half-wit, is a general in the Mexican army and is to be treated as such. I'll see that General Houston hears about this."

Miguel was grinning from ear to ear, enjoying every minute of Henry's bluff.

Henry turned to Miguel and saluted, saying, "General Gonzales, you'll need a horse." Handing Quicksand III's reins over, he whispered, "We'll wait for you downstream."

Miguel put his hand on Henry's shoulder and squeezed. "No, my brother, I cannot come with you. I must return to what's left of my army in Mexico. I just didn't want to leave until I could say a proper farewell. I will miss you."

In the silvery light of a waxing full moon, three generations of Stockmans sadly watched Miguel cross the Rio Grande.

Tears stung Henry's eyes and he wiped them away.

"Pa, don't cry, Miguel'll be back."

Henry smiled. "The hell with Miguel, boy. That Mexican just took my best horse."

On the other side, Miguel turned and waved, his face a mask of grief.

He had lost everything he'd fought for for over twenty-five years: Margarita, Texas, his country's honor—all gone. As he stared across what was once just a river, now a border, a familiar figure rode slowly to his side.

"So, Gonzales, what do you think of your Texicans now?" asked General Felipe de la Garza, contempt dripping from each word.

"I think, Felipe, that one day the sons of Texas and the sons of Mexico will fight in the streets of Mexico City."

EPILOGUE

NEW ORLEANS, 1838

Tears rolled down Margaret's cheeks as she read of her father's death.

Henry wrote that Frederick, almost ninety, failed to wake one morning, adding: *Sis, he had a big old smile on his face. I think he was happy to be joining Mama.*

She sat with Henry's letter in her lap, took a deep breath to stop her tears, then opened her escritoire and penned a reply:

My Dearest Family,

My heart is heavy to hear of Daddy's passing, and I am grieved that I did not see him in the past years. I miss you all so, and now that Texas is a Republic and no longer at war, perhaps I will come for a visit. I have a little surprise for you—two in fact—but you'll have to wait until I come to find out what it is. I love you all.

Your loving sister,

Maggie

Sealing her note with a wax seal she'd had made to resemble the lavaliere Miguel had given her as an engagement present, she rang for her manservant to take the letter to post, and sank back into a silk brocade armchair.

The envelope had left her hand destined for a long journey—one she herself might make soon.

She conjured up memories of her old home in Nacogdoches, with its beautiful rose gardens, and the way the light had entered her bedroom in the mornings. *Their* bedroom in the mornings. And Miguel.

She missed his handsome face, chivalrous manner and flowery speech. She missed him. She had loved Miguel most of her life, and he could never be replaced in her heart by another man..

I wonder what he would think of my life in here in New Orleans, posing as the tragic widow of a Spanish grandee. He'd probably be amused.

If one could possibly amuse a man one had treated so badly.

The sale of the lavaliere Miguel had given her as an engagement gift had allowed her to live handsomely, and, through wise real estate investments, she was comfortable financially.

New Orleans society had no reason to doubt Margaret's moneyed-widow status.

Smiling, she imagined herself and Miguel strolling along the fashionable boulevards of New Orleans—he blonde and virile, she dressed in her favorite ashes of roses silk. Their strawberry-blonde twins between them.

My, but wouldn't we make heads turn.

She frowned. *But he would never be content to live here in New Orleans, and there's no way in hell he's going to drag me and my children off to live in Mexico City! What a shame. Why does Miguel have to be so damned. . .Mexican.*

AUTHOR'S NOTE

The Texicans is a work of fiction based on the lives of Frederick and Katherine Stockman who did, in fact, immigrate to Spanish Texas in 1806. For a genealogical and historical accounting of my novel's characters, I offer the following:

Frederick Stockman 1749-1838
Katherine Disponet Stockman 1771-1834
Henry Stockman1782-1852 MyG-G-G-Grandfather.
George Stockman 1786-1815 Died in War of 1812
David Stockman 1784-1808 We don't know how David died—huge alligators did exist in those days.
John Stockman 1797-1869?
Peter Stockman 1800-1865
Margaret Stockman 1803-? We do not know what became of Margaret. She therefore became a fictional character in my novel.
Joseph Anthony Stockman 1806-1834 He was wounded in the Fredonian Rebellion and died the same year as Katherine.
Mary Sarah Stockman 1811-1865
Dorcas: ? Married Henry circa 1819. We don't know where she came from, or even if the Spanish spelling of her surname, Trebite, is correct.
Miguel Gonzales is a fictional character, as is the Indian, Jesùs. All others are historical figures.